HALF
SISTERS

ALSO BY VIRGINIA FRANKEN

Life After Coffee

HALF SISTERS

A NOVEL

VIRGINIA FRANKEN

Published by Lake Union Publishing, Seattle

www.apub.com

Amazon, the Amazon logo, and Lake Union Publishing are trademarks of Amazon.com, Inc., or its affiliates.

ISBN-13: 9781542037488
ISBN-10: 1542037484

Cover design by David Drummond

Printed in the United States of America

For Fizzle Pop, with great thanks.

CHAPTER 1

MADDY

She'd sat on the news for four long hours. Reined in the urge to divulge it via text. This was not news for texting. She'd held it in as Bee had bustled through the front door, Fergus and Robbie in tow, Robbie in full tantrum mode. Waited patiently for Robbie to calm down and, when requested, made a guess at what he wanted for his birthday. Then watched as Bee smoothed out the ensuing fistfight after Fergus blurted out what it was (a Nerf Blaster), spoiling Robbie's guessing game. But now, the boys were finally occupied, their hands full of the grass, dead leaves, and shards of old brick they were industriously collecting and dumping in a pile in the middle of the lawn. Dirt in their hair and under their nails. Content.

Now, both women had glasses of chilled rosé cupped in warm hands and had taken up their seats in the rockers. Always the same: Maddy on the right, Bee on the left. Maddy gently bit the rim of her wineglass as she listened to Bee talk and focused on the hazy landscape directly in front of them—her gaze lingering just above the final line of houses. She always thought those huge divots in the hillside looked like oversized eye sockets this time of day. The empty black eye sockets of slumbering giants. Bee reached a natural pause within her PTA rant, and Maddy opened her mouth to share her news, but Bee got there first.

"I mean it's not like I'm asking them to scrub public toilets for eight hours straight. It's two hours of selling books to children. Their own children! On *one* day. Maybe two days if they can possibly bring themselves to do it." Maddy had heard it before. Had taken a shift herself at the bookfair in the past, just to make it stop. But she didn't make the offer today, even though she knew that was why Bee had brought it up.

Instead, she stood, topped up Bee's glass and her own, then wedged the bottle back behind the big cactus planter. In lieu of a tabletop where a bottle would be safe from getting kicked over by little feet, it was what they did—they'd lost too many bottles in the early days. Of course, Maddy could have purchased a table. Just something small that could house a bottle of rosé and a couple of glasses. But whenever she'd start to eye one, not knowing what was going to happen with the house had always prevented the purchase. She couldn't sidestep the logic that there was zero point in furnishing a place that she might have to move out of at any moment. Because she knew that once she bought herself a tidy wine table, it wouldn't stop there. After the table, she'd need to swap out the too-hard rockers, and then with new porch furniture installed, she'd notice the paint on the railings really was too flaky to tolerate, and wasn't it time to replace the ancient doormat? And then into the front hall to fix the uneven parquet flooring, make the living room lighting less dungeony, and so on. And that would be how she'd end up refurbishing a house she had no idea whether she'd be able to stay in. But now she knew. There had been *news.*

Bee's monologue finally came to an end, and a short silence followed, silence that Maddy was supposed to fill with empathetic murmurs on the self-centered nature of the St. Novatus parent body. Instead, Maddy took a small sip and considered which words, exactly, she should use to spill the beans. But before she could compose the perfect sentence, Bee drew a breath to start into wave three, so Maddy decided she'd best just say it.

"We found her." The words finally spoken out loud caused some amorphous mix of relief and fear to unspool inside her stomach.

"Found who?" asked Bee, though from her face she could see Bee already knew *who*. She just couldn't believe it.

"We found Emily." The ensuing silence expanded until Maddy felt compelled to glance over at Bee to see what the deal was. To create an epic silence in the presence of her best friend was no small feat. But if there was any one sentence that was up to the task, it was the one that Maddy had just spoken.

"And where was she?" asked Bee finally, matter-of-factly, as if Emily were a lost belonging accidentally stuffed into the wrong drawer and not a person.

"New York. Joseph found her."

"*Joseph?* How?"

"They were at the same party last night."

"What? So she just walked up to him all: *Hi there, here I am, your long-lost sister-in-law?* Does she even know she's his sister-in-law?"

"I have no idea. The details were not forthcoming," said Maddy as she downed the last of her wine and headed for the cactus pot. Her husband was famous for failing to pick up imperative information. The few times he'd gone to social occasions without her, he'd provided shamefully sparse reports upon his return and had been unable to answer fundamental questions such as: *What did they name the baby? Had the bride worn pale blue, like she'd threatened to, or opted for fail-safe white in the end? Were Aunt Jan's eyebrows really completely paralyzed after her latest round of Botox, or had his mother been exaggerating?* Vital questions. All unanswered. But this one, this Emily discovery, was going to have to be the exception. Because Maddy had questions, major ones.

"There's got to be more!" Unlike her brother, Bee was an enthusiastic gatherer of all detail. "He didn't just say: *I'm at a party, I found Emily,* then hang up."

"He didn't *say* anything. He texted me. The next day."

"*Texted* you?" Bee was incredulous. And Maddy could see why. She'd been surprised he hadn't called her from the party, or at least afterward. Or just waited till he got home to tell her. A text seemed inappropriate, anticlimactic. Plain wrong.

"He said he'd had a crazy morning and his battery was dying." Those were the excuses he'd given Maddy, so she churned them out dutifully for Bee.

"Are we sure this is a real thing that happened? I mean, maybe he was hungover and he meant to say he *thought* he saw Emily."

"It's real. I didn't believe him at first either, so he sent a pic."

Maddy bent down and scooped her phone off the floor, but as soon as she had it, Bee took it out of her hands, unlocked it, and navigated to her texts. It was fine. Maddy and Bee's friendship predated the smartphone; they had phone-grabbing rights. Bee opened the text from Joseph, took a quick scroll to confirm that, no, there really wasn't any extra detail to be had, and then hit the photo he'd attached. Maddy pulled Bee's hand toward her so they could see the picture at the same time.

"My God," said Bee after a second. "Is there a filter on that?"

"I don't think so," said Maddy. "That's just what she looks like when she's not scowling." Emily stood at the edge of a rooftop garden, the lights of distant skyscrapers just visible through the mesh railings behind her. The expression of pained hostility Maddy remembered from their short-lived sisterhood was no longer visible and had instead been replaced with a smile that suggested its wearer had never known anything but good times. Neat fat curls had replaced the frizz that used to stick out at all angles, and she was wearing a diamanté headband nestled in among the curls. Maddy couldn't help but wonder how she herself would look wearing the same accessory. She'd look like a schoolgirl. But the way Emily wore it was both regal and bohemian. She was still so beautiful.

"Twenty years on and she looks just the same," said Bee. "So we know one thing for a fact, then."

"What?" asked Maddy.

"She doesn't have kids."

Maddy didn't know that to be a fact at all. It was true that Bee's face and body had aged in a way that Maddy's had so far escaped. But who knew if that was kids or genes or eating the right kind of kale or what. As far as Maddy was concerned, they still had no firm facts about Emily. She could be a mother to triplets for all they knew. But the not knowing would all change tonight, upon Joseph's return.

"So does this mean you're going to sell the house now?" asked Bee.

"I think we'll have to," said Maddy. "It's not like we can buy her out. Even if we somehow could, this place is a money pit." Though undeniably elegant with its gingerbread trim, half-moon windows, and wraparound porch, her parents' house needed work. Expensive work. Pile House, named after William Pile, the Civil War general who had commissioned it, used to be a reason to stop and stare. But her parents had bitten off more than they could chew with the purchase of a grand dame Victorian, and maintenance while they'd lived there had been cursory at best. These days the fish-shingle cladding that wrapped the exterior was dotted with dark spots, and the stained-glass window above the front door was cracked in three places. Inside, the wallpaper was peeling, the window beams were gently rotting, and parts of the bedroom ceilings were about ready to buckle. And that was just what Maddy could see with a layman's eye. God only knew what they'd find when professional inspections began. Sometimes Maddy called the place Pile Pile, though only to Bee. Joseph didn't need any further ammunition for his ongoing argument that the place was a dump.

"Joseph still not getting paid, then?" asked Bee.

"I mean, dribs and drabs. Nothing you could actually live on."

"How does it all just dry up overnight?"

It hadn't been overnight, exactly. But the flowing faucet that was the cash from her husband's career in music production had been slowly inching closed over the last couple of years, and now it was practically rusted shut. Bee's was a good question, one that Maddy didn't really have an answer to. She didn't know where the money had gone. Probably on to an industry that had worked out how to stop its consumers from taking its product for free. These days her husband still took gigs, but instead of getting payment, he got promises of payment. Promises that rarely seemed to be fulfilled.

But now that they could finally sell the house, there'd be a glorious, if temporary, reprieve from being broke. Pile Pile was a hot mess, but this was still Southern California. Property prices hadn't been much to write home about the last time she'd lived in Myrtlebury, but in recent years there'd been a mad gold rush on property here as the good citizens of Los Angeles had finally discovered that there was one last picture-perfect, affordable suburb with well-rated schools. And all within commutable distance of where the good stuff happened. Burbank, Glendale, Pasadena all lost to rampant house prices, but Myrtlebury had remained. The last bastion. That is, until recently, when it had been discovered and then rapidly developed. The original brickwork on Main Street, the unspoiled mountain backdrop, the art deco fountains dotted around town. Once one developer had had the idea, all the rest had followed, and Myrtlebury had transitioned from badlands to the darling of the San Gabriel Valley almost overnight.

After the sale, she estimated there'd be enough to bail them out of their tax issues, pay off the mounting debts, and start again. It was lucky—*very lucky*—that Joseph had bumped into Emily. Otherwise they'd have been saddled with three more years of waiting. Three more years stuck in her parents' world with its constant reminders of what she'd lost. The scent of her mom's perfume that still drifted around the drawers of the dresser. The way Maddy always pointlessly took care not to use the next-to-last stair when going up to bed in case its squeak woke her parents. The fact that whenever she heard the opening front door catch on the floor in the hallway, she expected to hear one of them calling up to her. *Maddy! Are you there?* Yes. She was here. Still here. But not for much longer.

"What time are you expecting Joseph?" asked Bee.

"Ten or so."

"Right. Guess I'll miss him, then."

"You could always put the boys to bed and come back."

"Could," said Bee. But they both knew she wouldn't. If Maddy had pushed her on it, she'd have cited the exhaustion of motherhood as her excuse. But that wouldn't have been the real reason. "I saw more of him when he lived half-an-hour's drive away."

"That's not true." But it was true. Embarrassingly true.

"I mean, it's fine," Bee went on, her tone belying the fact that it was fine. "But it's the kids I feel bad for. They're missing out on an uncle." Maddy considered protesting that Fergus and Robbie had the most loving and involved of uncles in Joseph, but that would have been a lie. It was Maddy who chose the birthday and Christmas gifts, Maddy who bought the poor-quality wrapping paper from the boys for their school fundraisers, who bent her schedule to pick them up after school whenever Bee couldn't. And she often couldn't. But Maddy's diligence couldn't cover up the missed opportunities to wrestle with someone who was unafraid of pulling at little legs and arms too hard, to fart at full volume and then pretend their mother had done it, to fill them in on all the embarrassing stuff Bee had done as a kid. The uncle stuff.

In response, Maddy did what she did best. She topped up Bee's glass once more, and then she changed the subject.

"You, however, will be an amazing aunt," Maddy said, and raised her glass in a toast to Bee's future greatness in the aunting department.

"You mean, if my brother ever manages to knock you up, I'll be an amazing aunt," said Bee. "Oh my God, what if you're pregnant right now!"

Maddy raised an eyebrow as if to say: *Who knows.* Though she knew. There was no chance. She'd been tracking her ovulation over the past year with more intensity than she'd ever tracked any other nugget of data. She knew when an egg was due, when it was in situ, and when its unfertilized empty sack floated down into the detritus of her uterine lining. Joseph had been out of town the last time she'd ovulated, so there was zero possibility.

It'd all been too easy for Bee, who'd fallen effortlessly pregnant on her honeymoon and then again when Fergus was eighteen months old. Not so for Maddy and Joseph. They'd done it and done it and nothing. But the money would change things. Health insurance could be upgraded, decent consultants could be consulted, IVF could be procured if it came to it. Anything and everything was possible now that Emily had been found. Bee didn't know about the year of not trying but not preventing, followed by the year of intense trying. Maddy, who preferred to keep her cards close to her chest, hadn't planned on saying a word about any of it until Bee had come across Maddy's stash of pregnancy tests in the bottom drawer of the bathroom cabinet when she was digging for a tampon. Bee didn't know the half of it, which is why Maddy let the comment go—even though it stung.

"Well," said Maddy, lazily considering the last couple of inches left at the bottom of the bottle. "If there is a baby in the middle of my middle, it's well and truly pickled by now."

"It's fine," said Bee. "It doesn't count till after the six-week mark. It's too microscopic before that to get pickled."

"Are you sure?"

"Positive."

"In that case," Maddy said, pouring half the remaining wine into her glass and then offering up the rest of it to Bee.

"Go on, then," said Bee, after thinking better of it for half a second.

"It's okay. We've just had two glasses each, and this is just the end bit."

"Two *big* glasses."

"A glass is a glass is a glass."

"If you say so."

"I insist so."

"I love you, Maddy."

"I love you too, Bee." And she did. Maddy truly loved Bee, and Bee truly loved Maddy. It'd been that way for nearly thirty years. Maddy's friendship with Bee was the longest relationship she'd ever had. And now that her parents were gone, it was also her most valuable. Not including Joseph, of course. He was number one. He was her husband. But his sister was a photo-finish second.

They considered opening up another bottle, but evening had undeniably turned into nighttime, and so a tipsy Bee scooped up Fergus and Robbie and trailed around the block, back home. After she left, Maddy stuffed down some aging lasagna, watched some random documentary on the invention of the lie detector, then eventually made her way to her perch on the window seat to await Joseph's arrival. No matter what time of night he got home, she always made sure she was awake and waiting for him when he arrived. It was their thing. Something she'd done in the early days that had stuck.

She pulled up the blinds, and her gaze found the mountains again, their dusty black outline stark against the nighttime sky. Beautiful. Calming. Familiar. She closed her eyes and dropped her head against the windowpane, still warmed from the sticky, hot day. Emily. She hadn't had a moment to think it all through. She'd been too intent on the mechanics of communicating the whole thing to Bee to really examine what this meant. She felt vaguely bruised over the way Joseph had casually texted her about it and undeniably raw about the whole thing in general, but she couldn't say that she felt threatened. So much time had passed. Things wouldn't, *couldn't*, be the same as they were before. Not now that they were grown-ups.

But these were the last few moments she'd have alone to consider how she'd present herself to the world on this, to Joseph and to everyone else who'd want to know how she felt about the locating of her missing half sister. She had to think about how she'd present herself to them, and then to Emily when she finally showed up. Because she knew, there was no question, Emily *would* finally show up here, whispering her version of events into any ear that would listen. Maddy flipped the situation and looked at it from Joseph's vantage point, and things instantly got clear. She'd rise above it. Stick to her story and stay out of the ring, no matter how hard Emily tried to pull her in. She'd be welcoming but cool. Professional. Sisterly, even, if it looked like things were going that way. How else could she be?

Outside, she heard a car pause at the corner and then turn onto her street. Dozens of cars had stopped at the corner and then driven down her street that evening, and this one sounded no more special than any of the others, but for whatever reason, the sound of its engine tugged on her attention. She looked up and saw that a car had indeed stopped out front. It was a generic-looking blah of a vehicle. The streetlight outside their house was broken, but even had it been broad daylight, she wouldn't have recognized the car. She didn't recognize the guy driving it either, but when she looked to the back seat, there was Joseph, tapping out something on his phone. He was home. Excitement rushed through her chest, and she jumped up from the window seat, ran to the front door, and pulled it open.

Joseph slid out of the back, pulling his carryall out after him. Maddy stood framed in the doorway, waiting for him to see her. He gave what one might consider to be the flank of the car a hearty pat to see it off and then bent down, concentrating on some detail of his bag. Surely he saw her? Why didn't he look up? She was standing right there, backlit, on the porch of their home. Finally Joseph started up the pathway, giving her a nod of acknowledgment before breaking into a smile. There it was. The magic smile that lit his face up and made him who he was to her. She couldn't help it. Four steps before he got to the porch, she ran down the stairs and wrapped herself around him.

"I missed you," she said into his chest.

"Missed you more," said Joseph, pulling her in closer and giving her a hard kiss on her forehead. But then she stepped backward out of his hug, and they stood in the middle of the path, bag abandoned on the ground, Maddy silently asking him if it was all still okay. Him answering that it was never better. And then he kissed her again, this time on the lips, and like he meant it.

"Come on," he said eventually, picking his bag up with one hand, then pressing the other to the small of her back and urging her toward the front door. "Let's get you inside so I can say hello properly."

Twenty minutes later they broke apart, and as was the normal way of things, Maddy felt her eyes heavy with the need to close. Between the sex and the wine, she was more than ready to plunge into the deepest of sleeps. Joseph's eyes were already shut, and she could tell he was drifting. She willed her eyes to stay open for another couple of seconds. She'd meant it when she said she'd missed him. She always missed him. They'd been in each other's lives since she was five years old, but all the years layered on top of years of him being around hadn't dulled her need to look at him. It was as if she had an eternal deficit.

Even though Joseph wasn't yet forty, his dark hair was streaked with gray, like a series of shooting stars. The gray had come on a couple of years ago, or rather, that was when he'd shaved his head, and the gray underneath the curls had become more apparent. His hair had grown back partially now and, in her opinion, had just reached the point where he'd have to decide whether to hack it or go long again. She looked at his ear, the left one, and noticed how the skin of his face slightly pouched outward as it rested there. Some parts of him were older. Some parts of him just the same. The skin under his eyes and over his nose somehow looked just as it had when he'd been a child. What was that part of the face called? The word *underbrow* popped into her mind. Joseph had an unchanged underbrow. That wasn't a word.

She closed her own eyes and began to feel her consciousness warp and slide, but just before she went, the floor dropped away from her in a cruel rush, and she slammed her eyes back open. Awake. Heart pounding.

Emily.

"Hey," she said, nudging his shoulder, then bending down to give it a firm kiss when the nudge got no response. "Don't fall asleep on me." Sex with Joseph had a way of pushing everything else out, but finding Emily was not a conversation that could wait until tomorrow.

"I'm not," he said, turning to face her, eyes still closed.

"Joe, come on! What happened with Emily?" He forced his eyes to open, willing himself away from sleep and back into the world of the waking. She could tell he wanted to tell her as much as she wanted to hear it.

"She's been living in New York," he said, blinking.

"All along?"

"Yeah, I think so. New coast, new start kind of thing."

"And you just saw her at some party? Wasn't it a work party?"

"She's a friend of Jodi's."

"Jodi *Khan*?"

"Yeah."

"How on earth is she friends with Jodi Khan?" Jodi Khan was the famousish singer Joseph had been in New York to record. Maddy had been hopeful that the fact he was now working with a singer she'd heard of might translate into actual payment.

"I don't know. I guess they know the same people in New York. Emily's different now."

"Different how?"

"She's together. She's really got herself together."

"Did you tell her we've been trying to find her?"

"I did tell her."

"And?"

"Yeah, she had no idea. She's just been doing her own thing. I don't think it crossed her mind to check in."

"Did you tell her about Mom and Dad?" This was the major question, after all.

"I did. She said she was sorry."

"Oh *really?*" said Maddy, and then reminding herself of her vow earlier, drained the harshness from her voice. "And how was she?"

"She seemed good. Grown-up. It's actually incredible how normal she is after everything she's been through." He paused here, and Maddy could tell he wanted her to press him for specifics. However, specifics were the very last thing she wanted, and so she remained silent. "Kids generally don't course correct out of juvie. She told me the stats. Seventy percent of the kids go back to crime. Another ten percent attempt suicide. Bleak stuff. She was in there with actual gang members, you know?"

"Gangs?" She'd thought very little about what her sister may or may not have experienced after she'd been extracted from Maddy's life almost as quickly as she'd been thrust into it. But the couple of times she had thought about where she'd gone, she'd pictured the facility as being more mildly correctional than jail-like.

"Yeah. Pretty wild. It'd never happen these days."

"Why not? I mean, she pleaded guilty, and so she went to juvie. What's so different now?"

"They shut them all down last year. They don't work, and they're too cruel. She told me she was in her cell twenty-three hours a day. Day in, day out. A face full of pepper spray if the wardens didn't like the way she answered their questions. When riots broke out, the kids would throw their crap through the bars and—"

"Did she ask about me?" She knew this interruption sounded ego-centric, but it was less about wanting to know the answer and more about making the information stop. It was too hard to hear.

"She did."

"And?"

"She gave me her number. She wants you to call her. When you're ready."

"Great," said Maddy, managing to inject her voice with more plea-sure than she felt. "And you told her about the house?"

"Yeah," said Joseph, that magic smile finding its way back to his face. "Farewell, money troubles."

"Farewell, indeed," said Maddy. They could have sold the house before now, even without finding Emily. They could have passed it on to the highest bidder, paid off the inheritance taxes, and then stashed Emily's half with the county comptroller. But if after five years Emily hadn't claimed it, what Maddy estimated to be about four hundred thousand dollars would have then slid into the coffers of the state of California. So they'd hung on, knowing that if they could get to five years without Emily being found, they could claim it all. And here they'd sat ever since Maddy's father had died, hoping for Emily to be found while hoping she'd never show up at all. But now she had been located—on Jodi Khan's rooftop of all places. The paradox had reached a natural conclusion, and both sisters were about to be at least a few hundred thousand better off.

"Wait here," said Joseph. "This calls for a toast." He slid out of bed, pulled on his discarded boxers, and headed downstairs. A couple of minutes passed. Then what felt like another five slid by. Maddy's eyes began to draw closed again. She turned over in bed, noticing that her legs were still pleasantly weak from sex. Her cheek found a new cool spot on the pillow, but instead of letting herself sink down into its softness, she forced herself out of bed, pulled on Joseph's T-shirt from the floor, and padded downstairs.

She found him in the kitchen, clearing away the remains of Fergus and Robbie's dinner. Chicken nuggets, peas, tater tots. The baking sheet was still half full. Maddy always cooked as if she had five nephews instead of two.

"You can leave all that," said Maddy when he turned around and saw her watching him from the doorway.

"I'm nearly done," he said, emptying the remains into the trash. "You had people over?" asked Joseph.

"Bee and the kids," she said, wondering if he thought she'd feed "people" chicken nuggets and tater tots. And what "people" would these have been? She hadn't reconnected with her old school friends since they'd moved back to Myrtlebury. She had Bee. Bee was all she needed. He knew that.

"She spends more time at our house than her own," he said, and hit the dishwasher button harder than he needed to. She should have lied.

"What shall we toast with?" asked Maddy. Distract, divert, deflect. It worked with her students. It worked with her husband. It worked with everyone. "We have scotch. That champagne."

"Scotch sounds about right," said Joseph. Maddy made her way into the living room and made her selection from the two Scotch whiskys in the bar. She chose the eighteen-year-old single malt, an Oban. Her father's. Not one for knocking back on a casual end-of-day basis. By the time she walked back into the kitchen, Joseph had two glasses in his hands, half-filled with ice. When he saw she had the Oban, he shook out the majority of the ice, took the scotch from Maddy without comment, and then poured. Maddy knew she'd only take half a sip, eighteen-year-aged or no. Scotch was the last thing she needed on top of half a bottle of wine.

"To Emily," said Joseph. Despite her earlier lecture to herself, Maddy felt her lips tighten for half a second before she could ease them into a happy smile.

"To Emily," returned Maddy. They clinked glasses, and Maddy took her half sip but stopped short as she felt something snag her lip. She pulled the glass back from her mouth. There was a chip on the rim. Sharp, but thankfully not so sharp that she'd cut herself.

"What?" asked Joseph.

"I almost cut my lip. This glass is chipped," she said, looking at it again. She recognized the glass. Her parents had had it for years. Not one of their "good" glasses but certainly one of the more sturdy ones. It'd been around for decades. "I wonder when that happened," said Joseph, picking it up to examine it. Still rubbing her lip where she'd almost nicked it, she opened the cupboard to look for her dad's Waterfords. They should be using those for the Oban anyway. She couldn't imagine what her dad would say about her and Joseph drinking Oban out of one of the old familiars. Nothing good. Joseph normally knew better. She opened the cupboard next to the sink, where they were kept. Not there.

"Where are Dad's whiskey glasses?" she asked. Joseph had grabbed another tumbler out of the cupboard and had already transferred her drink into it.

"You mean the crystal ones?" he said.

"Yes! Where did they go?"

"One of them smashed, remember?"

"No. When was that?"

"A couple of months ago? I dropped it. I told you about it."

"You never told me you broke one of my dad's glasses."

"Of course I did."

"So where's the other one?"

"You don't remember what you said?"

"Evidently no."

"You told me to trash it. You said it made you sad to see one of them on its own without the other. And that if you couldn't have both of them, you'd rather have nothing at all."

She froze. She didn't remember saying that, but it sounded exactly like the sort of thing she would say. Hadn't she actually said that about something else once? An earring. He'd probably broken both glasses, forgotten to tell her, and then made up this story to make it sound better.

"You don't need to lie to me, Joseph. It's only a stupid glass. I don't care."

"I know," he said. "Why would I lie about it?" And he was right. Covering up an error with something close to plausible was more her style. Joseph owned his mistakes just as confidently as any other man who'd never been taken to task for them. So then why didn't she remember?

"I'm going to take a shower. Wash off the New York," he said, and dumped the rest of the scotch into the sink, the remaining ice knocking against the porcelain. Then he kissed the top of her head and moved toward the stairs. Maddy watched him leave, now noticing the smells emanating from his dirty T-shirt she'd pulled on. Hot dogs. Onions. Street grime. New York indeed. She picked the last two ice cubes out of her scotch, throwing them in the sink after Joseph's, then downed everything left in two hard gulps.

CHAPTER 2

MADDY

The locating of Emily had triggered a new flurry of estate paperwork, and over the last week, figuring it out had taken up all of Maddy's spare hours. Unable to get her father's ancient scanner to work, she'd decided to hand-deliver the documents she'd had to sign to the lawyer's before class. She hadn't had much better of a time with the printer than with the scanner. It was a shitty printer. But weren't they all? When it wasn't busy complaining about its being in an error state, it often liked to print sheets out of order and sometimes slip in random blank sheets just because. To top it all off, she'd sent everything to print twice before realizing there was no paper stacked in the machine's flimsy little tray—which was truly ridiculous because she *knew* she'd filled it the day before. Joseph must have used the paper, but for what godly purpose she didn't know. And she knew that if she asked him, he'd just deny taking the paper or needing paper in his life at all, so what was the point. The whole printing thing had had her so frazzled today that at one point, as she desperately flipped printed pages back and forth, she swore they *all* had turned blank. It would be her undoing. This printer.

Eventually the document came together, and she signed it, then grabbed her workbag and purse and headed for her Jeep. But when she got there, she couldn't find her keys. This happened. It happened so often that she'd unconsciously baked a fifteen-minute buffer into her routine so she had enough time to walk to work if she had to. She let herself back in the house with one of the many spare keys she kept hidden for occasions like these, but her frantic search yielded nothing. She resigned herself to a long and hot schlep, but just as she was walking out the door for the second time, she slipped back into the kitchen and checked the microwave. She'd found her keys in there once, inside a half-composed cup of coffee. Even now, sometimes random grounds would work their way out of one of the ridges in the key ring and make her hands smell like she'd recently had them submerged in coffee beans. But her keys weren't in the microwave today. They were nowhere.

As she walked, the sun bit hard on her exposed shoulders and on the part in her hair. She'd forgotten to bring a hat. She was dressed for her afternoon of teaching tiny tots—and some not-so-tiny tots—ballet and already knew she was going to start her first class with sweat stains on her leotard. When it was like this, heat was normally all she could focus on, but today the image of Emily framed by the New York skyline sat in her mind, unmoving. The compact Craftsmans gave way to the blockier businesses and restaurants on Main Street, and eventually she reached the town's central crosswalk, the air-conditioned offices of Gonzales, Rae, and Swanson just on the other side. As she stood, overheated and waiting for the lights to change, her eyes drifted toward the waiting traffic, and she felt a leap of recognition as she saw Joseph's BMW join the back of the line. The car was the last relic of Joseph's financial glory days. Not long after he'd first gotten it, he'd had it fitted with ceramic brakes at what was these days a heartbreaking eight thousand dollars. Apparently the ceramic ones got less dusty, because God forbid the ultimate driving machine be bothered by a little dust. As she watched him, she wondered briefly if there was a way to swap the brakes out and get the eight grand back.

Joseph was four cars back, and he hadn't seen her. The lights changed, but instead of crossing the street, some instinct had Maddy stay exactly where she was. Joseph had left early to go hiking. One of the advantages of gig life was that he could hit the trails during the week when no one else was around. During the summer, he normally got back late morning before the heat really got going, and they'd usually cross paths as she left for work. But it was now early afternoon. Had he had an errand to run in the interim? She was about to wave when she noticed someone sitting in the car next to him. And then she saw exactly who the passenger was, and her wave froze in place.

Even without having seen the rooftop photo, Maddy would have recognized her. Because Bee was right, she looked exactly the same. The rough edges of teenhood were now blended out, but otherwise it was Emily. Her sister.

The lights changed again, and the line of cars drove on, Joseph's bringing up the rear. As they neared, Maddy took a step backward with half an idea about slinking inside the shop behind her. But she soon saw there was no need to hide—both their eyes were fixed on the road ahead, blind to anything outside the insulating bubble of the car. Neither one of them noticed the woman staring at them from the side of the road. For a few more seconds her eyes followed the back of his car as he drove up the street, clocking the ever-familiar dent on the back of his bumper. And then she tore her eyes away and forced herself to cross. The edges around her vision seemed lighter than they had been just a moment ago, and in contrast to the heat of the day, the skin over her face suddenly felt like an ice sheet. She picked up the pace, determined not to pass out in the middle of the intersection.

To see Emily here in Myrtlebury, though jarring, was no big surprise. She already knew she was in Los Angeles. For work, allegedly. As predicted, she couldn't keep away. The three of them had made plans to have dinner that night, or rather, Joseph had made the plans. But why would Joseph not mention that he was going to see Emily beforehand?

She supposed he wasn't obliged to tell her whenever he hung out with someone. Maddy certainly didn't notify Joseph every time she hung out with *his* sister. That would have been one constant notification. But then Bee hadn't been out of contact for the last twenty years; the last two of those, missing.

She reached the other side of the street, made it to a shady spot next to the front door of the lawyer's office, and sank into a squat. She needed a minute before she went inside and faced people. Had that really been Emily? She hadn't thought about her sister in years and years, but in the last week, she'd taken up more of her headspace than she had in the last decade. When she was a kid, Maddy had always known she had a half sister called Emily who lived far away. Her parents had never hidden it from her—though they hadn't exactly been brimming with intricate details either. She'd never been shown a photo. Never spoken to her on the phone. When Maddy had asked why they never went to see her sister and why her sister never came to visit, her dad had told her she lived too far away for any of that to be possible. And Maddy didn't think to question it. The questioning might have happened when she was older, but by that time, Emily had arrived. And after she'd arrived, the reason for any delay in Emily joining their family would have been the last question Maddy ever would have asked. She was too busy wishing she'd never arrived at all. But back when Maddy had been six, then eight, and even twelve, she'd happily believed that if her father said her sister lived so far away that she could never visit, then it must be true. What other possible reason could there be for a sister not coming to stay? The lack of letters from her sister was harder to understand. She wrote letters to Emily and gave them to her father to send, and he assured her he always mailed each and every one of them, but Maddy never got a letter or a photo in return.

The day that Emily had first shown up had been another gruelingly hot one. Maddy had been in the treehouse, reading, waiting. Normally she'd be inside on such a hot day, but there was very little her mom could have said that would have persuaded her inside that morning. She wanted to see her sister the moment she arrived, and from up in the treehouse, she'd be able to see them coming from three blocks away. However, Maddy's book turned out to be more interesting than waiting for her sister's arrival, and it wasn't till a car door slammed down below that she noticed her father's car was parked out front.

Emily.

Maddy practically threw herself out the treehouse door, her feet and hands barely touching the rungs of the ladder in her eagerness to reach the ground. She jumped past the last few and ran over to the front gate.

"Go back inside, Maddy," said her dad.

"No. I want to see her."

"Sophie," called her dad. But Maddy's mother didn't come.

"Why isn't she getting out of the car?" said Maddy, who could only see a dark pile of curls pressed up against the front car window.

"She's tired now. You can see her later," said her father.

"It doesn't matter if she's tired. She'll want to see me. I'm her sister."

"Sophie," her dad yelled again, but before Maddy's mom could appear, Emily turned and looked out the car window. She stared at the house with dead eyes, unmoved by the sight of picture-perfect Pile House. Then she looked back at Maddy, and Maddy saw why her dad had wanted her to go back inside. Maddy felt her knees give slightly underneath her. She'd just seen Emily's face for the first time. And it was a holy mess.

Emily didn't come out of her room for the next two days. Maddy noticed the tray on the floor outside her room always seemed to have a full bowl of cold tomato soup on it. Even though she'd been lectured at length about staying out of her sister's room, on the third day, Maddy snuck in there after she got home from school. Her mom was on the phone with the doctor, Dad was still at school for parent-teacher conferences, and so she seized her opportunity. As she eased the door open, she was hit with a heavy, dark odor, and she felt her face automatically crumple with disgust. Maddy hadn't smelled this before. All she knew was that the smell was sharp and that it was bad. Unfresh but interesting. Maddy took another sniff. The room hadn't smelled like that last week when she and her mom had been getting it ready. A week ago, it had been all potpourri and freshly vacuumed carpets. She walked over to the bed and looked down at the lump inside—half obscured by blankets. Then she quietly pulled the covers down so that she could see her sister's face. It looked different. Halfway to healed, which somehow made it look even worse than when she'd first arrived. The clearly defined blotches of navy were now vague washes of green and yellow that somehow made her face look dirty. Her lip did look a bit better, though. Emily was still sleeping, even though it was almost dinnertime. Maybe she was just sleeping because the blinds were still closed. Perhaps if Maddy opened them a little, she'd wake up?

Maddy fiddled with the blinds till she found the exact two slats that she was looking for. She pulled them apart and let the strong afternoon light shine right across Emily's face. After a few seconds, Emily's eyelids started to spasm in irritation. Bingo. Maddy pulled the cord and flipped the blinds, instantly letting the brightness and heat of the day in to merge with the funky stink of the room. Maddy was momentarily distracted by the thousands of dust motes suddenly visible in the air, but then her eyes sank to the floor, where she saw a pile of black fuzz by the head of Emily's bed. What *was* that? It looked just like a dead stray cat she'd once seen by the swings at the park. Maddy made her way over and squatted down to take a closer look. She picked the clump up in one piece by a tuft sticking up from its center. It was hair. A whole lump of hair. How had it gotten matted up like that? She stood up and looked down at her sister again, this time noticing that there was a raw spot on the side of her forehead and that the curls she'd seen smushed up against the window in her dad's car were gone. Someone, she presumed it was Emily, had hacked off all her hair and then dumped it at the side of her bed. The hair left on her scalp was long and short at the same time and stuck out in every direction. Did she not care? Finally, the new light in the room began to register, and Emily half opened her eyes. Maddy quickly pressed her lips together to hold in a scream. The white of Emily's eye—the one with the bruises around it—was now completely red, like it had filled up with blood. Maddy felt her entire body yearning to turn and run from the room, but it was too late now. Emily was looking right at her.

"I'm sorry."

"I was asleep," said Emily.

"I know, but I just wanted to say hi," she said, backing away from Emily and taking a seat on the end of the bed. "I'm your sister."

"You don't look like you're my sister. You've got red hair," said Emily, still groggy. Maddy didn't mention that she'd never imagined her sister having a red eye.

"I look like my mom. Do you look like your mom? You don't really look like Dad."

"He's not my dad," said Emily, rolling over onto one elbow. She slipped her hand under her pillow, withdrew a pack of cigarettes, then pulled one out along with a lighter. She lit up, sucked hard on its end, and tipped her head back to blow the smoke out above her in a hard, long line. Maddy was pretty certain that none of this was allowed. But she said nothing; she was too fixated on what Emily had said about their dad.

"He's *not* your dad?" she asked, confused. This was one of the very few definitive facts she had been given: that she and Emily shared a father. That her dad had been together with someone before he was married to her mom, and that his daughter from that relationship was Emily. And then, of course, that none of them had seen each other because Emily had lived so far away. But now her mom had died, and the rest of her mom's family was too busy to take care of her, so she'd finally made the epic journey, and here she was. Where Emily's bruises had come from, Maddy hadn't had any firm answers on, but the other facts of the matter had been made clear. But if Emily was going to start dismantling all the things that Maddy thought she *did* know for sure, then this was going to get really hard to piece together.

"He's only my dad by biology," said Emily.

"And he's my dad too, by biology," said Maddy. She didn't know what Emily meant by "by biology"—maybe it was just a way to refer to fathers. "And that means you're my sister. My half sister."

"True."

"By biology," said Maddy. Emily huffed a half laugh at that and then started to close her eyes again. "Don't go back to sleep. I've been waiting days for you to wake up. Where were you living before here?"

"Nowhere you want to know about," she replied.

"I do want to know," said Maddy. "I want to know what you've been doing all this time. I've missed you."

"How can you have missed me, you've never even met me."

"I missed you before I even met you."

"You're sweet," said Emily.

"What was your other family like? Were they sweet?"

"No. They were not sweet."

"I'm so sorry to hear that," said Maddy. It was her fallback phrase when she didn't know what to say to someone who seemed sad about something. She'd heard her mom trot it out, and it seemed to cover all the bases. "But you're with us now, so things will be better for you."

"For now."

"For always."

"For until your mom and dad get tired of me."

"They're your mom and dad too. And I'm your sister. And I'll never get tired of you. Bee has a brother. Everyone else in my class has at least one brother or sister. And now I've got a sister too."

"Having a brother or sister isn't this extremely special experience you think it is," said Emily. Maddy was quiet. How did Emily know that? Did Emily have other brothers and sisters? Some that she'd had to leave behind? Suddenly she didn't want to know. She wanted to be the only sister Emily had. Special. She wanted their newly forged family unit to be whole. Insular. She didn't want anyone hanging around the edges claiming Emily as theirs. Even if they *were* living far away. "My mom has a brother, and he's an asshole. I wish he wasn't alive."

Asshole. What would her parents say if Maddy had called anyone an *asshole*? She had no idea. She'd have to try it and see.

"Not all brothers are assholes," said Maddy. "Bee has a brother, and he's nice."

"Who's Bee?"

"Bee's my best friend. She lives in the house behind ours. We're all going to live together when we're grown-up."

"Who's going to live together?"

"Me, my future husband, and our five children, Bee and her brother Joseph, and you too if you like. We're going to live here and keep chickens in the front yard. We can all have our own rooms, and you can make the soup—if you like soup."

"The soup?"

"Yes. A big pot of soup. Enough for everyone. That would be your job. All you'd have to do is fill up the soup pot every morning and then make sure it was hot all day. Maybe feed the chickens too."

"I think I could do that," said Emily, rolling over in the bed and smiling. It was the first time Maddy had seen her smile, and it was dazzling, despite the fact that she could only use half her mouth because of the stitches in her lip.

"And maybe make some banana sandwiches too," added Maddy. "They're my favorite."

"Banana sandwiches sound better than soup. I don't really like soup," she said, and lifted up the covers for Maddy to get in bed with her. Maddy took one look at her sister's body and deduced that Emily must not like any food at all. She was rail thin. Maddy could see the outline of her ribs as high up as underneath her collarbone. It wasn't normal. She knew that much. But then so far, nothing about Emily was. Now that Maddy had opened the blinds, the air in the room had heated up, and Maddy didn't feel like getting under hot blankets. Still, she moved to get in. Just to be friendly.

Emily shifted over, and Maddy slid in beside her. The sheets were piping hot from where Emily had been lying on them, and when Emily pulled the blankets back, more of that strange dark smell wafted out from under the blankets. They both lay there in silence looking up at the ceiling, Emily tugging on a worn piece of leather looped around her wrist. Maddy noticed a strange pattern scattered over Emily's hands and down her wrists. As if one hundred ants had erupted out of her thumb and left tracks as they marched up toward her elbows. She also saw that her nails weren't much more than stubs on the ends of her fingers with blobs of Wite-Out applied where her mom usually had nail polish.

"What are those marks on your hands?"

"That's my stick and poke."

"What's that?"

"That's what you call tattoos that you do yourself."

"How do you do a tattoo yourself?"

"Not much to it. Just a sewing needle and some ink from a pen. I can do one for you if you like?" Maddy didn't answer, just felt herself clamp her hand around her wrist as if trying to protect it from a needle. Her armpits started to prickle with sweat. She didn't know if that was because of the stuffy room or the thought of her brand-new sister pricking at her wrists with a needle. "Or I guess you could just tell me more about these chickens instead," said Emily. And so Maddy did. She also told her about the swimming pool they'd build and how they'd all have their own personalized mailboxes, each one painted their own color. Emily had asked who was going to earn the money, and Maddy had told her that Bee had offered to suck it up and get a proper job to pay the mortgage. Probably as a vet. Joseph and Maddy, and Maddy's future husband, were going to earn extra money selling chicken eggs at the market and also tickets for the pool to the neighbors. Maybe Emily could set up a stall selling banana sandwiches too if things got tight. Emily said that would be fine.

"So tell me about your other family," said Maddy. She'd changed her mind. She *did* want to know about those potential other siblings after all. If Emily had siblings, then did that make them her siblings too? Maddy needed to know. After all, if more of them started showing up here over the course of the next few years, maybe they'd eventually all have to double up in their rooms in the future state of Pile House. These were the kinds of things you needed to take into consideration when making plans.

"What other family?"

"The family you had before you came here."

"I didn't have another family. Just my mom."

"You said you had an uncle."

"He was an asshole. Not an uncle."

"Were you in a car accident?"

"No. Why?"

"Someone at school had bruises on her face like you after she was in a car accident. I thought there'd been an accident, with your mom?"

"It wasn't that kind of accident."

"What, then?"

"I don't want to talk about it."

"Okay." Maddy decided she'd leave it for the moment and then ask again in a minute. That normally worked with her mother. "Why didn't you write back?"

"Write back to what?"

"My letters."

"What are you talking about?"

"I wrote you letters."

"I never saw any letters. The only mail Mom and I ever got from California was a check."

"Why did you get a check?"

"That's what you do if you have a baby with someone but don't want to stick around to be a father. You send a check."

"My dad sent your mom a check?"

"Yup."

"Like he was paying her to look after you?"

"Kind of."

"That's weird."

"Isn't it just."

"So what happened to your mom?"

"They didn't tell you?"

"No."

"It doesn't matter. It was a long time ago."

"No it wasn't. It just happened."

"It happened a year ago."

"Your mom's been dead for a year? So where have you been all this time?"

"I told you that I don't want to talk about it."

"Will your uncle come to visit, or is it too far away?" said Maddy, who wasn't slow to connect the dots on this one.

"Will you fucking shut up about my uncle!" yelled Emily. Maddy hadn't heard anyone use *that* word before.

"Why?" asked Maddy. She couldn't help herself. Emily didn't reply. She simply turned over in the bed, grabbed at Maddy's school shirt, and squeezed the tiny bud of breast that was right there, hard. She squeezed it until Maddy started to cry. And only then did she let go. Maddy clutched her throbbing booblet. It felt as if Emily had torn it off. As if she'd broken some delicate structure inside that tender dome. Maddy's school reports often said, "Talks too much." Her mom defended the trait as inquisitive. Her dad didn't say much about it, but she could tell he wasn't a fan of her endless questions. She'd never realized that talking

29

could have landed her in this much trouble. Perhaps this was why everyone had been trying to get her to shut up her whole life.

"Stop crying," said Emily. "You're making my bed wet."

"It's already wet," said Maddy, crying even harder. "Why did you squeeze me like that?"

"'Cause you were making me talk about things I didn't want to talk about."

"I didn't make you."

"Um. You kind of did."

"Did not!"

"Shut up yelling!" said Emily, and shoved Maddy's shoulder so hard that she smacked her temple into the corner of the dresser.

"Ow!" screamed Maddy, and started crying even harder, her hand clamped over her head. Emily pushed Maddy again, and this time she fell out of the bed and onto her hip on the floor. *"Mom!"* she screamed, and one second later Sophie had burst through the door and come running in.

Somehow it had been Maddy who had gotten in trouble for that entire scene. Not Emily. Emily was to be given the benefit of the doubt that first time, her mom had said. And then, seemingly a good many times after that first time, until Maddy had presumed that Emily was never going to run out of second chances. Maddy learned to hate her sister, and her dad just withdrew from the entire mess of it all. But Sophie, Maddy's mom, kept on trying. A little longer than the others, anyway, until Emily stomped hard enough over the tender shoots of love that Sophie had been trying to grow for her, and she turned her back on Emily too. The only person who didn't get pushed out or stomped on or sworn at was Joseph.

CHAPTER 3

EMILY

2002

The first time Emily saw Joseph was at the skate park. Emily didn't own a skateboard. In her opinion, watching was oftentimes better than doing. She'd been told before now that that was a weird way to approach life, but on that day, no one in the bowl seemed to think it was weird that the girl with the hacked-up hair was watching from the side rails. Or if they did, they didn't say anything. Polite valley boys, she supposed. They hadn't always been as polite back in New Jersey. There, leaning on the rails got her yelled at. But she still did it anyway. The vibrations of the wheels through her body as they roared and scraped over the concrete, the smack of bodies and limbs as they fell to the ground—it was how she got to feel something intense without having to risk a thing herself. It was her favorite place to be. Of course, it wasn't quite the same in Myrtlebury. The lack of river and Manhattan skyline views kind of took the edge off. And the flat heat was ever present, to remind you where you were and where you were not. But the railings were still railings. And she could still lean on them and feel.

That first day at the park, she instantly picked Joseph out as the only one worth watching. Not because he was the best, but because he was beautiful. Ghostlike and grounded all at once. Just like her mom had been. He didn't look her way once, though she watched him for hours—his face turned up to the fading sunlight and his unbuttoned shirt trailing behind him. Obliviousness itself. When he finally spoke to her, it was nothing more than a quick request for her to step back from the rail for a second. The directive was quick but well-mannered, and she was struck by how this way-too-cool, beautiful boy was so affable, even though he really didn't need to be. She'd stepped back, and he'd skated around the bowl and then downward, weaving to and fro, working up exactly the right speed, and then he'd gone for the rail right where she'd just been standing. He nailed it the first time. Leaped up out of the concrete pit and grabbed hold of the railing with one hand and was up and into a perfect handstand. His board skyward over his head, the rest of him underneath in a perfect line. Then he'd let go as easily as letting go of a door handle and smoothed back onto the ramp. He wasn't wearing a helmet, and if he'd messed up, he could have killed himself. It was clear that he either didn't care or was that sure of himself, and it was in that moment that she fell in love with him.

She watched him until midnight. Most of the kids drifted off around ten, but not Joseph. And not Emily. He kept swirling, soaring, flipping his board like he had magnetic control over the thing. If he'd been looking, he'd have noticed he had magnetic control over the girl watching him too. But he wasn't looking, yet. When he was done, he skated up and out of the bowl, and as if some kind of trance had been broken, he noticed her.

"Hey," he said.

"Hey."

"What are you doing out here? It's late."

"I'm watching you," she said. She'd decided that there was no need for her to try to act cool. He was cool enough for both of them.

"Do I know you?" he asked.

"I'm Maddy's sort-of sister."

"So *you're* Ivan's mysterious bastard offspring."

"Is that what everyone's calling me?" The tag didn't bother her particularly. But it was insightful. Everyone had been so *nice* since she'd arrived. Emily had a feeling the "nice" was like a thin-crusted layer on top of a molten lava flow: if she dared to apply any weight to it, she'd fall right through into what was really going on and get burned alive.

"Nah. That's just what Bee and I called you when we first heard. I won't call you that anymore now that I've met you."

"Comforting."

"I'm Joseph," he said, putting the board under his arm and extending a long, skinny arm to shake her hand.

"Emily."

"I know. Let me walk you home." And with that offer, she fell in love with him all over again.

In Emily's experience, walking naturally lent itself to talking. Walking had been the only time she and her mother had been able to get into a decent conversation, but on that first walk home, Joseph and Emily had started off silent. The silence went on for an entire block, and she'd just decided that actually she was totally fine with silence, when he spoke.

"What happened to your mom? All we heard was that she's dead. Was it cancer? Or something?" So it seemed like Joseph wasn't big on small talk. No bad thing in her opinion. Sometimes she'd listen in on Maddy and Sophie talking—making words for half an hour, and at the end of it, they'd not have said a thing. Not divulged one repeatable fact.

"Something. Not cancer."

"What, then?"

"She killed herself."

He stopped walking and turned to look at her then. Looked at her properly like no one had dared look at her since her mom had done what she had done. As if Emily had been infected with her mother's mental illness and if they made full-on eye contact with her, they'd catch it too. And as he kept on looking at her like that, like she was a person it was entirely safe to look at, she felt her entire chest relax. Tension she didn't know she'd been holding on to rushed out of every joint, as if she'd been tied together with a bundle of wires that had just become unraveled. Seeing her body sag, he grabbed her under the arms.

"Whoa. You okay?"

"Can we sit down for a minute?"

"Sure," he said. And so there on the sidewalk they sat, the moon high in the sky, their backs up against someone's white picket fence. Joseph put his feet up on his skateboard, and Emily thought he looked pretty comfy like that, so she put her feet on it too. Their legs were exactly the same length, so the skateboard-as-a-footstool concept worked out. And then Joseph picked up her hand, and she noticed that it felt strong and that he had the same sort of hands as Ivan. The same long fingers, but with none of the awkward bony parts.

"So, tell me," he said, and she decided she would. She had to tell someone.

"She stepped out onto the freeway, at one in the morning. Right in front of a freight truck. She was drunk. But she meant it."

"God."

"I know."

"Are you sure she meant it? If she'd been drinking . . . How drunk was she?"

"Not drunk enough to do it without meaning to. She'd talked about it before when she was super down."

"To you?"

"Yeah."

"About how she wanted to kill herself?"

"Yup."

"That's messed up."

"Isn't it just."

"Did you tell someone?"

"Who would I tell? Her friends knew, and they did nothing about it. She had meds. What else was there to be done?"

"So she had depression?"

"She spent a lot of time in bed. She said she had headaches, but that wasn't it. Headaches don't make you cry like that. Things were better when she took her meds. But every now and then, she'd try to 'detox,' and that's when she'd start talking about midnight strolls on the freeway."

"Did your dad know how bad it was?"

"I didn't meet Ivan till I got sent to live here."

"Are you serious?"

"Yup. A complete stranger."

"You never even *met* him?"

"Mom showed me a couple of photos once. I honestly didn't think about him that much. It wasn't like it was some big mystery. They were together and then they weren't. He said he wasn't interested in raising a child with her. She hired a lawyer who made him send a check each month. And that was how it was. No phone calls, no gifts. I don't know if he ever saw a photo of me. Zero interest."

"But you're here now."

"Until he can figure out another way to get rid of me. It's definitely not doing much for his kudos around town, having me here."

"Did your mom hate him?"

"Of course she did."

"She told you that?"

"It was her favorite topic. It was as if she still couldn't believe he'd left her."

"Did he break her heart, then?"

"No. I think she just never got over the fact that she'd been left with a kid to look after on her own. She never forgave him for being able to just walk away."

"So why didn't she just get an abortion? Sorry. That's a messed-up thing to ask."

"Apparently he didn't give her any reason to think that he wasn't going to stay. And then when she was too far gone to abort, he left. I think his plan was for her to give me up for adoption."

"But she didn't."

"I asked her once why she hadn't."

"What did she say?"

"That she was still making up her mind."

"Seriously?"

"I know. She thought she was hilarious."

"And what about your uncle? Same sense of humor?"

"You heard about all that?"

"Not really. Just that you'd been there awhile before you came here. And that it didn't work out."

"One way of saying it."

"What happened?" he asked. She didn't answer immediately. Instead, she ran her tongue over the hairline crack in her tooth at the front and made the decision to glide right over what happened. Marco didn't get to seep into what she had now and destroy it. He didn't belong here.

"He was an asshole is what happened. So I torched his motorcycle."

"You *what?*" Joseph turned to face her, outwardly more delighted than horrified, but she could tell a part of him was wondering if he'd bitten off more than he could chew with her. He had. But there was no need to let him know so soon.

"I stuffed a dishcloth in the gas tank, lit it, and pretty soon the whole thing was a wall of flames."

"You, my friend, are beyond badass."

"Thanks," she said, worried at his use of *my friend*—wondering if telling him what she'd done had nudged her out of the girlfriend zone.

"And then he kicked you out?"

"Kind of," she said. After the fire department had arrived, they'd taken one look at the state of her and she'd been placed in foster care within the hour. Then someone figured out she had a father, and two days after that, she'd arrived in Myrtlebury.

"Well, if it got you here, I'm glad you torched it."

"Me too," she said, and it was true. The way she already felt about Joseph, the beautiful ache of it, made everything she'd gone through to get here worth it.

"I'm sorry you had to deal with a group of shits for relatives. You deserve better than that. My parents are pretty useless too if it's any consolation."

"How so?"

"They don't care. Everyone at school's always going on about their parents being all over them, but mine don't give a crap."

"Ivan's barely spoken a word to me since I got here."

"I don't think he speaks to anyone if he can help it."

"Perhaps. Maddy's thrown a few cryptic comments my way about him being a normal father till I came along. She thinks it's all my fault that her dad no longer wants to tickle her and play baseball in the park. She's getting too old for all that crap is the real truth of it."

"I think they all stop caring once we get pubes and opinions."

"Are your parents wrapped up in each other?" she asked, thinking about how Ivan and Sophie were.

"God no. They barely even touch each other. I remember Dad holding my mom's hand once when she heard her sister died. Other than that, zero contact. When I see how other parents are with each other—like Ivan and Sophie—it's obvious something's not right. I want to be like those two when I'm married. Like it means something."

"Right? Otherwise, why bother?"

"Exactly."

Emily could tell that Sophie and Ivan were holding back a little in front of her. But even with them doing that, she could see that what they had was the real deal. She'd walked in on them kissing more than once. Real kissing. In the moment, she'd found it disgusting, of course, but she got what Joseph meant when he said he wanted to be in something like that when he got married.

And then, as if talking about Sophie and Ivan and what they had had given Joseph permission to try to find what this love thing was all about, he kissed her. She could tell he wanted to, even before she looked over at him. It wasn't her first kiss. But it was the first time it meant something. As he kissed her, he squeezed her gently on the back of her neck before moving his hands up through what was left of her hair, his fingertips gently tugging on the roots. She'd been considering shaving the rest of it off after she'd made a pig's ear of hacking the mats out, but in that moment she decided against it. Maybe she'd even relent and let Sophie take her to the hairdresser.

After the kiss, they walked, their feet moving in perfect synchronicity the whole way home, like two sets of swinging pendulums. It felt as if he were her reward for everything up to now.

"Why don't we go for a hike tomorrow?" he asked. "After school. We'll go see the waterfall. Anyone taken you up there yet?"

"No," she said, smiling, wondering if this was how California boys asked a girl out on a date.

"Meet you at the skate park at three?"

"Why not make it noon?" she said, because even though her new school life as the headmaster's bastard daughter wasn't as dire as it could have been, St. Novatus was in no way her chosen place to be.

"Noon it is," he said without a pause.

And that was how it began.

The first time they hiked in the hills, things didn't go any further than a kiss or two. But the next time, the kissing quickly became more urgent and then gave way to a whole lot more. The first time they did it was because she wanted to give him something back. Something for being the only person who'd been nice to her. But after the first time, it wasn't about him anymore. It was about them. And it was about sex. Overnight it became the only thing that was important and the only way she could feel a thing at all.

On the hottest day, on their longest hike yet, he pulled her toward the waterfall. She was reluctant at first, but the moment she'd agreed to it, everything moved fast. Too fast. One moment they'd been looking to see if it was even possible, then they were kissing, and suddenly she was under the water stream. It was different standing up. She had to hold on to him tighter with her legs and push herself up on the rocks with her hands so she didn't scrape the skin on her back raw. A couple of minutes in, her wrists started to ache from the pressure of holding herself up. She started to tell him it hurt, but that seemed to set off a chain reaction, and it didn't last much longer after that.

That was the first time they didn't use a condom. They didn't talk about it, but when they came off the mountain, she told him they should go get a tattoo. She said it was so they wouldn't forget their first time underwater, but really, she wanted to mark their first time with no protection. It felt important. Risky. He knew what could happen, but he'd done it anyway. To her, that meant that she was worth the risk. That *they* were worth the risk, and she didn't ever want to forget the way that made her feel.

They both got the tattoo that same afternoon. The tattoo hurt so badly she wanted to stop at just a couple of minutes in. The pain was different when you weren't the one controlling the needle. But she didn't stop. Emily got hers on her upper arm so she could turn her head and look at it whenever she wanted to. Joseph opted for the base of his spine. Emily knew that this was because he still cared what his parents thought of him—even though he pretended that he didn't. But hidden from the world or not, the matching tattoos were all she needed to know that they were in something real. Emily now had something her mother never had. She had love.

CHAPTER 4

MADDY

Maddy lowered the car window all the way down and let her elbow balance on the ledge, her fingers fluttering in the wind. The heavy heat trapped at the bottom of the hill was all but gone up here in the canyons. It wasn't completely fresh by any means, but the air was lighter and smelled of green. The last of the sun was hunkering down behind the hills, and it was one of those sunsets where the sky looked furious. Bright orange, dark purple. A warped reflection of the volcanic heat of the day. Joseph was leaning into the gas harder than she would have, given the winding nature of the road. Canyon driving always had her staring straight out the windshield in case the panoramic views on either side distracted her. Mountain roads were no place for distracted driving.

"Nervous?" Joseph asked.

"No," she lied. They'd both dressed up for dinner. It just seemed like the occasion—and the address—had required it. Apparently not just content with "passing through" for work after all, Emily had actually purchased a property up on Devil's Gulch Ridge with the intent of renovating it and then flipping it. Joseph had told Maddy that that's what her sister did for a living these days, property development. Maddy didn't love getting all her Emily information secondhand through Joseph, but so far she'd chickened out of calling her directly, so the only alternative to secondhand information would have been no information. Tonight was to fix all that. It was to restore things.

Joseph was wearing his "fancy" jeans, along with a gray blazer over a Jimi Hendrix T-shirt. He'd ripped his last left-eye contact lens the day before, so he was wearing his glasses. The glasses had large round frames, and when he'd first bought them she'd privately thought he looked like a grown-up Harry Potter, but they'd grown on her over time and now she thought they made him seem almost edgy. The look landed somewhere between wise owl and failed hipster, and she loved every bit of it. Maddy was in her favorite kelly-green shirt, with white skinny jeans that fit just right and a pair of ballet flats. As she had many times before, she mourned the loss of her mom's chunky silver bracelet that used to tie this particular ensemble together. It had gone missing just after they'd moved into Pile House, and in its place she now wore a thin gold one, which somehow downgraded the whole look. Her mom had always held that it was the small details that could make or break an outfit. Maddy hadn't really had much of an opinion on what made or broke an outfit until later in life, and by the time she'd discovered her mother was right, it was too late to let her know. Recently she'd been thinking about her daily. Even though her mom hadn't been her real self for years before she'd died, it seemed like the more time that passed, the more she missed her. Wasn't that the opposite of how it was supposed to work? Perhaps it was that the messier her life got, the more she missed her mother. She was ashamed to recall that she hadn't thought about her quite as frequently when she was freshly engaged and moving to Silver Lake, even though that was just about the time her mother was getting diagnosed and had begun her transition into someone else entirely.

"I saw you today," she said. She'd procrastinated over bringing up the sighting, but she supposed it would be smart to get it squared away before they got to Emily's.

"You did?" From the easiness of his tone, she realized he didn't know what she meant.

"I was walking into town. You were at a stoplight. Emily was in the car."

"Emily?" said Joseph, confused.

"Yes. Emily."

"The last time I saw Emily was in New York."

"I saw you both *today*."

"Where?"

"Driving down Main Street this afternoon."

"What time?"

"I don't know—about one?"

"I think I was driving back about then. But Maddy, Emily wasn't with me."

"I saw you together. You were driving. She was in the passenger seat." Joseph turned to look at her, despite their heading around yet another bend.

"I went hiking this morning. After that, I stopped at Wren's for an oil change, and then I drove back home."

"With Emily."

"No. Not with Emily." He turned to look at her again, and she saw from his expression, that as far as he was concerned, he was telling the truth. Or what he believed to be the truth. She opened her mouth again, this time to absolutely set him straight, but he got there first.

"This is like the thing with the socks," he said.

"Wow. We're finally allowed to talk about the socks," said Maddy. She crossed her ankles, realizing too late that she actually had the damn socks on. The socks in question had shown up uninvited in her top drawer. She still had no idea how they'd gotten there, and Joseph had refused to talk about it. They were no-show socks, and even though she'd never worn anything but "proper" socks before, it turned out these particular ones made her ballet flats fit just right. But still, they were not her socks, and she had no idea where they'd come from.

"I'm just bringing them up as an example of how, recently . . ."

"Recently, what?"

"Recently, it seems like you're getting confused."

"Confused?"

"Yeah, and it feels like it's getting worse. I haven't brought it up because I honestly don't want to think about what could be happening here. But now you're accusing me of driving around town with Emily, when I just wasn't . . . We have to talk about it."

"But you *were* driving around town with Emily."

"I wasn't. Maddy. I wasn't. And I didn't shove a pair of random socks in your drawer. I didn't put your keys in the mailbox or the fridge or the microwave. I didn't back my car into the Jeep. And I just wonder if this isn't the start of something."

"The start of what?"

"Could it be possible, in any way possible, that this is all leading up to the start of you developing the fuzzies."

The fuzzies. The euphemism her father had leaned on to make her mother's Alzheimer's sound cozier than it had any right to sound.

"Don't worry," said Joseph into the long silence. "I'm keeping an eye out. I've been keeping an eye out for a while now."

She didn't respond. He was completely mistaken. There was no reason to think what had happened to her mother was happening to her. Maddy had been moving through life under the assumption that what had befallen her mother was just an incredibly bad thing that had happened to an incredibly good person. But was that true? Neither she nor her mother had gone for genetic testing. Her mom had been old enough that it hadn't been deemed necessary. Chalked up to just one of those things. But the fact that no one had been sent for testing in no way guaranteed Maddy's DNA was free from the same flaw that her mother's had.

"Are we on the right street?" asked Maddy. If you could even call what they were driving along a street. More like a lane, or even a trail.

"I think so." By silent mutual agreement, they had dropped the subject. Up ahead a doe and her fawn stood by the side of the road, heads bent to the grass, grazing. Joseph slowed almost to a stop as they passed them in case the deer should jump out into the road. They didn't, and after one glassy-eyed stare from the mom, after which she went back to eating, they virtually ignored their admirers. Joseph slowly drove the car off again, but Maddy turned back in her seat, watching them until the car slipped around another corner and they disappeared from view.

She bent down and pulled her phone out of the purse at her feet to see if she could get a rough idea of where they were. No bars.

"How do you even know which way to drive?" she asked. "There's no signal."

"You found your phone, then," he said. She'd been frantic looking for it on their way out, only to find it on the floor of the passenger seat of Joseph's car. She had silently slipped it into her purse, embarrassed at how manic she'd been.

"How do you know the way, Joe?" she said, a tightness creeping into her voice. Had he already been up here without her? He kept his gaze on the road in front of them, but she could see his expression harden.

"I know the way because the house she bought was where we used to go." As soon as he said it, Maddy felt a dot in the center of each of her cheeks grow hot. When she'd first gotten together with Joseph, images of him having sex with Emily would hijack her mind's eye at the worst possible moments. But she hadn't thought about Joseph and Emily naked together in years. It definitely wasn't the image she needed in her head when she was moments away from seeing her. "I'm sorry," he said, eventually. "I don't want to make this any harder on you than it already is."

"It's okay," she said, and meant it. It wasn't her husband's fault he'd been flung into this situation.

"Just try and put it out of your mind." *Fat chance,* she thought but didn't say. Because who could ever forget that their husband had been to bed with their sister.

The road had become straighter and was now more or less a tunnel of green leaves, with occasional flashes of epic views across the hills when the trees thinned out.

"I didn't even know you could live this far up. It's crazy," said Maddy. They rolled along in silence for a couple more minutes, and then Joseph, seemingly cognizant of a building approaching, slowed down. A few seconds later, Maddy could see a splash of lights across the road, then the trees came to an end, and Joseph rolled to a stop.

Maddy didn't know where to look first. Joseph's face as he stared at the house or the house itself. In the end, she settled for the latter. It was a vast, *huge* house. Almost vulgar in its size. In fact, with those blocky turrets bookending the building, did it perhaps qualify as a castle? Who had any idea that *this* was up here?

"Is this it?" she finally asked.

"This is it," he replied.

They drove across the driveway, the car crunching satisfyingly along the gravel as they went. Finally they pulled up, Joseph turned off the engine, and there they both sat, listening to the engine as it ticked at them in disapproval at the difficulty of the bumpy terrain it'd just traversed for their benefit.

"She *lives* here?" said Maddy, breathlessly.

"For now," said Joseph. He dropped his hand behind her head and gently squeezed her neck. As she always did when he did this, she felt a ripple of goose bumps blossom along her arm. Joseph got out of the car and then opened Maddy's door. This was normally a date-night move, but the unexpected romance of their current setting seemed to almost require it. She passed him the bottle of wine they'd brought—a

Napa cabernet sauvignon, one from her father's collection—then took his offered hand and got out. The sun was all but gone, and the wind had picked up, as it often did in the canyons after dark, and was busy bullying the trees.

As they walked toward the front of the house, Maddy did some subtle deep breathing to combat her nerves. How, exactly, was this going to go? Maybe Emily had forgotten all the clammy details of their short-lived sisterhood. Perhaps she'd want to relive it all again—talk it through in exquisite detail. Or perhaps she was Buddhist now, and tonight she'd tell Maddy to forget everything that had ever happened between them, that it was all good. Unlikely.

She held on tighter to her purse and started up the flight of stairs leading to the front door. The stairs were made of polished stone, narrow and worn. Stairs made for slipping on. The front door was sturdy, set at the back of an arched brick porch that was three times the length of Pile House's. Joseph passed in front of her to get to the front door, where he gave the doorbell a hearty press, then turned to give her the thumbs-up as a cheery clanging sang out through the house.

"What's wrong?" he said, seeing she still stood by the stairs. What was wrong was that the moment was here. It was finally time to see Emily, and all she wanted to do was drag Joseph back into the car and drive as far away from here as possible.

"I don't think I can do this," she said.

And then Emily opened the door, and twenty years drained away, as if they had never happened at all.

CHAPTER 5

MADDY

"Watch out," said Emily, pulling the last of the containers out of the oven and dumping it heavily on the table. "It's all superhot. Hold on, there have to be some spoons somewhere around here." She started opening and closing every drawer in the kitchen. "Nope," she said, as Maddy and Joseph caught each other's eye. "Endless piles of mouse poop, but no spoon on the premises. Aha!" she said as she pulled something heavy and tarnished out of the back of a drawer. It was huge, like something you'd use in some abstract veterinary fantasy to spoon medicine into a willing horse's mouth. Maddy and Joseph watched as Emily turned on the tap and started scrubbing at the massive spoon with an old dish sponge. In contrast to Maddy's big dress-up effort, Emily was in leggings and a tank top. Zero makeup. No bejeweled headband today. In fact, her curls were all piled on top of her head and seemed to be fixed there with nothing more courageous than a blunt pencil. Maddy tried to push aside the feeling that, even in a tank top, dusty leggings, and no makeup, Emily was still the one out of the two of them who would hold the eye. The one whose features were arranged in that mystical way that caused everyone to read the exact same thing: beauty.

Joseph was right. Emily *was* different now. She was together. She was almost funny. She was almost warm. If she hadn't looked all but the same, Maddy would never have believed it was her sister at all.

"You know," said Maddy, getting up and rifling through the takeout bag, "I bet we can work it out with what we have in here." She grabbed a couple of extra spoons and a stack of napkins out of the bag, then folded the napkins into a makeshift oven glove. She picked up one of the containers and started persuading uncooperatively sticky rice onto each of the plates.

"That works," said Emily. Despite the dingy state of the kitchen, and the lack of utensils, Emily looked totally at home. Maddy didn't think she'd ever seen Emily look so comfortable, but then she'd only really ever seen Emily in places where she was so obviously the outsider. Maybe that was all Emily had ever needed to take the spike out of her personality—to be somewhere where she could be herself. It was a reasonable assumption. Wasn't that what everyone needed in order to feel human: to belong.

"So how long do you think it'll take to get the place up to snuff?" asked Maddy, helping herself to some curry. Even though it was an alarmingly loud shade of orange, it smelled tangy and delicious. She carefully put the curry back down next to her plate, in between her and Emily. The table was tiny, so they were eating practically on top of each other. Ironic that in this house that was composed of nothing but vast echoes of space, they were all sitting together in such a cramped situation. To say that the house was a fixer-upper didn't even come close to the reality. It was practically a shell. As they'd learned during their grand tour, Emily was in the middle of taking the house down to the bare bones before building it up again, and the place was nothing but soaring ceilings and cavernous rooms. It made Pile House's flaws look like minor fixes by comparison. Emily was living out of a tiny apartment in the back of the house. It was the only part of the house not covered in grime and dust—not that the apartment was particularly clean.

"Six months or so."

"That's it?"

"Well, it's not just me. There's a whole crew of guys who show up here every morning."

"So when it's done . . ." Maddy knew what she wanted to say, she just wasn't sure how she was going to say it.

"I'll sell it," finished Emily. "So don't get too attached."

"It suits you," said Joseph. And he was right. The house did suit Emily. Broken, magnificent, out of keeping with everything else for hundreds of miles around.

"You've done this before, I take it," said Maddy.

"Several times. It's what I do. What about you?"

"I'm a dance teacher. I have a studio in town," said Maddy.

"So was that the fallback option?" asked Emily. Maddy kept her face flat to cover up the hurt she felt at the assumption behind Emily's question. *If you can't do, teach.* But Maddy *had* been doing. She'd been doing just fine until she'd fallen in love with Joseph and the six-month contracts away from home became an issue. Dancing was not a relationship-friendly profession. She could, in fact, *do* very well, but teaching . . . Turned out that Maddy was a highly average teacher.

"Depends how you define *fallback*," said Maddy. "I was dancing professionally before Joseph and I got together."

"Really?" said Emily, surprised and suddenly genuinely interested. "Where?"

"Cruise liners. Mostly around the Caribbean," said Maddy, avoiding looking at her sister when she said it so she wouldn't have to see the reaction. She caught it out of the corner of her eye anyway. Emily had pulled a face that seemed to simultaneously transmit *Not bad* and *That's not so impressive.* Maddy knew Emily was right on both counts, of course. It wasn't like she'd been dancing on Broadway, but it wasn't exactly like she'd been working the local strip pole either.

"Cool. I wouldn't have imagined you ending up as a teacher, though."

"Why not?" asked Maddy.

"I don't know really. Just doesn't seem like it would suit you. What did Ivan think about it?"

"*Dad* never expressed that much of an opinion on the matter." That was a lie. Her dad had had quite a few things to say about it. Finally backing off the topic in resigned disgust once he saw she wasn't going to change tracks, follow his advice, and head to college. One of the only things she'd ever seen him get passionate about was his insistence that she *not* become a teacher. He knew the gig after all; he was one himself.

"Right. No. Teaching. That's good. It's a really *good* thing to do. You should do what makes you happy. Good for you."

The passive-aggressive nature of the swipe surprised Maddy. At least you knew where you stood with teen Emily. Turned out this version waited till your guard was down before she took a chunk out of you. Wine would help. She looked over at the counter where the unopened cabernet still sat.

"You have a corkscrew?" said Joseph, reading Maddy's mind.

"Nope," said Emily.

"It's okay," said Joseph. "I think I can do it with this." He stood up and grabbed the bottle from the counter and set to work with his pocketknife.

"You got glasses?"

"I have cups," said Emily, and grabbed a couple of coffee mugs from the cupboard and placed them on the table in front of Joseph and Maddy. Maddy's bore the mark of an old coffee ring halfway down.

"None for you?" asked Maddy.

"I'm sober."

"Oh," said Maddy. "Then we shouldn't—"

"Not at all. You can drink in front of me."

"It's fine, honestly. I—"

Emily grabbed the opened bottle from Joseph and began to pour into Maddy's cup. As the liquid neared the old coffee ring, Maddy opened her mouth to say that was plenty, but before she could, the bottle dropped out of Emily's hand and fell hard to the table. Before Maddy could get out of the way, a bold line of red had surged across the tabletop and onto her lap.

"Shit!" said Emily as Joseph righted the bottle, then grabbed a wad of napkins, damming the flood as best he could. The liquid could not be contained, however, and his efforts sent another wave of wine running over the side of the table. The second splash managed to hit Maddy once more, even though she'd already jumped backward.

She looked down at her front. Both her top and formerly crisp white jeans were now soaked—crisscrossed with deep purple slashes and blotches, as if she'd just taken part in some kind of grape slaughter.

"Great." Joseph offered her the saturated napkins, even though they would clearly do no good. "Do you have a bathroom, Emily?" With the state the house was in, she wasn't making any assumptions.

"Out of here, first on the right."

"Okay." She paused, waiting for an apology, for some kind of appropriate reaction on the part of her sister. She didn't know why it mattered to her that she got one.

"You need something to change into?"

"That would be nice," said Maddy, pretending to herself that that offer was all she'd been waiting for. Emily disappeared into a back room, where they heard her sliding hangers along a rack. A second later she emerged with a handful of silk.

"Here. This might work."

Maddy took the material—goodness knows what she'd given her. It looked like it might be lingerie.

"Thanks." As Maddy walked out of the kitchen, she could feel the wine had reached as far as the insides of her shoes, even saturating the infamous socks. She turned right as instructed but halted a couple of steps down the corridor. Her excuse to herself was that she'd suddenly become fascinated with the grain on a particular patch of wood panel because it was slightly paler than the others. She heard nothing and after a couple more moments kept walking. However, just as she stepped into the bathroom, she heard a bark of laughter. It was Joseph. She didn't want to know what it was that Emily had just said that had made him laugh so loud that she could hear it at the other end of the corridor. It was a long corridor.

The bathroom wasn't in any better a state than the dilapidated kitchen. She stripped off her clothes, dumped them in the sink, turned on the water, and then stared at the purple-splotched material as the water rose around it. She didn't know why she was bothering to soak her clothes. They were ruined. The ballet flats were ruined too. She peeled off the socks and dumped them in the trash, glad to see the end of them. Then she rinsed the flats out in the bath, opened the French doors leading out to the garden, and perched them on a stone step. She didn't know why she thought the evening air might dry them any quicker than leaving them inside, but it was worth a try. The silky number turned out to be a generous-sized kimono, which actually fit her pretty well. She wrapped it carefully around her body, tying a knot at the side. The material slid against her skin whenever she moved, and she suddenly felt vulnerable. No shoes, no real structure to her outfit. She could be made naked in the mere pull of a knot.

She walked quietly back up the wood-paneled corridor. Almost tiptoeing, but not quite. If she *had* been tiptoeing, she would have had to admit to herself that she was trying to sneak up on the conversation. However, she heard no voices on her approach. Maddy sped up and then crept into the room as silent as a ninja. But there was no one there.

The dinner wasn't any more eaten than when she'd left. Anxiety rising, she moved deftly into the back room where Emily had gotten the kimono. No one. Just a rail of clothes, a shapeless purse dumped on the floor, and a camp bed with a sleeping bag on it. She wondered if Emily squatted like a hobo in all the houses she flipped. What kind of a life was that? Maddy halfheartedly pulled the first few items on the rail out to take a look. Nothing sensational. Skinny pants. Silk shirts. Blazers. Gym clothes. Where *were* they?

She checked her phone in case she had a message from Joseph. Nothing. She tried to call him but was met with a sour-sounding "The wireless customer you are trying to reach is not available. Please try again later." Not ready to acknowledge that she had no way to communicate with her husband at all, she slid her phone into the kimono's pocket and went back through the kitchen. She started up the stairs that led into the main house. The staircase light was on, where it hadn't been earlier. So they must have come up this way. But why? Why had they abandoned their food, abandoned her, and disappeared off into the house? Maddy didn't know. And she didn't want to even start to make a grab at guessing.

She opened the door at the top of the stairs and stepped into the dark, intimidated. Suddenly feeling as if she had no right to be there. She paused for a moment, considering scurrying back down the stairs to the safety of the basement apartment. But then she closed the door behind her with a firm click. Really, go back downstairs and start eating her orange curry alone? No. She had to find Joseph. She started down the corridor, her bare feet stepping carefully on the rough sacking material that covered the flooring. Twilight was on the cusp of turning into evening, and the last of the light falling through the windows wasn't quite enough to see by. However, the lights at the front of the house were still on, and she moved down the corridor toward them. Finally, she found her way into the main hallway. The hub of the house.

Even with the detritus of scaffolding and dust cloths slumped everywhere you looked, there was no hiding it: this house was going to be a beauty. It *was* a beauty. How on earth had Emily pulled together the money to buy a place like this? Maddy took a few steps into the hallway, onto a sea of delicate black and white tiles that felt cool and smooth underneath her bare feet. She could see at least eight rooms leading off from where she now stood, each one framed by a soaring arch carved of wood. But which way to go? And then she heard them.

They weren't quite shouting, but their voices were definitely raised. She crossed the hall to reach the room with all the noise. The door was half open, and so she stood there, hidden by the gloom around her. Listening.

"You're as fucked up as she is. It's sick." This was Emily. Who did she think was fucked up?

"So what. Nothing? Be like you and just let people do things to me?" There was a short, sharp silence before she heard Joseph's voice again. "Hey!"

"Let go of my wrists," said Emily.

"I'll let go when you stop trying to whack me."

At this, Maddy rushed into the room in time to see Joseph release his hold on Emily only for her to give him a hard shove. He stumbled backward, finding his footing just before he fell. Emily and Joseph were now both silent, the atmosphere in the room so intense they hadn't even noticed her come in.

"Having fun?" she asked. They turned to face her then. "What are you doing in here? We're supposed to be having dinner."

"Just taking a quick trip down memory lane," said Emily. Maddy didn't like the sound of that.

"What were you arguing about?"

"Actually, we were arguing about the fact that—"

"So this has been fun, but Maddy and I are leaving now," said Joseph. *Thank God,* she thought. He was right. It was time to go. She'd reached her limit for tolerating Emily's uncouth behavior years ago, and she wasn't interested in sticking around to witness more of it tonight.

"Oh come on. Don't get all 'Maddy and I' about it," said Emily.

"What's that supposed to mean?" said Maddy, feeling the glow of the upper hand. Silence. No one wanted to address what *that* meant.

"Can you just admit what you did and say that you're sorry about it?" Emily said. And quite incredibly, Maddy saw that Emily was directing the question to her.

"That I'm sorry about what?" she said. The space and silence dragged out between them. Did she mean for her to say she was sorry for marrying Joseph because Emily had had a crush on him twenty years ago? She would not apologize. She'd done nothing wrong. "I have nothing to be sorry for. What do you mean?"

And then Maddy watched as Emily's entire face changed. Her sister had decided something. But Maddy had no idea what it was.

"Forget it. So before you two scuttle on back to your love nest, we should talk about the will."

"Now?" asked Maddy, incredulous. The reference to their "love nest" made her think that, yes, it was getting together with Joseph that Emily wanted her to apologize for. It was ridiculous. Emily had been gone years by the time they'd gotten together.

"So . . ."

"So?"

"So Ivan and Sophie left me half the house. Were you ever planning to bring that up? Or were you hoping I'd just let it slide?"

"Of course not. If it makes you feel any better, before all the shoving and yelling and spilling of wine, I had planned to bring it up at some point this evening."

"Well, consider it brought up."

"I will."

"So. What do we do about the house?" asked Emily.

"I don't know," replied Maddy. And she didn't know. In all the time they'd spent looking for Emily, she hadn't really thought through what would actually happen if they found her. Obviously the house would have to be split, but exactly how and when she wasn't sure.

"How about I buy you out?" said Emily. "Unless you want to buy *me* out?"

"No. I . . . I don't know," said Maddy. And she didn't. Her half-formed ideas on what might happen to Pile House if they found Emily had centered around Maddy selling the place and then sending Emily a check for half the value. She'd never considered that Emily might want to—or would be able to afford to—buy her and Joseph out. That changed things. She tried to poke at *why* that changed things, and words like *territory, family,* and *mine* shot into her consciousness. Not logical words. But those were the words, even so. Pile House belonged to *her* family. And even though Emily was technically family, and certainly more so than some anonymous buyer, Maddy didn't want her to have Pile House. Maddy wasn't saying *she* wanted it. But she sure knew she didn't want Emily to have it. Emily didn't deserve it. And even more than that, from where Maddy was standing, in the heart of Emily's grand-scale mansion—she didn't particularly need it.

"I'll buy it. Simpler than selling to a third party. I'll get it valued. I'll transfer the funds to your account, you can give me the keys, and we can all move on with our lives. I'll call my appraiser tomorrow," said Emily.

"Wait!"

"What?"

"I mean, that's pretty fast. We live there right now. It's our home."

"It's technically my home too."

"But we can't just move out tomorrow."

"No one's talking about you moving out tomorrow. How about . . . a month?"

"A month?"

"Well, how long do you need?"

"A month should be fine," said Joseph, ignoring Maddy who was looking at him, mouth open, appalled.

"Emily . . ." started Maddy, knowing what she wanted to say but not quite having the gumption to say it. Or at least not enough balls to say it in a way that would make it ring true.

"What?" said Emily. "Was there another way you wanted to do it?"

"Emily, you have all this already," said Maddy, sweeping her arm in a motion meant to encompass the entirety of the vast house they were standing in.

"So what are you saying? Because I'm working on this house, I should gift you the other one?"

"Of course not," said Joseph, in his special "Here I am, the voice of reason" tone. Sometimes Maddy *really* hated that tone. "I'm sure this renovation is costing a fortune."

"It is."

"But do you really need our house too? It's all we have left. And it's the only thing left of my family."

"It's not the only thing left of your family. If you're that attached to the place, you buy me out. I really don't care either way," said Emily.

"How do you even have the money to buy us out?" It came out wrong. Or rather, it came out right. Maddy couldn't fathom how her sister had stepped into enough wealth to buy the house they stood in, let alone another one.

"I was married for a while. Then I wasn't," said Emily. She looked wistful, and Maddy saw that whomever this short-lived marriage had been with, it was someone important to her. She saw Joseph notice too.

"What happened?" she asked. If nothing else, it would be good for Joseph to hear what happened to men who tangled with her sister. Financial ruin at the very least.

"We met in rehab and got married right afterward. An extraordinarily bad idea. But we meant it. Or at least I did. Anyway, a couple of months in, it was clear we'd made a mistake. He wanted to make it go away, and so there was a settlement."

"How much?" asked Maddy. She knew she had no right to ask, but she needed to know.

"Four million."

"Are you serious?" said Maddy, who looked at Joseph for confirmation that, yes, this was next-level insane. But he'd pulled his glasses out of his pocket and was busy examining them for damage, which was apparently more absorbing than the revelation about Emily's financial circumstances.

"Somewhere around that mark. Depending on how you count it." She directed this last part to Joseph, despite Maddy being the one who had asked the question. Maddy stood completely still. This was a hard one to take in. Four million in the bank that she hadn't even earned, and she insisted on taking more. Just because she was entitled to it. Just because it belonged to Maddy.

"So you're adding our house to your stack," said Maddy.

"You're looking at me like I just said I like to drown puppies on the weekend. It's not that bad. I'll write you a check. It'll be the most cash you've ever had in your pocket at one time."

"That's pretty patronizing," said Maddy.

"Well, it will be, won't it?"

"And what are you going to do with Mom and Dad's place? Are you going to flip it?" Maddy didn't think she'd be able to bear that. All her parents' ancient but beautiful carpentry hauled out of the house and thrown in a dumpster. The ivy dragged off the front of the house. The white clapboards painted gray or whatever other blah color Emily chose to paint them.

"I'll probably fix the roof, and all the other things that were falling apart last time I lived there, but other than that, I'll probably keep it the same old home sweet home."

"But what will you *do* with it, Emily?"

"I'm going to live in it."

CHAPTER 6

MADDY

The car bumped over an endless river of divots and potholes as they drove away from Devil's Gulch Ridge, back down to the real world. Considering what had gone on that evening, they'd actually managed to leave relatively gracefully. Maddy and Joseph weren't saying much to each other now, however. Which wasn't like them. Maddy was holding back. Knowing that if she started bitching about Emily, she wouldn't be able to stop. She still wasn't completely sure where Joseph stood with the whole Emily thing. He hadn't had much of a reaction to her insisting she take half of Pile House, despite the fact that she clearly didn't need it. He hadn't had much of a reaction to her wealth at all.

What Maddy couldn't work out was exactly why Emily would want to live at Pile House. It wasn't as if she'd had a grand experience the first time around. It hadn't been a happy place for anyone when Emily had been living there. Was it that she simply had a hankering to live in a crumbling Victorian on the crappy side of Myrtlebury? No. Emily wanted it because Maddy had it. And that was all the reason she needed.

Eventually, Maddy could no longer stand the silence.

"What are you thinking about?" she asked. Kind of juvenile, but this conversation had to start somewhere. One of the disadvantages of their knowing each other since they were kids was that it was too easy to revert back to their childhood selves with each other. Or at least their teenaged selves. They could get away with it, not being grown-ups. They didn't take that kind of behavior out into the wider world. But with each other, they were often childish. It was one of the things Maddy both loved and hated about their relationship. Their being together meant that they had never fully grown up. No one had ever demanded it of them.

"Nothing." The inevitable response. She held in a sigh. Since when was anyone ever thinking *nothing*?

"What were you two arguing about?" He didn't answer immediately. If he said *nothing* again, she was going to grab the steering wheel and plunge them both off the side of the canyon. She took a silent breath in and then all the way out. Then she compressed the urge to grab the wheel into a small hard nut at the bottom of her stomach. Calm. This needed calm.

"Just about someone we both know. Emily didn't like what I was saying about her."

"Who?"

"Jodi."

"Jodi Khan?" He nodded. Of course. Their big celeb mutual acquaintance. "What were you saying about her?"

"I can't really repeat it," he said.

"Why not?" she said.

"She's a person of interest. You can't tell people things you know about celebrities. It gets out, they start looking for the leak, and then you're out of the circle."

"I'm not 'people,' Joseph. I'm your wife." He didn't respond to that. She did not even slightly like the fact that Emily and he had friends in common, the particulars of which could not be shared with her. But she opted not to push it. There were other things to discuss.

"So, what are we going to do?" said Maddy.

"Do?"

"About the house?"

"I guess we'll move," he said.

"What if I don't want to move."

"You want to move," said Joseph, and this time yesterday he'd have been in the ballpark of correct. But how things had changed in twenty-four hours. Emily wanted the house. Perhaps Emily also wanted Joseph. Maddy hadn't been able to dismiss her telling him not to get all "Maddy and I" about it. As if Emily and Joseph's ancient teen history still held some sway. Surely Emily didn't think so. Not over an actual marriage.

"I never definitively said that I wanted to move out," said Maddy. "I always said I didn't know. I think I was just waiting to see what was going to happen before I got attached to the idea of raising a family there."

"And now that Emily wants it, all of a sudden it's the only place you could possibly ever be happy."

"It's not like that." It was a bit like that. But weren't most things you wanted in life colored by how much someone else wanted them? What other people wanted always mattered. That was how value worked.

"Maddy. It's a cute place, and sure, if money were no object, it'd be fun to do it up and raise kids there. But fundamentally, the house is a disaster. You know that. It's not just the roof, it's the everything. The bats in the attic, the mold in the beams, all that wallpaper your parents painted over. It's kind of amazing she'd even consider renovating it. Most people would just knock it down and start again."

"They would not! It's beautiful." Maddy felt instantly pissed at the reference to her parents' subpar attempts with the wallpaper. He had no right to say one negative word about her parents. Not about what they had or hadn't done to the house. Not about anything. Not when they'd been alive and certainly not now that they were dead. Those were the rules.

"It's beautiful but rotting where it stands," said Joseph. "You've said a thousand times that it's not where you'd actually choose to live." A thousand times was an exaggeration. She'd made that point once or twice, and only halfheartedly. And she hadn't meant it. He was supposed to know that she hadn't meant it. Who could mean it of a place like Pile House?

"Then we should leave Myrtlebury," said Maddy. If she couldn't have it her way, then she didn't want to have it any way. They'd go. Head back into town. Start again with the money. Away from Pile House and away from Emily. "We only moved here for the house anyway."

"We'll stay. Your school's here. Bee and Sam are here," he said, and she wondered exactly when Bee being nearby had become a plus for him. She also wondered when exactly she started to get to make the choices here. All this because her volatile sister couldn't stay away.

"Do you think she would have hit you?" asked Maddy, remembering how hard he'd been holding her wrists when she walked in on them. Joseph shrugged; he clearly didn't want to talk about it.

"Four million dollars richer, but looks like nothing much else has changed."

"What do you mean?" said Joseph.

"I mean she was insane then and she's insane now."

"Was she insane, back in the day? I don't remember that side of her."

"Because you were the only one she never terrorized. How can you not remember? She was violent."

"I remember she smacked Bee once, but wasn't the general consensus that that was somewhat provoked?"

"She attacked *me*. More than once. You know that." He squinted out into the darkness and slowed slightly as if he saw something up ahead, then relaxed his gaze and sped back up again. He didn't answer the question. "She used to come in my room at night and terrorize me. I'd wake up, and she'd have her knees on my chest, squeezing the air out of me. I'd have to scream until my parents came in to pull her off."

"Must have been hard to scream with the air getting squeezed out of you."

"Yes. It was." Was he questioning her? "And don't forget about this." Maddy held the inside of her forearm out for Joseph to see. He glanced over and then nodded. It wasn't possible to see what she was showing him in the dark, but he didn't need to see. He'd been shown it before. "You know what she was like, and she's the same way now. The only difference is she's older and apparently richer. But she's still the same person, underneath."

"Still, doing pretty well considering what she's been through," said Joseph. Maddy bit her lip and turned to look out the window into the dark beyond. Not *this* again. "She really struggled for a while, you know. Before she found her feet." *Before she found some guy to bail her out*, Maddy thought but didn't say.

"How do you know?" she asked. Between the Jodi Khan thing and him seemingly knowing Emily's entire backstory, it was as if they had a whole shared world she knew nothing about.

"We talked. In New York. We had a lot to catch up on. There were huge chunks of her life that I knew nothing about. I expect you'll want to get caught up too at some point. On everything that's happened to her."

"Hmm," said Maddy.

"She was homeless for a while, you know."

"That had to have been hard."

"Yes. It was. New York is no place for a woman to be homeless." His voice now had an edge, and she could tell that he was mad about it. Mad with her? That made no sense.

"That's not our fault. We looked for her."

"Did you know my dad took the stand at her case?"

"I didn't know that," said Maddy. She hadn't been anywhere near court when Emily had been on trial. That had been her father's burden to bear alone. He'd been clear about that.

"He was a witness for the prosecution. Basically told them that she'd been out and about trespassing on property with yours truly."

"Wow."

"I know. Thanks, Pops."

"I've zero idea why she's come back here. Doesn't she have a life to get back to in New York?" she asked.

"Does it bother you, her buying us out?"

Maddy shrugged. It did bother her. But she had no justification for saying so, so she sat on it.

"It doesn't matter who buys the place, Maddy. A sale to Emily will be cheaper and definitely quicker, but if the thought of her living there feels off, we can put it on the market and sell the place to some rando. It's whatever you want. Really."

Reverse psychology. She could read it for what it was. But that didn't make her any less susceptible to it. But it was true. Did it really matter who lived there if they no longer could?

"You're right," she said. "It doesn't make a difference."

"It won't make a difference. But the money will. And getting that money this month rather than months from now, that's huge. We can start to get things going, you know?"

Maddy felt these words snag her attention. Recently it had felt as if he'd been pulling back on the baby thing, which made sense considering their financial situation. And also considering the fact that the sex had gotten to "that" stage. The stage where it was an utter drag. Every time he returned from a work trip, the first round would be fast and tinged with a feeling of urgency, like he was trying to fuck his way right through her. But outside of those rare flurries, he had little enthusiasm. The thought of sex getting even one step more medical wasn't something their relationship needed, at all. But. A child. That made it worth it.

"Get things going as in . . ."

"With the IVF. Or at least see if we need IVF. I think it's time. Right?"

"Yes, definitely time," she said, hearing how excited she sounded and for once not trying to drain it out of her voice. It was happening. Finally. "You okay with me setting up a couple of appointments, for tests?" Despite what he'd just said, she felt nervous. The tests were always where he'd drawn the line up till now.

"Sounds like a plan," he said, and smiled. A relaxed smile. A real Joseph smile. Thank God. They were good. It was all good. She was going to be a mother. This time next year, her whole life might be completely different. She wasn't sure what her rush was, exactly. At thirty-four it wasn't like her time was running out, but then it wasn't exactly stacking up either. When Bee had been pregnant, she'd talked at length about how motherhood wasn't going to define her—even though in the end it had swallowed her whole. But Maddy sometimes wondered if that was one of the reasons she wanted to have a child. Perhaps she wanted something concrete to define her. She knew it was a bad reason for wanting to become a mother—but in an overheated, overpopulated world was there any good reason?

The trouble with conception had been a mystery up till now. She'd privately put it down to stress. The stress of losing her dad so soon after her mom, the stress of trying to find Emily, the stress of Joseph's money evaporating into nothing out of nowhere, the stress of starting a dance school and trying to fool her hometown into thinking she knew how to teach when the truth of it was that she didn't have a clue. As Emily had so helpfully pointed out, teaching just didn't suit her. So, yes, there had been stress galore. Egg-shrinking, sperm-withering, baby-denying stress. But now there was money. The kind of money that had the power to eradicate the stress, or at least to mitigate it—to fix the damage that it had wrought. This money had the power to fix everything. And it would. She just had to not think of it as Emily's.

CHAPTER 7

EMILY

2002

"What's the point in trekking all the way up here if we're going to be put off by a bit of pointy metal?" Fucking in the forest had become a total drag. Emily wasn't tired of sex with Joseph. She knew she'd never get tired of that. But trying to get comfortable while being ground into a tree or having her spine crunched into the hard grass just wasn't working out. An alternative was needed. Joseph said he'd heard of a series of abandoned miner's cabins somewhere up in the hills—he didn't know exactly where—so today they'd hiked higher and farther than they'd ever been before in an attempt to find them. So far they hadn't found the cabins, but they'd stumbled across *something*.

"That bit of pointy metal's a pretty universal signal that someone wants to keep the public out," said Joseph.

"It's a universal signal that there's something in there worth hiding. I'm going over."

"Emily, don't."

"Just pass me the sex mat."

"Why?" he said, holding up the ugly orange mat Emily had pilfered from the bathroom. The mat proved a handy barrier against the stones, leaves, and general mud underneath them, and so they always brought it with them when they visited the woods. Turned out, it was also handy for flinging over the top of barbed-wire fences.

She was over in less than thirty seconds, with Joseph up and over shortly after. They walked south for a while, and as they wandered, the ground flattened out and the softening light began to turn the trees peachy gold wherever it touched bark. The longer they walked without finding anyone or anything, the more they zoned out, almost forgetting they'd hopped a fence at all.

"So. How are things at home these days?" asked Joseph.

"Now, why'd you have to go and ruin our magical walk through the woods asking about that?" she said.

"You don't have to talk about it if you don't want to." His tone was the ever-reasonable Joseph she loved, but she could tell he felt rebuffed. It was a habit, butting everyone out of her business. But he'd more than earned a place in the center of her world, so if she wanted him to stay there, she knew she had to try to let him.

"It'd be better if Maddy wasn't such an epic pain," she said.

"She's normally pretty chill, no?"

"Chill's not how I'd describe her," she said, already annoyed that he wasn't open to seeing Maddy the way she saw her. This was why you didn't talk to people. "You hear her do that baby-voice thing?"

"What?"

"She does this weirdo baby voice whenever one of her parents are around. It's truly bizarre."

"What's all that about?"

"Sophie's theory is that Maddy's regressing."

"Isn't she a bit old for that?"

"Fourteen next week. Sophie says she's resentful of the time she's spending with me. Maddy's not used to sharing her toys."

"I guess it's an adjustment."

"Sure," said Emily, her voice flat. No one seemed bothered about the adjusting she'd had to do. Emily searched for something to say to get them off the grim subject of Maddy's regression and back on the purpose of their trip. "You think this could be army land?"

"It's not army land."

"What if we get shot for trespassing?"

"I won't let anyone shoot you, Sisu," he said, and looped his fingers between hers. That was better. Sisu was what he'd started occasionally calling her when he was feeling extra protective. Apparently, Sisu was Finnish and didn't have a direct translation, but he'd told her it was something to do with strength in the face of adversity, which made sense. Emily didn't have a name for Joseph. To her, he was just Joseph. Her Joseph.

As they walked deeper into the woods, Joseph held her fingers a little tighter. Even though she'd been all gung ho about going over the fence, now that she'd imagined hordes of soldiers streaming through the trees toward them, bayonets at the ready, he could tell she'd become scared. He could read her shifting moods as easily as he could read the weather. If they'd still had the sex mat with them, he'd have suggested they throw it over the fence and climb back out again. But it had gotten snagged on the barbed wire when they'd climbed over, so they'd left it behind.

But then they saw something that meant that the endless walk through the woods had been worth it. The shack was made of nothing but flaking wood and was barely the length of the both of them. The bottom of its door looked like it'd recently been mauled by wolves, but what it did have was a roof. Also walls. Joseph went up on tiptoe to try to peek in one of the windows, but he couldn't see past the rusted grate fixed over the front of it.

"Come on," said Emily, pulling him through the ruined door. This was exactly the type of thing they'd been looking for. Something they could call theirs. Inside wasn't much to look at. Rubble and trash over the floor. Some half-rotted cabinetry. Joseph pulled a board back from where it leaned up against one of the windows, and some of the evening light filtered in so they could see a little better. But apart from a tired couch against the side of the wall, there wasn't much more to see. Emily walked over to see what state the couch was in. It was dated—puffy corduroy cushions with a pattern of roses—and kind of dusty. But not in too bad a shape, considering.

"Don't touch it, Emily. It might have fleas."

She poked at it to see if that'd disturb anything living inside it, but it didn't seem to be riddled with bugs or fleas or anything else. She pulled the cushions off the frame just to be sure and saw that the couch was actually a sofa bed. She pulled at the frame, expecting it to be stiff, but it was so old and loose that the bed fell straight open. The mattress was practically anorexic, and the blankets looked like they'd last been used sometime in the seventies. But it was a bed. She didn't even bother to look over at Joseph before she started to take her clothes off.

"You've got to be kidding me."

"What?"

"That thing's disgusting."

"It's cleaner than the leaves, twigs, and dirt you've been pounding me into."

"You didn't seem to mind at the time."

"I didn't. But this is better. Come on."

"Sisu, it's gross."

Keeping her eyes on him, she took off her shorts and T-shirt, then her panties, and lay out over the top blanket, naked but for her bra. Wearing just her bra made her feel more exposed than if she'd had nothing on at all, but for some reason, she couldn't bring herself to take it off yet. He stood watching. Still not moved enough to forget the ancient covers. Suddenly self-conscious at being the only one naked, she ran her hands over her stomach. It wasn't concave as it had been when she'd first arrived. Every part of her felt fuller, her thighs, definitely her breasts. Emily knew this was because she'd more or less stopped smoking, which had meant she'd started eating. She didn't smoke around Joseph as he didn't like it, and she hadn't felt quite as entitled to raid Sophie's wallet for cigarette money as she had her uncle's. Sophie had taken her shopping a couple of times, tactfully saying that it looked like she'd "grown out" of her old clothes. Emily had been glad to get rid of all of them. Now, instead of the bra she'd lifted from a thrift store, she had a sweet broderie anglaise one that fit her perfectly and smelled of nothing but laundry powder and herself. Joseph was still standing by the door, so she took the plunge, unclasped the bra, and dropped it on the floor. He didn't need any more encouragement after that. It was, after all, the first time he'd seen her completely naked.

Afterward, she cried. She had no idea why. She didn't feel sad. In fact, for the first time in her life, she felt close to happy. Almost whole. Connected. After the tears stopped, they lay face-to-face, looking into each other's eyes. They didn't talk. They didn't need to. She loved him, and he loved her. And it would be that way for the rest of their lives. It was understood.

When they woke later it was pitch black. The only light came from the green glow of Joseph's watch as he checked the time. Almost midnight.

"Crap," he said, already half up. She put her arm over his chest and pulled him back toward her. She hadn't meant to fall asleep, but it was the first time they'd curled up together, him snug around the back of her like the world's warmest spoon. She'd never known any sensation so cozy and luxurious as limb on limb, skin on skin. How could she not have drifted off?

"Let's just stay here for the night and go down in the morning," she said.

"Are you kidding?"

"They don't care what we do."

"They don't care if we get in late, but if we're not home when they wake up, and they don't know where we are, they'll call the cops. And that's a whole lot of extra hassle I don't need."

"We'll never get down the trail in the dark."

"I'm pretty sure there's a fire road just south of here. We can follow it back down."

"Can't we just stay here? I'll wake you up at five, and we'll go down then."

"You'll just somehow wake up at five?"

"Sure. If I bang my head five times on the mattress before I go to sleep, I'll wake up at five on the dot."

"Does that work?"

"It worked the one time I tried it."

"I'm not betting my future freedom on it happening again."

"Are you sure?" she asked, brushing one hand over his penis.

"Stop!" he said, grabbing hold of her wrist. She twisted out of his grip, hurt. Did he really care more about what his parents thought than having sex with her? And if that was the truth of it, did he even love her at all? "I'm sorry," he said, not needing to see her face to know what she was thinking. "I just don't want to spend the night here. It's creepy." So it was the dismal state of their accommodations, not the thought of upsetting his parents, that had him on the move. She knew then that they'd never come up here again. God knows what they were going to do about finding a place to be together. There was no way she was going back to having sex behind some tree.

They headed out, fumbling along in the dark till they found the fence again. With one hand each trailing along the chain link, they moved carefully forward. They didn't talk. Between the sex and the trek up there, they were beat. Not long after they started walking, the trees came to an abrupt end to reveal an epic-sized backyard, with an equally epic-sized house sitting at the end of it.

Tall and gray in the moonlight, the house was a vast, flat expanse of stone. Its face a sea of unlit windows, each one tucked into its own arched pocket. Emily took in the flood of slate steps leading up to a veranda and imagined how they'd feel under her feet. Reassuring and solid. The solidity of this structure made her think of New York. This was the opposite of the "one-story and painted an optimistic shade of bright bullshit" houses that filled the streets of Myrtlebury, every step and door and wall made from ever-flaking wood. This was a real building. And as she looked at it, she had a sense of a beginning. A feeling that if she didn't end up living in this house of stone at some stage in her life, then what would have been the point of anything? Out of nowhere, she had a goal. The stone house.

"My God," said Joseph.

"Who lives here?"

"Don't know. You want to go knock on the front door and ask?" he said.

"Sure."

"I'm joking. Let's walk down the side and see if we can get out the front. I bet the road's right there."

They moved across the lawn toward the house. The closer they got, the more she wondered what on earth could be inside a house that large. Would it be filled with furniture or just broad expanses of uncluttered open space? As the lawn turned to gravel, she drifted toward the back steps, compelled to know if they'd feel as solid under her feet as she thought they would. But before she could reach them, Joseph pulled her back toward him, and together they moved down the side of the house. They were almost to the front drive, Joseph cringing at the sound of their feet on the gravel, Emily too distracted to care, when she saw the thing she didn't know she'd been looking for. An in.

"Joe, look," she said so sharply he had no choice but to turn and see what she saw.

"No."

"We'll be in and out in thirty seconds. Don't you want to see what's inside?"

"Not if it means getting charged with breaking and entering."

"We're not breaking anything. The window's completely open. The house is inviting us in."

"The house is doing no such thing. Emily, it's time to go." She'd never heard outright tension in his voice before, and she realized that about now might be when Joseph Moth found out exactly how much more she was than he could handle. But she didn't let him in on this revelation, just twisted out of his grasp before climbing up onto the flat of the window ledge. A second later she was under and inside.

The room she landed in was large. She couldn't make out much detail in the moonlight, but she could tell there was no furniture to speak of, perhaps a fireplace on the far side. She made her way across the expanse and into the hallway, stepping onto a mass of tiny black and white tiles that squeaked beneath her sneakers. The ceiling here was so far away she lost sight of it in the dull darkness above. This hallway was even gloomier than the room she'd just come from, but at the center of all of it, she could make out a staircase wide enough for at least twenty people to stand side by side. She wondered for what earthly purpose would anyone create a staircase that expansive. She took a step toward it, imagining herself standing at its base, perhaps wearing a long cocktail dress and bathed in soft lamplight. What was at the top of those stairs? Perhaps a bedroom that was finally worthy of how much she and Joseph loved each other. Somewhere clean. Somewhere where they could be themselves. Maybe this was it. Their haven from the rest of the world, simply waiting for them to claim it.

She heard a soft tap back in the room she'd just come from and turned to find Joseph now inside, having just climbed in the window—his eyes as wide as she'd ever seen them.

"You *have* to come see these stairs. They're vast." He motioned for her to keep her voice down. Former Emily would have given a loud whoop just to show she didn't care, but instead she silently held out her hand, and then when he reached her, gently pulled him into the hallway.

She watched with pride as he took in the wide stairs and the wood-paneled walls. As if this was all hers and she was showing it off to him for the first time.

"I don't think there's anyone here. This could be our place," she said. She could see he wasn't convinced yet, but she'd get him there. But then, she saw his expression change. And then she heard it. The unmistakable snap of a cocking gun.

"What do you want?"

Emily felt all the blood bubble away from her face as she turned to see a figure at the top of the stairs. A woman in a thigh-length slip, all white silk and pale skin. If the woman hadn't spoken, she'd have sworn she was a ghost. But she was as real as they were. And much deadlier. The gun she pointed straight at them and the unshaken tone of her voice proved that.

"Move," hissed Joseph, bolting for the window like he thought it might close before he'd reach it. Emily went to follow him, but her feet wouldn't shift. She was stapled to the ground. Time froze as she stood staring at the woman in front of her, unable to breathe, but then she felt Joseph's rough tug on her hand, and whatever was holding her in place released. She half stumbled to the window after him, then forced her numb body under the pane. Her hair caught on the hook of the window latch as she went under, but she tugged hard and ripped it free. She landed hard on the gravel on both knees, and Joseph pulled her to her feet and dragged her toward the road just as the porch lights were turning on.

As soon as the house was out of her sight line, Emily was able to move again, and they ran—their footfalls landing on the sand track below them in dual thuds. She'd forgotten how her body shut down when she was scared. Despite all the negatives about living with Sophie and Ivan and Maddy, she had to acknowledge that she hadn't become trapped inside herself like that since she'd arrived at Pile House.

When they ran out of breath and were forced back to walking, she turned to ask Joseph how close he thought they'd just come to actually being shot, but he was staring straight ahead, and something in his glazed look told her that if she asked her question, she'd get no answer. He'd shut her out. She'd finally pushed him too far. Rather than admit that he'd gone to a place where she couldn't reach him, she let him have his silence. As they walked, she wondered if the woman in white had been real at all. Despite her hard voice and the click of the gun, now that they were away from there, something about her didn't seem of this world. The house had seemed so empty, so unoccupied at its very heart. It didn't seem possible that it was someone's home. But that was the truth of it; the house belonged to someone else. It wasn't Emily's. She wouldn't be going back there any time soon, but nevertheless, she could somehow feel it waiting for her return. Waiting for her to be ready to claim it. As if it knew she hadn't yet earned the right to be its owner, but that in time, she would. And even though it seemed wildly unlikely now, she knew that one day, the Stone House would be hers, and when it was, she'd move Joseph in. And then the two of them would never leave.

CHAPTER 8

BEE

Bee's phone sat on the table in front of her, its scratched-up, kid-proof case the shabbiest thing in the bar. Despite the phone's outward appearance, she didn't have the courage to put it away in her purse, as much as she'd have liked to. She checked it again, telling herself she was only looking to see what the time was. It was ten to eight. Still no texts from home, which meant the boys were either already asleep or keeping Sam so busy he hadn't had a chance to text her to complain about the impossibility of the task of putting them to bed without her. She hoped it was the latter. The boys attached themselves to her in a way they didn't their father, and she had cause to both love and hate that fact every single day. Tonight was the first time she'd ventured more than a couple of miles away from Fergus and Robbie since they'd been born. She'd hopped out for a quick glass of wine in Myrtlebury plenty of times with various collections of school moms—a quick three minutes' drive home if things went south with the bedtime routine. But tonight was different. Tonight she was in Silver Lake. Too far to go home for anything less than an all-out emergency.

It had been Maddy who had suggested the big night out. Now that her days living at Pile House were numbered, Maddy appeared to be weighing the pros and cons of moving back "into town." She hadn't said so explicitly, but nevertheless, Bee could tell she was mulling the idea over. This evening was Bee's first Silver Lake bar experience, and she was stuck somewhere between enchanted and feeling completely out of place. She'd only come to visit Joseph and Maddy in Silver Lake post-kids, and so they'd gone for marches around the reservoir, and visited achingly cool coffee shops, but never ventured into bars. This was a first.

They'd gotten a spot out on the patio. It was so pretty out here with its checkered floor and its pillow-topped benches, the brightly colored cushions luxuriously soft compared with the nut-hard wood underneath. The evening air was gently warm, and the wall in front of her, which bore a mural of macaws, toucans, and cockatiels, was washed in a light peach glow from the final rays of the sun. This didn't feel like the California she knew. It felt like someone else's secret and exotic dream. Maddy's dream.

The first drink had gone down way too easily, and Maddy had gone inside to get them a second. The others on the patio looked like they belonged on a movie set, and not behind the camera. Even with blue hair, nose piercings, microbangs, arm and neck tattoos, and wearing plaid of all things—they looked beautiful. And Bee knew enough to know that it wasn't the edgy styling that made them attractive. They just were. She drained the last of her drink and looked through the glass doors to where she could see her best friend leaving the bar, a fresh round of gin concoctions in hand. Maddy was in a cropped T-shirt and skinny jeans with a bulky belt and a bag Bee hadn't seen before. All black. She had no tattoos, no funky hair, not even a fedora, but even so, Maddy fit in. She looked happy. And no wonder. This was where she belonged. She was one of them.

A blast of hip-hop followed Maddy out of the bar and then quit as the glass door closed behind her. Bee took the cocktail Maddy was holding out to her, noticing her hands now smelled of just-cut citrus.

"Okay—two more bee's knees!"

"Is this . . . *lavender*," Bee said, pulling the sprig out of the chilly bronze mug. "Am I supposed to eat this?" Bee knew she wasn't supposed to eat it. She was playing up her role as basic white girl from the burbs. She didn't know why. Bee took a sip. Pure flavor heaven. Bee took two more quick sips, and as the good feelings finally hit, she released her sucked-in stomach. What was the point. It was what it was.

"Cheers," said Maddy, holding out her mug.

"Cheers!" said Bee as they clinked. "This place is amazing. Like, next-level people watching."

"I know. I love it. I used to hang out here all the time. It just feels right, like home—you know?"

"Totally. So this'll be your local again if you move back?" said Bee, hoping the question seemed more casual than it was.

"I suppose so." Maddy glanced around the patio at the yoga instructors and the graphic artists and the art directors, and Bee could tell that she was imagining it. Her grand return. All of a sudden, Bee didn't want Maddy to move back to Silver Lake. She didn't want to have to drive twenty miles and leave the boys to the mercy of Sam's second-rate bedtime story–reading skills in order to meet her for a drink in a bar where she didn't fit in. She wanted to make it stop.

"So I guess if you're going to be here downing sexy cocktails, and Emily's the one left puttering around Pile Pile, she'll have to be my new hang buddy." It was a joke. A half joke. But Bee instantly saw she'd hit a raw spot. For half a second, Maddy looked so stung, she almost regretted saying it. Almost. But then, Maddy was flaunting a new life in front of Bee. Admittedly a life that Bee didn't want, but even if she had wanted it, it was a life she could never have. That hurt. And she'd wanted to hurt her back. Just a little.

"Girl, you'd better watch your back if you're lining Emily up to be your new bestie. There's layers of stuff going on with that woman."

"*More* layers?" Maddy had already told her about the money, the vast house, the mysterious argument over Jodi Khan. What else was there?

"All I'm saying is, think twice before you start buddying up with her. You have to think of the boys, you know. She's not exactly the kind of person you want around kids."

"Maddy, it was a joke. I'm not going to start buddying up with her just because she's living in your old house. I'll probably never set foot in the place again after you move out." This seemed to settle Maddy, but Bee was suddenly struck by the idea of never setting a foot inside Pile House again. That beautiful house where she'd spent most of her life walking in and out the front door as easily as if she lived there. She supposed she'd still be in and out of there all the time if it had been Emily who Joseph had married instead of Maddy. "Imagine if they'd never split up and *she* was my sister-in-law." Bee said it out loud before she even thought about it.

"God. I mean, first off, never would have happened," said Maddy, looking at Bee like she'd just insulted her.

"I know, but what if it had? I'd be forced to be nice to her." No response was forthcoming from Maddy. Was it that hard a thing to imagine? Bee could quite easily imagine Sam married to someone else. Or maybe that was just because *she* occasionally fantasized about being married to someone else. She didn't necessarily *want* to be married to someone else. But she thought about it. All the time. Who didn't? Evidently Maddy. Bee took another swig. This cocktail was already two-thirds gone. At fifteen bucks a pop, these things needed to last longer.

"I mean, you *couldn't* be nice to her. Who could?" said Maddy, finally. Bee shrugged; she could feel her thoughts getting sloppy.

"She wasn't all that bad when she first got here. You almost had to feel sorry for her, right? After what she'd gone through with her mom and all the rest of it."

"After what she'd gone through, sure. But Bee. She *was* that bad. From day one she was that bad. She slapped you, remember? Hard."

"I know." She thought about it, the slap. Amazingly, as she relived the moment, she could still feel the slight tingle of it across her cheek. Bee rattled the ice at the bottom of her mug. A third was definitely in order. "Another one?" Bee said, and stood up. She'd already decided on another one, whether Maddy was into it or not.

The inside of the bar was just as decadent as the patio. All low lighting and even lower leather sofas. Bee placed her order with a bartender, or mixologist as Maddy had gently corrected her earlier, and then climbed up onto the velvet barstool. The bar was busier than it had been an hour ago, so she got ready to wait. She let the effects of the gin wash over her and thought about how her life might be different if Joseph and Emily had stayed together. Then she thought about how Emily had been when she'd first arrived and how things had gotten off track between them all and why. Bee felt as if she'd almost have everything in one long line—all the memories and motivations clear, the lines of fault as obvious as red blinking arrows. But then she'd get distracted by someone or something and the past would swirl out of reach, and she'd have to restack it all again from the beginning.

"Hello, stranger," said a voice, way too close to her ear. She whipped around in her seat. As if he'd sensed that he'd startled her, the whisperer was now standing a couple of feet back.

"Neb!" she said, jumping off the stool and giving him a hug he didn't seem to be expecting. "Oh my God. How are you?"

"I'm good. You look great," he said.

"I don't at all, but thank you," she said. Last time Neb had seen her was two kids and ten pounds ago. He, however, looked amazing, if very different. His hair was now shaved at the sides but scruffy on top. No facial hair, thank God, though there was a hint of a tattoo peeking out of the neck of his T-shirt. What hadn't changed about him was his general vibe of good times to be found within. He still looked like he'd tell you where all the fun stuff was happening if you would just ask. He smelled good too. But then, he always had.

"How are you?" he said. He said it like he meant it, as if he wanted to know every single thing that had happened to her in the ten years since they'd seen each other. What was there to say? That she was broke. Tired. How could she say any of that when here he was, looking better than ever, living on the Eastside. Literally the one who got away. She corrected herself. She'd let him get away. Sent him away. Big difference.

"Are you here with Joseph?" he asked.

"No. He doesn't live around here anymore. He moved back home."

"He did?" said Neb. "Why'd he move?"

"Maddy's dad died, and . . ." Neb looked at her expectantly for the rest of the sentence. Did he want her to spell it out for him? Maddy's parents died, so they'd had somewhere to live for free, and as Joseph's career was broken, the move had been a no-brainer. "And so they're living in his old house," she said diplomatically.

"Sorry to hear about her dad. Did they move back to Myrtlebury for good?"

"I don't know. Currently under debate, I think. But unless Joseph's career comes back from the dead, then probably?" She felt a bit disloyal talking about Joseph like that. But this was Neb. They'd grown up together. And Neb was in the same line of work, so she was sure nothing she was saying to him was new news. She'd heard enough of the details via Maddy to know the general music industry story. The friends who'd had to move back to Michigan to work in coffee shops or move out to Bali to work at surf resorts, not for the ocean breezes but for the cheap living. The only thing that had stood between Maddy and Joseph and that fate had been Pile House. She watched Neb, expecting him to nod sympathetically and then launch into a story detailing his own difficulties. But he just looked confused.

"I thought Joseph was doing pretty well, no?" he said. And she could tell he wasn't just being polite; he meant it. Most likely Joseph didn't want the whole world to know he was sinking in quicksand so had gone to great lengths to hide it, and now she'd blown it. Great. One more nail in the coffin that was her relationship with her brother.

"I mean, he's been working a few gigs here and there, but I think they've just been super slow in paying up."

"Gigs? I didn't think he was doing gigs anymore," said Neb. Bee shrugged. It irked her that Neb, who didn't even know where Joseph lived now, seemed to have more information on the particulars of how he spent his time than she did. Most of all, it irked her that her brother shut her out. On this. On everything. It was embarrassing. Perhaps it was time for Joseph to learn that there were consequences to giving his sister half the information and none of the story.

"All I know is what Maddy told me, which was without her dad's house to stay in, they'd be more or less homeless. Things have been bad. The whole industry's bad? I thought?"

"Not for Joseph. The rest of us are getting by on scraps. But he was one of the few who saw it coming. I mean the Apple placement alone—"

"Apple placement?"

"The music for the AirPods ad. You know, *I saw you once, I saw you twice.*"

"Yeah, yeah, I know that song." Bee had seen the ad in passing, but what was more familiar than the specifics of the ad was that first line. Everyone knew the song. It was part of the national consciousness.

"He brokered the licensing deal for that. That track is one of his massive library of goodies. All those unsigned bands, man. No label to get in the way, no manager to make a stink over publishing rights, he gets half the cash. The bands don't know any better. They're just grateful to have some money to supplement their barista jobs and make their next album with. I'm just surprised to hear he's struggling. I would have thought that the cash from Apple alone would have been enough to set him up, at least for a while. And that's just one of the deals he's done."

"All I know is that they've had a really rough couple of years, and Maddy's been the one who's been keeping everything afloat." She could hear her voice getting icy.

"Yeah, I don't know what's up with that," said Neb. But she could tell from his body language that wasn't actually the case. That he'd clocked exactly what was up with that and was backing off the topic. She wanted to ask more about these supposed advertising deals, but she could tell that the unclimbable walls had gone up.

"And what about you? Are you doing okay?" Behind her, Bee heard the drinks being placed on the bar. She turned around and picked up the closest one.

"Hanging in there. I'm a music editor now. Corporate bullshit, but it pays the bills." He looked at her drink, curious, and she held it out toward him.

"See if you like it," she said. The nonintimate thing to do would have been to politely refuse. But he didn't refuse. He took her offered glass and had a long taste, raising his eyebrows in approval.

"Gorgeous," he said softly, before handing it back to her. "So, if you're not here with Joseph, who are you here with? The husband?" said Neb. He sounded upbeat as he said it and looked around the bar, apparently seeking Sam. Neb had been invited to their wedding but had declined, saying that Abbie, his cousin who now lived in Phoenix, was getting married on the same day. But Bee had tracked Abbie down on Facebook and found that not to be the case.

"No," she said. "Not the husband." The way she delivered it was all wrong. She said it like there was more to the story. There was no more to the story. She was a mother of two, and Sam was the father of those two. Why was she opening the door to flirtation like this?

"What's your drink called?" he asked, taking it out of her hand again, his fingers against hers for a brief moment.

"Bee's knees." He took another sip, this time staring into her eyes as he did so until she felt that hard, long-forgotten knot at the bottom of her stomach think about unraveling. Oh shit. Time to shut this down.

"Think I'll have one too," he said, relinquishing her drink and looking down the bar to see who he could summon.

"Neb, can I ask you something weird?"

"Of course," he said lightly, as if he could already sense that what was coming was on the delicate side.

"It's a thousand years ago. And so stupid. When we were like, fourteen."

"Go on," he said, looking serious now. Ready to hear it. His seriousness was what made her decide it would be okay to say it. If he'd been all buoyant and teasing, she wouldn't have felt safe enough.

"Did you ever say"—she tucked her hair behind her ear, suddenly self-conscious despite the amount of gin she'd already consumed—"that I looked like a candy corn with a couple of oversized lemons stuffed down my shirt?"

"What?" She'd expected him to laugh, but he didn't.

"Did you ever say that? I know it was a long time ago. It doesn't—"

"I never said that. I know the dress you mean. I remember it—the one with the wide stripes. But I never put it together with a candy corn, and the thing with the lemons, just no."

"Are you sure?" she said, narrowing her eyes and adding a bit of laughter back into her voice. Despite how much it'd hurt her feelings at the time, she wanted to make it okay for him to admit it if he had said it. She wanted to know. Genuinely.

"Bee. That's a pretty specific burn. I'd remember if I'd said anything like that."

"Did some other guy say it?"

"No. I never heard anyone say that. Bee. Why are you asking me about this? You really think I'd say that?" She looked up at him. Yes, she'd believed that he'd said that. And as silly as it sounded now, it had been all she'd needed to blank him for the next four years till they both left town for college. She'd had a tough time believing that he liked her in the first place, despite how he'd acted. But then that comment, right when she'd been at peak paranoia about her body shape, had stepped in and confirmed what she'd suspected all along, that she just wasn't good enough for him.

But what if she had been?

Behind Neb, she saw that Maddy had come inside. Neb turned to see what Bee was looking at.

"I'm here with Maddy," said Bee finally, feeling ridiculous for stringing him along. So pointless. All of it was. She picked her cocktail back up and waved her over. Maddy smiled and began to walk quicker toward them.

Neb turned back toward Bee. His expression was flat, all the bounce and easy flirtation of earlier drained away.

"What's wrong?" said Bee.

"Nothing," he said, and then smiled a second too late and too light for Bee to believe him. "I have to split. I'm late."

"Late for what?" she said, suddenly achingly disappointed. "I thought you were going to get a drink. Stay to say hi to Maddy at least."

Maddy had almost reached them.

"I have to go," said Neb, and to her great surprise, he moved in and kissed her lightly, dead in the center of her mouth. She felt herself responding for a whisper of a second. And then he was gone.

"My God," said Maddy as she reached Bee. "What was *that*?"

"That was Neb," said Bee, still reeling from the kiss. His lips were hot and softer than they looked, and the second they'd touched hers she'd been struck by a *Sliding Doors* moment—imagining a second life. One where she lived in an apartment here in town with Neb. And . . . she forced herself to stop.

"Um. I could see that! Did he just *kiss* you?" said Maddy.

"Just saying goodbye. A peck on the cheek," she lied, passing Maddy her drink.

"Didn't look like it was on the cheek from where I was. What were you two talking about? It looked intense."

Bee made a split-second decision. Despite Joseph being a pain, despite his shutting her out, and despite Maddy being her best friend, when it came to it, her loyalty lay with her brother. Some instinct told Bee that if she didn't know about these ad deals he had going on, Maddy wouldn't either and that he might have some reason for wanting to keep it that way. She'd ask him. If she didn't like his answer, if she didn't like his attitude, she'd tell Maddy everything she knew. But she'd give him the benefit of the doubt first. Give him a chance to make it right.

"Just his career and stuff," Bee said.

"Ahh yes. Another poor soul suffering through the great music industry implosion."

Bee took another mouthful, and though the drink tasted and smelled exactly the same as the last one, for whatever reason, the feeling of it in her mouth suddenly made her want to throw up.

CHAPTER 9

BEE

Bee stood in the middle of the kitchen, in what she'd always considered to be the heart of Pile House, its outdated expanses of terra-cotta tiling and wall-to-wall honey-oak cabinets as comforting and familiar to her as her own home. But this room didn't look like the heart of anything today. It looked like a cross between a Daliesque nightmare and a hoarder's den. The counters were piled high with mismatched dessert bowls, mixing bowls, oven dishes. Every item of cutlery had been laid out in a series of neat lines as if it were about to head into battle; every type of knife ever imagined, every size of spoon and fork. It was impossible to think that these cupboards had contained so much. Surely they had never used all this stuff? It looked like someone crazy lived here. It looked like other people's garbage. Which was what it was.

Bee wandered into the living room, which was no less cluttered. Sets of dusty crystal ware, cocktail shakers, holiday decorations, half-burned candles, and various other bits of crap that Bee couldn't imagine any reasonable person wanting layered every surface. Bee didn't know how Maddy could stand the thought of strangers trawling through her parents' everyday items, discarding most of it for the useless crap that it was, and then taking home with them the few parts of her parents' life that they had deemed worthy enough for reuse. Well. They hadn't gotten through the day yet. In all likelihood, Maddy may *not* be able to stand it.

Bee had offered to do the estate sale for her. Had told her to get out of town for the weekend and come back when it was all done. It was a generous offer, and one that she hadn't made without some consideration, as it would have meant the boys would be stuck with Sam all weekend, which would have had repercussions one way or another. But Maddy hadn't taken her up on it. She'd insisted on doing it herself.

Greg walked into the living room, head bowed to his iPad as if he were in silent worship.

"You get that thing working yet?" asked Bee. The thing she was referring to was a credit card reader. Greg had spent most of yesterday trying to set it up, leaving Bee, Maddy, and Joseph to haul boxes of crap out of the attic and pull every item out of every cupboard, then display it all around the house till the place resembled a swap meet. If anyone else had spent all day sitting on the couch messing around with a piece of tech, she'd have thought they were trying to get out of the harder stuff. But not Greg. He was one of the good ones. And one of Joseph's oldest friends.

"Yeah. Want me to set yours up? I've got it figured out now."

"Too late for that," said Bee, and nodded to the front window. It was a few minutes till eight, which was the advertised start time, but even so, *they* were arriving. Two couples stood on the lawn. Eyes on the house, hungry.

"And the dead shall outnumber the living," said Greg.

"What?" said Bee.

"It looks like they're here to feast upon our brains. That one's drooling." He gestured to a woman with bottle-black hair who'd moved closer to the window, squinting to see what was happening inside.

"I'm pretty sure their hunger is purely for the trash of the newly deceased," replied Bee. Maddy chose that moment to enter the living room.

"Hey, Maddy," said Bee. "Shall I let them in?"

"Hold on a second," said Maddy. She walked over to the bar and opened it up, scanned the space inside, and closed it again quickly. Then she flipped open the ancient trunk next to the sofa. There was nothing in there. There was nothing inside anything. They'd already pulled every single item out of every single box, cupboard, and dresser in this house. It was what they'd spent the last day and a half doing. Did she not remember?

"What are you looking for?" asked Bee.

"Mom's hairbrush." The doorbell rang. "My dad's barometer's missing too."

"So let's find them," Greg said, putting down the iPad and opening up a closet that they all knew had nothing in it, but Maddy had given up her search and now stood in the center of the room, one hand over her mouth, silently crying. Bee watched as Greg abandoned the closet, then maneuvered around the piles of junk to pull her into a hug. She noted that Maddy's head fit in the space under his chin just perfectly. She'd never seen them this close to each other, and she had to admit that the two of them wrapped around each other like that looked weirdly snug. Greg looked over at Bee to see if she knew what this was all about, but she just shrugged in response. This was Maddy these days. He hadn't been around as much as Bee since she'd returned to Myrtlebury and didn't know how scatterbrained she'd become. Or how distressed it made her. Bee swatted away the unkind thought that Greg looked as if he was enjoying comforting Maddy in her moment of need a little too much.

"Where did you last see them?" asked Bee, not sure why she was bothering to ask. Since when did anything ever come of asking that question? Maddy abruptly broke out of Greg's hold.

"I put them both in my car," she said. "Yesterday."

"Oh." Unexpected. "Why?"

"Because I thought that'd be the one place they'd be safe." She wiped hard at her eyes with the heel of her hand, and Bee wanted to tell her to ease up but didn't. Maddy's whole face was now a sea of red blotches, and Bee privately marveled at how a face could go from normal to more or less wrecked so fast.

"Safe?" said Greg. *Safe* was an odd word choice. He patted his back pockets searching for a tissue, but the expression on his face told Bee that none were to be found. What dude carried tissues in their pocket on the regular? Greg was way too much.

"Safe from whatever it is that happens to any object you care about in this house," she said, turning to face Joseph, who'd just walked in. "But when I went to look for them, they weren't there. You moved them, didn't you." It was a statement, not a question.

"Of course I didn't move them. They probably got swept up when we were packing. I bet they're in the garage." Bee noted Joseph had *that* tone on. The placating tone that Bee happened to know irritated the fuck out of Maddy.

"How do you sweep something up from the trunk of a car? You don't. You move it. That's the only way things disappear from the inside of a vehicle. Someone unlocks the door, takes things out, and puts them somewhere else."

"Then I don't know. I'm sure they'll turn up at some point," said Joseph.

"Right. Like my bracelet did?" said Maddy. Bee realized she was biting her lower lip, hard. This was what she'd started doing recently in lieu of yelling at the kids when they drove her crazy. Maddy used to be so chill growing up. But she'd changed since she'd returned. Was it losing both parents practically back-to-back that had done it?

"Maddy, you're just going to have to let that one go," said Joseph.

"It was my mother's. How can I let it go?"

"Because we've talked about it and talked about it, and I can't talk about it anymore."

"We talked about it a couple of times two years ago."

"More like twenty times over the last two years."

"What?"

"Okay. Last time we do this. Your mom's bracelet dropped off your wrist when we went out to dinner. Remember?"

"What are you talking about? It vanished from my jewelry box."

"No. You wore it out on our anniversary dinner. Our first anniversary in Myrtlebury. The first time we went to Embassy. And when we got home, it was gone. You don't remember me tracking down the Uber guy and going through his car?"

"No. That was for my phone—an entirely separate time."

"You sure?"

Bee watched Maddy's face, and in the hard silence that followed, she could tell that Maddy wasn't sure. Bee knew the bracelet they were talking about; it was chunky and made of silver links that gently clinked as it moved up and down your wrist. She remembered Sophie wearing it. If she had to call it, Joseph's losing-it-while-out-at-dinner story made more sense than the thing spontaneously disappearing from Maddy's jewelry box, but it didn't matter either way—what mattered was how to deescalate this situation.

They all turned at a sound at the window. The woman now had her face up to the pane, the sides of her hands pressed white up against the glass as she cupped her eyes to get a better look inside.

"Maddy, we have to let them in before they crawl through the windows," said Greg.

"Okay fine, but if you see someone trying to buy a barometer or a hairbrush, don't let them."

"I promise," said Greg, opening the door.

"I'll go check the garage," said Joseph. And as distant as Bee was from him these days, she could tell he was relieved to have an excuse to leave, even though he was trying to hide it. This whole estate-sale thing wasn't his scene. The woman from the window had hustled to be first through the door, and Bee now watched as she rifled through some crafting supplies laid out on a picnic table. This wasn't particularly Bee's scene either.

"How much for these?" the woman asked, holding up a yarn ball she'd just picked out of a tired Ralphs bag. Maddy opened her mouth to reply, but nothing came out.

"They're a dime each. Everything on here is ten cents," said Greg, pointing to the sign taped onto the tabletop.

"I'll give you a dime for the bag."

Maddy closed her eyes. Bee needed to stay to oversee this. Maddy wasn't going to last more than five minutes without her. But this was her big chance to talk to Joseph alone. And so she decided to take it.

When Bee got to the garage, she saw that Joseph was not dutifully sifting through the many packed boxes. He was texting. He had the garage door raised to see by, and the brightness of the day didn't quite reach all the way to his corner, but even so, she could see that he hadn't made a start.

"Hey," she said.

"Hey," he said, shoving his phone into his back pocket. He then picked up a knife from the top of a box and sliced open the tape covering it. When had she last been alone in a room with her brother, without their spouses, or their parents, or her boys there as a buffer? Had it just worked out that way, or was it because that was how Joseph had wanted it?

"No barometer yet, then?"

"Not yet," he said lightly. Clearly she was being obtuse. But instead of telling her to get off his back, as would have been a fitting response, he tolerated the question. He was formal with her, like he always was. And she hated it.

"May I help?" she asked. Great. Now she was talking like a third-grade English teacher.

"Sure," he said. Short. Lean with his words, like every one of them cost him a quarter. Why was he like this with her? She knew why. But it was stupid. The real reason was that he'd just gotten in a habit of shutting her out. He hadn't adjusted to make up for the fact that they were both adults now. Adult siblings. Two people with a symmetrical history who were supposed to understand each other like no one else on earth could. She tugged at the tape on top of one of the boxes, but it wouldn't budge. He didn't offer to help.

"Can I borrow your knife?" she asked. He didn't answer. Just paused his own search, moved over to where she stood, and slit the top open. The box was packed full of china plates. There clearly wasn't going to be a hairbrush in here. This was a ridiculous task, and they both knew it.

"I saw Neb last week," she said. He looked up at her then. Properly *at* her.

"Where did you see him?" he asked, in the same polite voice as before. Too late for that. She'd seen that look. She had him.

"Silver Lake."

"Why were you in Silver Lake?"

"Maddy and I went for drinks. Didn't she tell you?"

"She said you were going out. I didn't know you were going that far."

Bee let this sit for a moment. She had the upper hand here, and she was going to play it. She could feel him waiting for her to say more. But she wasn't going to. She was going to let him come to her.

"So how is Neb?" he asked.

"Seems to be hanging in there."

"Yeah, I heard he was working at Warner Brothers now. Benefits, all that. What else you guys talk about?"

"Just stuff," said Bee. She was torturing him, and she was enjoying it. This was the most interested her brother had been in anything she'd had to say in years. "He did say this one weird thing," she said eventually into the silence, giving in to the urge to have his attention.

"Yes," said Joseph, looking up at her, all ears.

"Something about you and the music for an Apple ad. You know that song, *I saw you once, I saw you twice.*"

"Oh right." He pulled down another box, stacked it on top of the first one, and slit it open. That was all he had to say on the matter? *Oh right.* Now he had *her* on the back foot.

"Okay, are we really going to look through every one of these boxes for a hairbrush?" said Bee, closing the one she was looking through.

"I won't tell if you won't," said Joseph. She sat down heavily on the nearest box, which was slightly soft on the top. She moved, feeling whatever was underneath poking her in the butt. Not a pleasant sensation. Joseph looked like he wanted to tell her not to sit there, but he didn't say the words, and so she didn't move.

"Neb seemed to find it hard to believe that you and Maddy were broke."

"Oh God. Did you tell him that?"

"I may have alluded to it."

Joseph tipped his head back to stare at the ceiling, which she knew meant he was trying to hide how exasperated he was. Not so polite now.

"What? I'm sorry, do I have the wrong impression? I mean, there were times over the past year when I brought you guys a pot of mac and cheese because I was worried you literally wouldn't have anything to eat otherwise. But here's Neb telling me you made a bunch of cash on an Apple ad, and now I don't know what to think. I'm sure it's none of my business if you've got a secret chunk of cash stashed in the bank. But I think Maddy probably deserves to know."

"Can you just—"

"What?"

"Can you just do me a favor and not say anything about it to her." Joseph had his arms crossed, fingertips stuffed all the way up into the armpits, thumbs urgently pointing forward at her, like they were trying to make his point for him. As if he was trying to show that he was stubborn and reasonable all at the same time. But it wasn't going to work on her. The business-savvy body language, the conversational backtracks and switcheroos designed to twist you around so you didn't even remember the question you were asking in the first place. Even though he might not think much of her, she was still his sister. She'd grown up with his bullshit.

"So is it true?" she asked.

"Would you mind sitting on another box? That one has breakables in it." She ignored him.

"Is it true that you made a ton of money from an Apple ad and then forgot to mention it to anyone in your family?" This was the only way to deal with Joseph. Keep asking for what you wanted. He knew she had him pinned, and he didn't answer. Instead, he'd picked up a tape gun and closed up the box he'd just opened. "You can't stonewall your way out of this."

"I'm not," he said, applying an unnecessary third layer of tape.

"Joe. It's all you ever do to me. It's like you're eternally trying to work out how to be in my life as little as you have to be—how to speak to me as little as you have to. It's some stupid, petty habit you got into somewhere along the line, and it has to stop."

"I'm sorry. I don't mean to come off as standoffish." *Standoffish* was something of an understatement. All she had to do was walk into a room, and it was as if he was compelled to walk out of it. This admission was a start at least. But she was also wide-eyed enough to see it for what it was. A distraction. He knew that if he seemed open to talking about their relationship, she may well wander off down that conversational alley. But Bee wanted to know about the money. It was why she'd abandoned Maddy to the estate-sale zombies and trekked in here in the first place. And the only way she was going to get the info out of Joseph was to crawl forward in a straight line, eye firmly on the conversational prize.

"Maddy's my best friend. I'm going to have to say something. You're not—"

"You notice a change in Maddy, recently?"

"She's been spiky, sure, but she's been through a lot." *Spiky* covered it. Most of the time Maddy was fine. But every now and then she'd flare up. Not at Bee or the boys. But whenever she talked about Joseph, or the house, or the future, she was on edge.

"It's more than spiky, Bee."

"Then what?"

"I'm pretty sure she's getting sick. Like her mom."

"Alzheimer's? She's way too young for that."

"Early onset, then. All I know is that I'm seeing her do exactly the same sort of things that Sophie used to."

"What kind of things?"

"Losing stuff all the time. Forgetting where she's supposed to be."

"We all do that."

"This is different, Bee. She puts things in bizarre places and then blames me for it. And she gets so mad. Like, she put a basket of wet laundry in her trunk and then blew up at me for doing it. And I'm pretty sure she hit my car with hers, then just forgot."

"No. That dent in the bumper? She told me she found it in a parking lot like that."

"Not the case. I was the one who noticed it. I also noticed the matching dent on my bumper. It's like she sideswiped me reversing out of the drive, then forgot to mention it. Or perhaps she didn't even realize. She probably shouldn't even still be driving."

"If you truly think she's developing Alzheimer's, then you have to take her to a doctor."

"I don't think she'd go. I brought it up with her the other day, and it hadn't even occurred to her that something might be up."

"You think she's too close to it?"

"Probably. She understands about things going missing. And she knows that she'll be halfway through something and forget what it is she's doing, but I don't think she realizes that her personality's changed.

You know?" This was not where Bee had seen their conversation going. It killed her to drop this and bring them back to her original question, but he knew that—which was why he'd done it.

"And the money?" Bee asked. Joseph gave her a sad smile, and this time she knew she'd won.

"I'm thinking about leaving her."

"What? Because she got sick?"

"Bee, this isn't just sick. It's not like she needs to be driven back and forth to radiation a few times a week. You saw how it was with Sophie and Ivan. I can't do that. The upstairs bathroom still reeks from when Sophie forgot how to use a toilet and her pee sank into the floorboards. *You* know, you joined in enough Sophie hunts. Remember when she took off that last Christmas, and when we finally found her, Ivan had to wrestle her to get her back in the car? She didn't turn into some sweet old dear who couldn't remember her name. This thing with Maddy could go on for another twenty, thirty years. If Sophie hadn't had a seizure, it would all still be going on now. Decades and decades of things getting worse and worse. It's not like *The* fucking *Notebook*, Bee. I can't do it."

She wanted to judge him. She wanted to tell him that this was the response of a sociopath. That if she were in the same position, she would never make the shameful choices that he was now. But was that true? She who fantasized about being married to Neb just because he lived in a cool part of town and because her own perfectly healthy husband didn't listen as much or perhaps love as hard as he used to. But that was fantasy. It wasn't reality.

"Joseph, you married her. She's your family. You don't just get to ship out because something bad happened."

"Is she my family, though? It's not like we have kids together. I mean, sure, I wrote my name on some paper, people ate cake, but—"

"And so this money you're funneling away. That's for your big new start, I suppose?"

He looked away from her, out toward the drive. So here was the crux of the matter. She'd finally gotten there. He didn't answer her. He didn't have to.

"Wow. So not only are you going to leave her because she's losing her mind, you're also going to fuck her over for money as you walk out the door."

"She won't be fucked over. She keeps all the money from the sale of the house. I'm not entitled to any of that in a divorce—and I wouldn't even try to touch it. But even though she gets all the house cash, I'd still have to pay her something like ten grand a month. For years. I went to see a lawyer, and we did the math. Ten grand a month, Bee. It's not nothing."

"You mean alimony? Joseph, she's not going to sue you for ten grand's worth of alimony. You don't have kids. She's a grown woman. She runs her own business."

"Believe me. When this all comes out, it's the first thing she's going to do."

"You need to be straight with her. About all of it."

"I've already told her I think she's getting sick. She doesn't believe me. What more can I do?"

"You can tell her the truth."

"I'm asking you for a favor. As your brother." She felt her face change as he said that and hated how transparent she was. He knew that that was what she wanted. To be his sister again. His real sister. She didn't know whether something had genuinely shifted between them, or whether he was talking to her again because he wanted something from her. But either way, she had him back. And she didn't want to lose that. "Besides, it's not like she's the total innocent," he added.

"What do you mean?"

"I can't say," he said, looking down at his hands. "I'm sorry. It has implications for Greg."

"Greg? Did she have an affair with Greg or something?" It seemed unlikely but not impossible. Maddy had always held Greg a little too far at arm's length, and Bee had always half wondered if she was pretending she didn't like him in order to cover up some inconvenient feelings.

"I can't say. I would if I could. Believe me, I would. Can you just trust me on this one?"

Trust him? Trust the man who was about to all but push his sick wife over the edge of a cliff. Bee considered what it was that she wanted. Despite his flaws, she wanted her brother back. He was the only one she had. She wanted an uncle for her sons. She especially wanted to reclaim him if things were going to continue to fall apart with Maddy. She'd come to rely on Maddy way too much. Bee's parents kicking back in their retirement in Shangri-la a couple of hours' drive away weren't nearby enough to help out with the kids. Of course, she had other friends outside of Maddy, but they all had families of their own, and it was understood your own family came first, and if you or your kids had needs that clashed with what their spouse or kids or great aunt needed—too bad. Maddy would have gone the same way too—if she'd ever had kids. Bee wondered if she'd even have kids now. If Joseph was right about what was happening to her, she well may never.

"What do you say to dinner next week, wherever the boys want to go. My treat," he said, seeing she was on the verge.

Too right it would be his treat. Bee wondered how much money, exactly, he was making right now. And then he did something he hadn't spontaneously done in years: he moved over toward her and pulled her into a hug. They hadn't hugged in so long that his body felt different to her. Still Joseph, but there seemed to be more meat and fewer awkward angles than the last time they'd hugged. He was a good hugger when he meant it, she'd forgotten about that. But then he started to talk, and she felt her stomach tighten.

"You don't have to lie. Just don't tell her what's up. Just for the next few weeks. It's not the right time. The move's enough for her to cope with. We have to go slow on all this. These things are fragile."

"What's fragile?" They both turned, caught in their hug. It was Maddy, standing just inside the garage door. The bold sunlight behind her made her face a dark shadow, but Bee didn't need to see her face to know what she was thinking. She could hear it in her voice.

"Your mom's china," said Joseph, breaking away from Bee and flipping open the box she'd been sitting on. Thankfully, it hadn't yet been subjected to one of Joseph's triple-retaping efforts. "I should have wrapped this before it was boxed up. If these movers are anything like our last set, it'll never make it."

"You booked the last movers," said Maddy.

"I did," conceded Joseph. Bee looked at Maddy. Old Maddy never would have blamed the crappy job the last movers did on Joseph. She'd have placed the fault firmly with the movers. Joseph closed the lid of the box again, but something about the way he paused before he did so caught Maddy's attention, and she made her way over and opened it up again. She moved her hands over the china inside and then picked up what appeared to be a gold-rimmed milk jug missing most of its handle. Then she picked up a curved piece of porcelain and held the two together. It was a match. Bee opened her mouth to apologize. But Joseph got there first.

"Sorry, that was me. I knocked it over when it was on the ground." Bee waited for the reaction from Maddy. Old Maddy would have smoothed it over, made a joke, changed the subject. Who knew what New Maddy would do. But it turned out New Maddy didn't seem that bothered about the broken jug. She'd moved toward a long filing cabinet that stood against the wall. She gave the top drawer a hard tug. For half a second it looked like the cabinet was going to open, and then it tugged on back. Locked.

"Why did you lock this?" said Maddy.

"So it doesn't pitch open in the moving truck," said Joseph. He picked up the discarded milk jug. "You want me to try and glue this?"

"Where are the keys?" she asked.

"Why?" asked Joseph.

"Those newsroom photos of Dad's typewriter are in here. I'm in an argument with some woman about exactly how old it is. You have the keys?"

"Somewhere," said Joseph, moving over to his desk and opening the top drawer. He rifled through the junk inside and then, not finding them, opened the drawer underneath.

"Are they not on your key chain?" asked Maddy. Joseph patted his pockets.

"Maybe. My keys are in the house if you want to go check."

"I'm not going back into that insanity. You go check," said Maddy.

"Hey," came a voice from the drive. It was Greg, drained of all his earlier easygoing humor. The shoppers had gotten to him. "Someone wants to know if you'll take fifty bucks instead of two-fifty for some china dogs."

"Those are nineteenth-century Staffordshires," said Maddy.

"She also wants to know if you'll take fifty for the dining room table instead of two hundred."

"Should I just parcel up the rest of the house and give it to her for another fifty?"

"You need to put the antiques and stuff on eBay," said Bee.

"I know. I just thought I might be able to get some of them taken care of today," said Maddy, who looked so totally deflated and so totally like her old self that Bee felt her heart melt a little. But then she pulled it back—if she was going to be on her brother's side, she was going to need to stop melting every time something bad happened to Maddy. Otherwise, she was going to wind up as nothing but a puddle on the floor.

CHAPTER 10

MADDY

"It's really not that bad," said Bee, throwing herself down in the middle of the couch.

"Bee, it's awful," said Maddy from the bed, where she sat cross-legged on top of the covers. They now sat eye to eye, which was made possible by the bed and the couch being in the same room. This fact, among other things, had brought Maddy to the conclusion that the new digs were more or less unlivable. It was the size that was the issue. But the more Maddy complained, the more Bee felt a duty to endorse the place. And now they were caught in a conversational loop. *It's fine. It's not fine. It's fine. It's not fine.*

The current digs were supposed to be temporary. Despite, thanks to her sister, suddenly having more dollars in their account than Maddy had ever had at one time, it turned out that potential landlords were really into things like salaries and credit scores. With the chunk of cash they had at their disposal, they might have been able to sidestep the need for a decent set of financials with a good reference from their last rental. But the end of their last tenancy had coincided with Joseph's bank account emptying out, and so they'd used the deposit in lieu of paying the last month's rent and then bailed. They could have had

Joseph's parents sign as guarantors—not that two retirees living off a fixed income in Big Bear were exactly the big leagues—but Joseph had put his foot down at that one, and so here they were. In Greg's guest house. They'd find something decent soon enough. But what with the difficulties with red tape and the one-month turnaround time, they'd been short on options.

Greg was doing them a favor letting them rent his guest house at all. Greg had been living in it for about a year now while he slowly, so slowly, renovated the main house. But he'd generously put his tortoise-paced refurb on ice as soon as Maddy had mentioned her and Joseph's predicament and let them move in. Greg was now living in the main house that had no working shower and boxes of wood-effect tile everywhere you looked. He hadn't even been going to charge them rent, but Joseph had insisted on that one. Joseph had presented his eagerness to pay as all about him being a good and generous person. But really, Maddy knew it was because if they didn't pay Greg rent, Joseph would get roped into the refurb, and after successfully avoiding doing any work on her parents' house for the past two years, Joseph wasn't about to start ripping up kitchen floor tiles and smashing jackhammers through bathroom walls on a property that wasn't even his.

The place was fine, even though trying to find a place to put anything was like a never-ending game of Tetris. But the thing that had *really* sucked about moving out of Pile House was that there was no longer any Bee on tap. Bee was now on the opposite side of town. It shouldn't have mattered. Not to a friendship as long and strong as theirs. But it did somehow. It had changed the dynamic completely. No more casual dropping by. No more barefoot boys ready to dig up her garden in a valiant search for pirate worms. In fact, she rarely ever saw the boys now. Bee seemed to have somehow developed the ability to pick the boys up from jujitsu and a swim class that finished at exactly the same time, and Auntie Maddy's Taxi Service, as she'd always called it, was no longer required. She hadn't seen much of any of them. This was, in fact, the first time she'd been able to get Bee over to see the place, and the boys hadn't come with. A microspace with boxes of stuff stacked in tenuous piles was no place for kids. Despite the stacks of crap everywhere, a good percentage of their belongings was actually stashed in the storage unit they'd had to rent to house the bulk of her parents' furniture. Her unwillingness to let it all go for a fraction of its worth meant that the estate sale hadn't been the success it might have been.

It wasn't a huge surprise to her that Bee had taken so long to come visit. In all honesty, the vibe had been off between them from before the move out of Pile House. There had been a series of odd things. No response to a voice mail left asking Bee what clothing size Robbie was after she spotted a T-shirt at Target she knew he'd love. Zero response to a text asking Bee if she wanted a latte when Maddy had gone on a Starbucks run. And, of course, the fact that Maddy was no longer called on to shuttle the boys around when she knew that she needed *someone* to do it. Something was off. In general. And today was her chance to find out what.

The debate about whether the guest house was livable or not had drawn to a close, and they now sat in silence, Bee's eyes flitting over the boxes piled up against the wall. Maddy framed a question in her mind, though the thought of actually having to ask it had her feeling humiliated before she'd even said the words. You shouldn't have to beg someone to let you do them a favor.

"So how come Fergus doesn't need picking up on Wednesdays anymore?" There. She'd said it. She couldn't take it back. She could guess what Bee was going to say here. That the jujitsu class time had changed or that the swim class had. But they hadn't. She'd called both places to check. If Bee told her any different, then she'd know that something was up. Majorly up.

"Rose said she could pick him up. Her son's in Fergus's class, so they all go back to her house for twenty minutes or so till I can get there. Baked-in playdate. The boys love it."

"Really? Nosey Rosey?" Nosey Rosey had earned her name during high school for her skill in picking up gossip. Or rather, her lack of skill, hence the nosey part.

"That was a million years ago. She's fine now." But Maddy knew that one mom spontaneously helping another out wasn't what had happened here. Bee hated to be in anyone's debt—except for Maddy's, she didn't count. She wouldn't have rigged up this playdate arrangement unless she was desperate. Especially not with Rose. Even if she was no longer nosey, she was surely still obnoxious. That trait didn't just evaporate with age.

"Everything okay with you?" asked Maddy.

"With *me*? Sure," said Bee lightly. Maddy didn't care for the way she'd put an emphasis on *me*. It seemed to insinuate that whatever the fuck was up, the issue lay with Maddy.

"I mean with *you and me*?" Bee didn't respond. Bingo.

"Okay," said Bee, getting ready to spill it, whatever it was. "Can we get real for a minute here?"

"Real about what?"

"Real about what's going on with your health."

"My *health*?"

"I talked to Joseph, and—"

"Bee." This was serious, and she hoped her voice conveyed exactly how serious. He couldn't just go around telling everyone that she was sliding into dementia. That was the way that things that weren't true became true.

"What?"

"I'm fine. Joseph's being paranoid."

"You don't think there's any chance at all that what happened to your mom could be happening to you?"

"Bee, he's talking about one or two tiny, minimal things. Like, there was this random pair of socks in my drawer that I didn't recognize and then—"

"He said you put a basket of wet laundry in the trunk?"

"What? That never happened."

"You sure? You used to go to the laundromat, right? When you lived in Silver Lake?"

"Yes, but—"

"You think maybe you spaced out and—"

"Forgot I'd moved to another part of LA and gained a dryer? No."

"The dent on your Jeep—"

"I found it like that, in the parking lot."

"He said there was a matching dent on his car. Like you backed into him and—"

"That's just a coincidence. I've no idea how a dent appeared on his car. Or the Jeep. Maybe there's some dick on Peach who can't park and then doesn't leave a note when they crunch someone's bumper."

"But you parked in your driveway at Peach, not on the street, and I thought you said it happened in a parking lot."

"You know what I mean."

"He said you've been forgetting things, losing everything."

"I don't forget anything important, and we all lose things."

"Maddy, I need you to hear what I'm saying. I'm worried about you. One or two of these things on their own doesn't add up to much. But when you combine them, it starts to paint a picture."

"There's nothing wrong with me. I'd know if it was something more than just me ditzing out."

"Would you, though? Did your mom know? Or did she need other people to tell her?" This one stopped her in her tracks. Her mom. Maddy and her dad both sitting around the dining room table—the one that she'd just handed off to some stranger for fifty bucks—trying to convince her beautiful mother that something was wrong. Trying to make her understand that Dad wasn't trying to get her committed, he just really needed her to come to the doctor with him. But her mom couldn't see that she was already halfway to becoming lost, because the

106

part of her brain that could have recognized that it was happening had already died. There was a term for it. Maddy reached for it but couldn't recall what it was. The word was similar to amnesia. *Ansong*-something. Whatever it was, it meant that when her mom one day didn't recognize the hairdresser she'd had for the past fifteen years and then when she'd mistaken her husband for an intruder and tried to push him down the stairs, even then, she still couldn't grasp that something was wrong with her. She told anyone who would listen that it was Ivan who was responsible for the things that were happening, that it was Maddy who'd somehow accessed her bank account and spent all the money, even though she hadn't lived at home in years. Was it really outside the realm of possibility that Maddy was already knee-deep in the sludge of the same battle and didn't even know it? She *felt* fine. But was she?

"There was one thing that freaked me out," said Maddy. Ever since Joseph had brought up "the issue" on the drive out to Emily's place, Maddy had been privately obsessing over each point he'd made—analyzing each one until she could more or less explain it away. She'd come to the conclusion that socks she didn't remember buying, a minor dent on her Jeep, and things ending up in the wrong place didn't mean she was afflicted with what her mother had. But there was one incident that she couldn't explain away.

"What?"

"I saw Emily in Joseph's car. They were driving down Main Street, but when I asked Joseph about it later, he said it never happened." Bee sat with this one for a second, her head cocked. She looked concerned. But it wasn't the kind of concerned that meant Bee sniffed a rat. It was the same breed of concern she'd had for this entire conversation. Concern for Maddy's sanity.

"You sure it was Joseph?"

"Yes. I even saw the famous dent on the bumper. It was them." Now that she'd said it, she realized that she'd just given Bee ultimate power. She would be the decider here. She now got to tell her whether she was hallucinating, or if maybe, just maybe, something else was going on. "Do you think he could be lying about it?" Maddy prodded as Bee's silence dragged on.

"Did he seem like he was lying?"

"No." Maddy suddenly had an unwelcome flash of her mother railing against her dad for something similar, again, just before they found out what was wrong with her. She'd been convinced he was cheating on her with her own cousin. And then equally convinced he was sleeping with the deputy head at St. Novatus. All false. But Maddy *had* seen Joseph and Emily in the car. And as much as using the same script as her mother made her want to push the words back down inside her, she had to say them. "Do you think he could be having an affair? With Emily."

"An affair with your fucked-up sister? I don't think so," said Bee. And the way she dismissed it, without even snagging on it for a second, Maddy knew that Bee didn't think it was true. Whatever inside intel Bee had on this situation, Joseph having an affair with Emily wasn't part of it.

Bee's phone trilled from inside her bag. She grabbed it and shut off a calendar reminder that was pinging at her.

"I've got to go," she said, getting up off the couch. "Bookfair."

"Okay," said Maddy, slightly frosty. Was this not more important to her than that damn bookfair?

"I'm sorry. I want to help you work this out, Maddy, but I've got about fifteen minutes to get to the school, and I have to shove at least some makeup on my face before I get there, or no one will recognize me."

Normally Maddy would object and tell Bee that she was beautiful just as she was. But today, she didn't say a thing. Truth be told, without eye makeup on, Bee did look radically different. Her eyebrows had been overplucked back when they were teens, and now things had to be done with pencils to alert the general public as to where they could or should have been. If she turned up like she was right now, half the women on the PTA probably wouldn't know who she was.

"So will I see you soon? Or are you going to disappear into a black hole again?" asked Maddy, hoping they'd repaired things enough between them that they were back on track. That they were healed enough to talk about why they'd been off track in the first place.

"What do you mean a black hole?" asked Bee, giving Maddy her answer. No, they were not back on track, not even slightly.

"Bee, I'm scared. I don't know what's going on."

"Try not to dwell on it. It's all early days," said Bee. Something about her best friend falling back on a puffy cliché in this desperate moment made Maddy angry. Was this all not worth a more genuine response? "You need to talk to Joseph. *Really* talk to him. Please. Let him know how you're feeling. He's your husband. He should be helping you with this."

"Yes, my husband. At least there's someone legally responsible for making sure I don't end up wandering the streets like a bag lady if my mind *is* turning into pus." She was joking. But Bee didn't answer. At least, she didn't answer verbally, but what Maddy saw flit across her oldest friend's face made her stomach turn over. Because for a split second, Bee looked scared.

"Why did you look like that?" Maddy asked.

"Like what?" said Bee, heading toward the door. Maddy wanted to physically pull her back. To superglue their hands together like they'd done when they were seven. But most of all, she wanted to shake her until she affirmed that blood was not thicker than water and that Bee's loyalty was to her before her brother. She wanted to shake her until the truth fell out. "I have to go. I'll see you later." Bee leaned over, gave Maddy a kiss on the cheek that didn't quite connect, and then walked out the door.

CHAPTER 11

BEE

The weather was a betrayal. For the conversation she was about to have, there should have been rain, or at least a chill in the air. Instead, it was punishingly hot. Clouds a thing of memory, the sky the flat, solid blue of a California valley summer. Bee stood across the street from the fire station. Despite having just taken the world's shortest walk from the city parking lot, sweat cupped the underneath of her boobs and her inner thighs clung to each other like they were lined with Velcro.

This was it, then. She'd looked in Greg's windows on her walk down to Maddy's. He wasn't home. His car wasn't home. Which meant he was at the only other place he ever was—the fire station. She'd already texted Rose to say she'd be late for her shift at the bookfair. Truth was, depending on how long this conversation went on, she didn't know if she'd make it to the bookfair at all. Rose had said she'd cover. She was in uncomfortably deep with Rose at this stage, and the payback would come at some point. An obligatory sleepover for James so Rose and her husband could get away for the weekend. Dog-sitting. A request for a grocery run when it wasn't really convenient. Something. But it was worth it. Maddy was worth it.

She took in the fire station, which wasn't much more than a squat stucco building. The only thing of any charm, the freshly washed fire trucks themselves. She eyed the front door. Were you even allowed to just walk into a fire station? She'd never been inside one before. And then she saw him, walking toward one of the trucks with a leaf blower, a towel in his back pocket. If drying a truck on a day as hot as this one was all he had going on, then he could certainly spare twenty minutes to talk. He saw her when she was halfway across the street and waved, pleased, then slightly concerned.

"Hey, you," he said, setting down the blower and coming out onto the sidewalk. "Everything good?"

"I'm not sure," Bee said. "Can I talk to you for a minute?" An older guy in suspenders and the beginnings of a belly walked over to the leaf blower and picked it up. Sensing someone behind him, Greg turned back around.

"Can I steal him away for twenty?" Bee asked, instinctively knowing that Greg would never agree to leave but that if this man said he could go, he'd be obliged to.

"You bet," said the guy, flicking the blower off and on again. "Have fun." He said it with a touch of something that Bee couldn't quite place. He turned his attention to the truck, and Greg looked back at her, pissed but hiding it. She had a feeling he'd pay for her visit later. Something along the lines of epic teasing over someone else's wife coming to the station for a heart-to-heart.

"Coffee?" said Greg, pointing toward The Myrtle on the other side of the street.

"Perfect," said Bee. Maddy hadn't offered her coffee earlier like she normally did, and Bee was currently undercaffeinated. She added the coffee oversight to the pile, along with all the other small things that on their own meant nothing but added together might mean *something*.

The coffee shop was only half-full, but even so, Bee could feel the subtle ripple reaction from almost everyone inside. She'd walked into places with Greg in his uniform a couple of times before now, and it always went the same. Navy pants and a navy shirt with a small patch on the shoulder. Not exactly the stuff of hot dreams, but nevertheless, she got it. She'd turned to stare herself whenever firefighters came into the grocery store. You couldn't help it. One of them or a group of them, either way, you had to look. For reasons unknown, it was compelling. They slid into the nearest booth and were quickly poured coffee "on the house" by the waitress.

"Sorry to drag you away like that," said Bee, and took a sip of the coffee and thought that it was just as well it was free.

"It's fine. It's not like me having a woman come visit me at work will lead to any speculation at all," said Greg, dumping a third pack of sugar into his cup. He obviously had experience with this brew.

"I'm not *a woman*, Greg. I'm your friend."

"I know that," he said. "And I'll tell them that. But even so, my big morning coffee date will now be a running topic for weeks. Maybe years. Anyway. What's up?"

"You get many women coming to visit you at work?"

"As you're asking, no. You are the first. Which is why they'll have such a fantastic time with it."

"No visits from Maddy, then?" she said, and watched for the reaction. There was none.

"Maddy? No. Why?" Bee was good at digging for nuggets of information. But that was because, when you got down to it, people were always ready to give them. Everyone loved to know that someone else was interested in what was really going on with them. But Greg wasn't playing. Bee had the feeling he didn't even realize he was in the game. Over the last week, she'd kept coming back to Joseph's "not so innocent" comment. Bee knew that whatever Maddy had gotten up to with Greg in the past should have no bearing on whether or not she told her about the gobs of money Joseph was stashing away. She was her best friend. But Joseph was her brother. So if whatever Maddy had done was *that* bad, maybe she could find a justification for not cluing her in. Or at least delaying until it was too late to make a difference. She was hunting for a way to keep the moral high ground *and* stay on the right side of her brother. If Maddy had cheated on Joseph with Greg, then it could be argued that she deserved everything that was about to happen to her. Not really. But at least Bee could then find a way clear to be on her brother's side.

"Something's going on with Maddy. And I'm trying to work out what."

"Okay," he said. "What's the scoop?"

"Are you and Maddy having an affair?"

"What? No!" The woman at the booth opposite theirs glanced over at them and then back to her food. No expression on her face, but they could both tell she was now contently eavesdropping. The magical *affair* word had been dropped after all, and now that the glint of sex had been introduced to the conversation, there was something worth listening in to.

"Joseph said that she'd done something. That she wasn't 'so innocent,' whatever that means, but he wouldn't tell me what because it was something to do with you."

"Can you keep your voice down?" he said. Bee shrugged. Keeping her voice down wasn't something she could commit to under the best of circumstances, let alone a discussion like this one. "If it was something Joseph thought you needed to know, then he'd have told you."

"Whatever it is, it's not his secret to tell. It's yours and Maddy's. And I need to know, because if you two have been having an affair, it changes things. It changes how I feel about things that I know are about to happen. Even if it's not going on right now—even if it was a while ago—it's important."

Greg slid to the end of the booth and stood up. She turned to watch him go, thinking he was headed for the door. If he thought she wouldn't follow him back to work, he was mistaken. They could have this conversation in front of the entire fire crew if that was his preference, she really didn't care. But then she saw he wasn't headed out the door, but to the counter. And a second later he returned with two takeout cups.

"Let's walk."

As they stepped outside, Bee felt the heat clamp down around her again. She wished she hadn't been so flippant about keeping her voice down now; the air-conditioning inside the café had been strong enough for the wet patches on her shirt to turn cold. Greg turned away from the fire station and headed toward Main Street.

"Where are we going?" asked Bee.

"Away from other people. You can't take me to the coffee shop across the street from work and then start yelling into a megaphone about how I'm having an affair with my best friend's wife."

"I wasn't on a megaphone."

"You may as well have been. It'll get back, you know."

"To the firehouse? Is that all you care about? There are bigger things at stake here."

She waited for him to ask what things, exactly, were at stake, but he didn't. They walked another block in silence, then crossed the street and headed into the park. It was pretty empty—only a couple of parents with their kids at the far end attempting to run the energy out of their offspring before the day inside got started. But the fountain in the center had no one on the benches dotted around it, and so that was where they took their seats. Greg handed Bee her coffee, and she immediately leaned over him to pitch it straight into the trash can. She waited for him to make some wry observation about her trying more sugar next time, but he said nothing. He was pissed at her.

"I have never had an affair with Maddy. I promise you. If she's cheated on Joseph, it wasn't with me. I'd tell you if it was."

Bee knew that the whole Maddy-and-Greg-affair idea hadn't seemed that likely in the first place. Not because Greg wasn't attractive.

More because infidelity wasn't his style. Greg took the whole firefighter thing very seriously—a bit too seriously in Bee's opinion—and though Bee knew that the ability to put out a fire didn't necessarily guarantee that person would never have sex with someone else's wife, she did know that he was old-school. He'd told her more than once that his biggest aspiration was to be thought of as a pillar of the community. And unlike Joseph with his "I signed some paper and people ate cake" ideals, Greg put a lot of weight on marriage as an institution. He believed in it. Even though he hadn't done it himself. Perhaps because he hadn't done it himself.

"So what, then? What did you and Maddy do that wasn't innocent?"

He didn't respond. Just took a sip of the coffee and then flung his into the trash too. He may not have been lying about the supposed affair, but she could tell that he knew exactly what she was talking about. Up till now, she'd wondered if Joseph had only said what he'd said about Greg to divert her attention. But no, she could see that something was there, but he was going to need it prodded out of him. She'd ease him into a trade. Give him her nugget so that he'd be obliged to give him hers.

"If I tell you something about Maddy, can you sit on it?" she said.

"Sure." Anyone else and he probably would have told her to keep her secret to herself. A pillar of the community wasn't interested in gossip, after all. But when it came to Maddy, he was happy to bend the rules.

"Joseph's going to leave her."

"What?"

"I know."

"Why?"

"He thinks she has Alzheimer's like her mom, and he doesn't want that to be his life for the next twenty years." She could have framed it better, she knew that. But she'd said it that way to stoke a reaction.

Make it seem like whatever Greg had gotten up to with Maddy, Joseph was capable of much worse.

Greg was now staring straight into the bubbling water in front of him, which would have seemed like something of a nonreaction to most, but she could tell that he was livid. His eyes had turned a bright blue, practically the same hue as the mosaic at the bottom of the fountain, and she wondered if that was down to the intensity of the morning sun or the intensity of his rage. If it had been Greg married to an ailing Maddy, he'd have brushed her hair when she forgot how, shielded her from the fact that both her parents were dead when she asked where they were for the eight hundredth time; he'd have held her hand extra tight when they crossed the road, wiped her crap from the walls when she took to smearing it on there, and done everything else that needed to be done until the day she died.

"It's a diabolical choice," said Bee. No one was denying that. "And I know it's not what you would do," she said.

"You're right about that," said Greg, and he said it with such heat that Bee wondered if her thoughts about Greg being in love with Maddy for the past two decades were right on the money.

"Joseph asked me not to tell anyone. Just for a few more weeks. And I'm still hoping to change his mind. But if she was cheating on him with you, I'd at least be able to see why he was doing it. I want to be on his side. He's my brother. But he's making it very hard." She didn't mention the money. There was no need. Joseph's plans to leave Maddy had been more than enough to get the response she'd wanted.

"It's not an affair," said Greg.

"So what, then?"

"I'm not sure if this is exactly what Joseph's talking about. But it probably is. Either way, it's time for it to come out."

"Okay?" she said.

"You cannot tell anyone that you heard this from me."

"I won't."

"Bee. Promise me. It's important. It can't get back to Maddy that I told people about this."

"I promise. Whatever it is, I won't say you told me. Anyway, this is just for me—so I can get my head straight." She could see he was still reluctant. "I promise. On my kids' lives, I promise." She hadn't wanted to say that. It had slipped out. But it was the one thing she'd never go back on, and he knew it. "So what is it?"

"Okay." He took a huge breath in, held it for a second, and then blew it all out. "This was almost twenty years ago, Bee. We're all different people now."

"I know that."

"You remember the fire, at your school?"

"Um. I'm pretty sure I do, Greg," she said. Of course she did. It was town legend. The fire, and everything that had followed it, had defined half her teenhood. It had shaped all their lives in ways that were both obvious and murky.

"It was Maddy."

"What do you mean?"

"It was Maddy who started the fire. And me."

For a second, Bee didn't understand. It made no sense. And then it made all the sense in the world. The consequences immediately began to list themselves, one stacking on top of the other until her brain gave up on processing them all. What had they *done*? She felt her face flush hot with the shock of it, as if *she* were the one who should be ashamed.

"Why?" she asked.

"Bee. It was a complete and total accident. Just a knocked-over candle."

"What were you even doing at school?"

"Just messing around."

"Messing around doing what?" she asked. He didn't answer. And then she figured it out. They'd been doing *that*. So her idle speculations about Maddy having had feelings for Greg once upon a time weren't off base. She couldn't believe that Maddy had never told her. But then, if what Greg was saying was true, her one-time fling with Greg was the least of what Maddy had omitted to share. "Greg. You destroyed—"

"I know. But Maddy was so scared. I was too. We were just teenagers. Clueless. But then one day you're not a teenager anymore, and suddenly you know exactly how wrong and stupid you were. But then how do you make it right?"

"Is that what you're doing now, making it right?"

"I don't think there's anything I can do that'll make it right. Do you?"

Bee didn't answer.

"There were certainly things you could have done back then," she said eventually.

"I know. But I didn't."

"Why the fuck not?"

"For Maddy. She made me promise. I keep my promises, Bee." Bee stared at him. Was he going to try to twist this up into him actually being honorable? "And when I got older and knew better, I still didn't say anything. Because, as you said, it was too late. Way too late. Then she married Joseph, and so there was no way. But if they're over, then there's no reason to sit on it anymore. People should know the truth."

Bee looked up toward the mountains. Faded black in the morning heat and covered in beige haze, they looked exactly the same as they had forty seconds ago, despite the fact that her whole world had just turned itself inside out.

"And how are *people* going to find out, exactly? I thought you didn't want anyone to know this came from you?"

"I'm sure it'll find its way out somehow," he said, looking at her sideways.

"What, you think I'm the town crier or something?"

"Aren't you?"

"Gregory. You're already on thinner-than-thin ice."

"I'm sorry! All I'm saying is, it is generally known, that once Bee Hooper comes into possession of a piece of information—that information often finds itself liberally spread from one end of town to the other."

"Well, thanks." She sounded what she'd classify as upbeat sarcastic, but she felt hurt. Bruised that she'd been labeled as the town gossip. Depressed by the realization that at some point she'd become the person who did the talking and not the person who was talked about. She supposed she would have to have done something vaguely interesting in order for the latter to be the case.

"You okay?" he asked. She shrugged. Greg wasn't like her ice-cold brother or her oblivious husband. He could tell when he'd said something that sent the other party reeling. That's what was so crazy about all of this. No one would have expected this of Greg. He was supposed to be one of the good ones. If one of the good ones had done what he'd done, what could the less shiny men in her life be hiding?

"But what about your job, Greg?" she asked. He was a firefighter, for God's sake. How did he think this was going to go?

"I already talked to my chief about it, a couple of years after I first joined the fire department. I had a feeling it'd get out at some point, so better he heard it from me. He listened to my side of things, and he didn't love it, but he was okay with it. I'm not going to lose my job. And it's technically too far in the past for there to be any legal consequences. But . . ."

"What?" she asked. Wondering what on earth else there could be.

"I've been looking at jobs, with other fire departments. Out of state. I'm in the final round for one in Idaho."

"You're moving?"

"Might be. I finally got my ass in gear to finish off the house. It won't be hard to sell it." Bee was quiet. He was right. He'd make a killing on his house, and then, like so many before him, he'd pocket the profits, pack up, and leave. Away from the heat, and the fires, and the expense.

Another one of the original crew gone. And despite just learning what a total ass of a thing he'd done, she would miss him.

"Leaving's probably a good idea," she said. "I doubt you'll be in line for boy scout of the year when this gets around." Out of the corner of her eye she saw him dip his head slightly in acknowledgment that he deserved what she was saying but that he didn't like it. She was being cruel. But he'd been crueler. He'd ruined lives. She was just pointing out what was true.

"Things will be hard here for a while, I'm sure," he said. "They'll be hard on Maddy as well." Bee nodded. Maddy was sick, and her husband was abandoning her over it, and now this. And to think that this time last week she'd envied her. "She may find she needs to get out of town too," he added. Bee turned to look at him. Was he proposing what she thought he was?

"And you think she'll want to hitch a ride with you to Idaho?" she asked. She was joking, but he didn't laugh.

"It'd be a new start for her." She opened her mouth to tell him that he could not be serious, but he got there first. "She'll need to get away from all this. She'll need to get away from Joseph. Emily. All of it."

So this was why he'd done it. To trigger this big mess and then be the one to sweep Maddy up and out of it. To finally, *finally*, claim her for his own.

"So this isn't just a karma cleanup. You have something of a long game here."

"Can't it be both?"

"And does Maddy know anything about these plans of yours to airlift her out of her life?"

"She doesn't. But I expect she'll come around. When all this gets out, she won't have a whole lot of choice."

◆ ◆ ◆

Bee pulled up a few feet outside the back entrance to St. Novatus. Normally she parked in the lot, but today she needed time before going inside. Time to think. She honestly didn't even know if she'd make it in to the bookfair—Rose may well be stuck doing the shift alone. More dog-sitting. More sleepovers. But there was no way that Bee could push the details of what she'd just heard to the side and walk into school as if nothing had happened.

She still didn't have a complete handle on the new information. Her thoughts were like a hundred rubber balls bouncing around her head in several directions at the same time. There were implications to this news, ways that it twisted and turned current events, but she couldn't wrap her brain around any of that yet. All she could think about was the past. And how Maddy had lied so hard and so deep that she'd rewritten people's lives. And how one of those lives was Bee's. She could feel the initial shock lifting now, like a fog reluctantly burning off in the mid-morning sun. And underneath the soft fog of shock was anger.

And had there been other lies? A memory that had been trying to bubble up for a couple of weeks now came shooting to the surface. *A candy corn with a pair of oversized lemons rammed up its top.* Now she remembered. Maddy had been the one who'd told her Neb had said that. Maddy who knew how paranoid she'd been about the size of her breasts. Breasts that Bee could now see hadn't been much more remarkable than any other ninth grader's.

But what about Emily? Maddy had lied about who she was too. She'd painted her from day one as being subversive, twisted, evil even. And without questioning it, Bee had taken everything Maddy had said and had felt, then magnified it and taken the action she knew that Maddy wouldn't. Because *that*, she had thought, was what friends did. It had felt loyal. But had she misplaced her loyalty? And without a doubt, bouncing balls inside her brain or no, the answer came back in an instant. Yes. She'd taken Maddy's side over Emily's. And Emily's side had, of course, been Joseph's side, which meant she'd stood with

Maddy instead of her brother. And the moment she'd chosen Maddy over Joseph had been the start of her brother walking out of a room whenever she walked into it.

And now, even now, when the ugly thing that Maddy had done was about to come out into the light, she had been gifted an escape hatch through Greg, ready to spirit her away to a new life so that she didn't have to experience any social fallout. Handsome, home-owning Greg, who was happy to have her despite the fact that her brain was turning to mush and her personality was turning one degree more toxic every single day. And, of course, she'd sat on her evil lie for so long that any legal consequences that might have taken her down had crumbled away to nothing. A typical Maddy Moth soft landing. She always got away with it.

And Bee, her supposed best friend, wouldn't even have known about any of this but for the fact that she'd been tapped in her capacity as town gossip. There were, of course, people she'd love to tell. But how could she speak with any kind of credibility when she couldn't say where or how she'd heard this news? It'd sound like she was making it up. She couldn't say that Joseph had told her. That'd get straight back to him, and she didn't want to ruin what they'd tentatively started to get back on track. She couldn't say it was Emily, because who'd ever believe this info with Emily as its source? And then she decided. She wasn't going to say a word. She was done with being manipulated. Greg had only told her so he could get his hands on what he wanted faster. He could spread his own gossip.

Bee's gaze fell on a raggedy-looking crow perched on top of the wall, its head sternly inclined, seemingly fascinated by something far below. Apparently unable to tear its eyes away, the crow started sidestepping along the wall before giving up and taking flight. It then changed its mind and settled on the roof next door to what used to be a dive bar. The teachers notoriously used to stop in there for at least one stiff one after school, but in recent times, that whole notion hadn't gone over well with the parents, so now they went home to drink their whiskey sours alone. The bar had since been gutted and converted into Maddy's dance studio. Rumor had it Maddy wasn't much of a teacher. Nevertheless, her classes were still busy. Probably something to do with the price of them, though Maddy had raised her rates recently. She'd only managed to start off cheap because she paid a negligible amount to rent the place, the owner apparently being the last one in Myrtlebury to realize she was in possession of real estate platinum. Dear, sweet, broke-ass Mrs. Trumbly who only owned this studio by virtue of her parents getting to California a bit before everyone else did. In the modern world, there was no way someone so scatterbrained would be in a position to own one property. Let alone two.

Bee's phone pinged. A text from Rose.

Okay. I just caught two fourth graders with graphic novels stuffed up their shirts. Gave them the smackdown and sent both to Lovano. You need to get your blonde butt here along with some more petty cash. How long?

Wow. Where other people thought things but didn't say them, Rose said them and then expected you to like it. Maddy was right, Nosey Rosey was no substitute for her. But she was someone. Bee began composing a text back saying that the office had more petty cash and that she'd be there in two minutes. But then she stopped. Her mind suddenly clear of any thought except the one that had just popped up inside it. Text half composed, Bee dropped her phone back into her purse, depressed the brake, and turned on the engine. Time to give Maddy's space cadet of a landlady a quick rundown on the basics of a little term known as *gentrification*.

CHAPTER 12

MADDY

Maddy hesitated for a moment before knocking on the door. Should she have sent her customary check-in text before coming over, even under the current desperate circumstances? Despite her and Bee's friendship predating the dawn of the cell phone, Maddy always sent a text before coming over. That had started when Robbie had been a baby. She'd knocked on Bee's front door, her signature four-bang knock, and woken the slumbering infant when he'd apparently been asleep for a solid two hours—his first proper stretch in over two days and nights—and had still been going strong. Bee had let her in, ashen-faced, and when Maddy had asked her why her face had looked like that, she had just started crying and then told Maddy exactly why her face looked like that. Sleep. Bad things happened when people didn't sleep. Ever since then, Maddy had sent a check-in text before coming over. Bee extended Maddy no such courtesy in return, but then Maddy didn't have kids—yet.

In lieu of an "I'm coming over" text, the four missed calls would probably serve as a good indication that something was up. Nevertheless, she considered shooting a text off now as she stood on the porch, but that was the path to pedantic ridiculousness, and so she picked up the knocker and gave it four evenly spaced hits. As she knocked, she noticed that her hand was still shaking. In fact, she could feel her whole body gently trembling as if she were cold, even though the evening air was still heavy with the heat of the day. She hadn't told Joseph where she was going. When he finally realized she was gone, he'd have no idea where she was. She'd liked to think that that would worry him, but given what she'd just uncovered, she wondered if he'd even care.

Maddy stood there, waiting, the street behind her seeming artificially quiet. No response to her knock. She pressed the doorbell. It hadn't worked for the past two years, but perhaps today was the magical day. Nope. Still not working. The sun was all but down, but the kids wouldn't be in bed yet. Would they? She checked her phone. Half past seven. The start of the bedtime routine. Though from what Maddy had seen, it wasn't so much a routine as a series of gentle suggestions that maybe it was about time to put pajamas on, which slowly ramped up into all-out war. It wasn't a good time to drop by. But when *was* a good time to get hold of Bee? Not in the morning when she was getting the kids to school, not after school was over, certainly not during the day when she was volunteering in class. There *was* no sanctioned time. She knocked again.

She heard footsteps inside, and a second later, the door opened. And there was Bee in one of her stretched-out rompers, her hair bundled on her head in a severe topknot. Bee had several similar rompers that she lived in during the summer. The Hoopers didn't have air-conditioning, and Bee had told her it was as close as she could get to wearing nothing.

"I'm sorry. I tried calling," said Maddy.

"What's up?" said Bee, half closing the door behind her against the chaos Maddy could hear coming from the living room. Bee was polite, but only barely.

"I saw something on Joseph's phone," she said.

"What did you see?" she said, coming out onto the porch and closing the door firmly behind her. As if sensing their mother's complete withdrawal, a second later they heard the sound of two sets of little fists and palms banging on the door, along with shouts of "Mama! *Mama!*" Bee opened the door again and spoke to someone just inside. "Can you handle it, please. Two minutes." Without waiting for an answer, she closed the door behind her again.

"I'm sorry," said Maddy again. "I just don't know what to do." She sank onto the porch steps, and a second later Bee sat down next to her. The Hoopers' front steps were tight, so there were only a few inches between the two of them. She could feel the heat coming off Bee's arm, could smell her deodorant. Smelled like dude deodorant. She knew Bee sometimes "borrowed" Sam's when she ran out. Maddy looked out onto the cracked path and the dried-out grass. Bee and Sam had turned the sprinklers off last summer to conserve water, and the lawn had never recovered and was now just a stretch of pale dirt with a few hardy patches of yellow here and there.

"I'd offer you a drink, but if I go inside, I'll never get back out again," said Bee. "What was on his phone?"

"Photos."

"Of what?"

"Of Emily." Bee raised both her eyebrows, ready to be scandalized. "Not that sort of photos," Maddy added. There was nothing spicy about these pictures. Or not to the casual observer anyway. She shifted her butt and felt the wooden ridges of the steps dig in.

"How'd you even get into his phone?" asked Bee, more interrogative than curious. She didn't believe her. That was about to change. When she heard the rest of it, she'd have no choice but to believe it.

"There's about thirty seconds after you finish using your phone before it locks. If you can get there in time, you're in." Bee inclined her head, reluctantly impressed.

"So how long did you have to wait for that to line up?" asked Bee.

"A while," said Maddy. That was all she was going to say. She wasn't going to tell Bee about the attempts to hack in that went horribly wrong. Or about the hours wasted, hanging out in the background while Joseph tapped away on his phone, waiting for the moment he'd leave it unattended. It'd only happened in the end because he'd been distracted by an ambulance pulling up outside the house across the street.

"So if the photos weren't racy, then what's the issue?"

"Would you like it if Sam had photos of his ex on his phone?"

"No, but—"

"The issue was the amount," said Maddy. Why couldn't Bee take her words at face value, for once? "Twenty of them. At least."

"And what was she doing in them?"

"Nothing much. Drinking coffee. Standing on some bridge. Look." She pulled her phone out of her pocket, opened it up, and started scrolling through the photos she'd texted herself from Joseph's phone. She paused at the one of Emily on a bridge. There wasn't much bridge in the picture—the frame was mostly taken up by Emily—but what she could see of the background and the dark sky above her didn't have a West Coast vibe, and it was somehow clear the shot was taken in New York.

"Why'd you send them to yourself?"

"I wanted to look at them properly. It's too many pictures. It's not normal, right? You think I should say something?"

Bee took Maddy's phone out of her hands and swiped through the pics herself. She paused at the last one, a selfie of Joseph and Emily together. They weren't looking at each other but directly at the camera, matching wide smiles in place. Two old friends catching up? Or a new couple out on a third date? If you looked at the picture with no context, it could have been either. But Maddy had the context, and so did Bee. Bee seemed to be stuck on the image of Joseph and Emily together, busy making some kind of calculation. Maddy was about to say something when Bee clicked off the photo and handed Maddy back her phone.

"It's nothing. If you're worried, you should talk to him about it. But people have pictures of other people on their phone. I have pictures of people on my phone." Bee's answer was smooth. Too smooth? Didn't

Bee at least smell a bit of a rat? She was always the first one to poke, to question, to accuse, to stir up. This diffusion of trouble was new. Was it because Bee really thought it was nothing? Or because she knew that it definitely wasn't?

"Really? You have a stash of selfies of you and your ex in a bar?" Her tone said she was pretty sure Bee did not have this.

"I don't have an ex," said Bee lightly. Maddy had forgotten that Bee had only ever been with Sam. She'd had that stupid crush on Neb at one point, but after that whole thing had fizzled out, she'd never really gotten back into the swing of dating until college.

"Okay, so the pictures on their own, perhaps that's nothing more than a big *whatever*. But there was also this text."

"About what?" said Bee. Maddy would have expected her interest to be sparking again, but it was as if Bee was already gearing up to dismiss the text too. How could she when she didn't even know what it said? Bee was about to get either majorly defensive or majorly talkative when she heard who the text was about. And Maddy was ready and watching to see which.

"It was about you, actually," said Maddy.

"Me?" said Bee, glancing back toward the front door. Planning her escape? Or suddenly concerned about her children?

"Yeah." This was the real reason she'd come to track Bee down at her house. She didn't really need a secondhand opinion about whether it was okay or not okay for her husband to have pictures of Emily on his phone. What she'd really wanted was to see Bee's reaction to the text; she wanted to see her eyes when she told her.

"What, then?" asked Bee more urgently.

"It was from Greg. It just said, *Bee knows.*"

She looked at Bee's face, so neutral. Too neutral? "You know what?"

Bee closed her eyes for a second. And for the first time ever, Maddy didn't know what her friend was thinking.

"I guess that's it, then. The jig is up," said Bee, snapping her eyes open.

"What?" said Maddy, confused.

"Does somebody have a birthday next week?"

"Oh. Right." Was that it? It didn't feel like her and Joseph's lives were in the birthday party zone right now.

"Greg said something to me about your surprise party in passing, but I hadn't heard. So he filled me in."

"That's super weird," she said, wondering exactly when and why those two were having passing chats. Bee and Greg weren't proper friends. They orbited around Joseph and Maddy like the sun and moon, but they didn't have a friendship in their own right. "Why wouldn't Joseph have told you about a party?"

"He said he was worried about me blowing the surprise, and now I guess that's come to pass." She'd flipped it. Bee had flipped the script, and now she was pissed at Maddy for digging. "Joe's put a bunch of work in, so when you walk in the room and we're all '*Surprise,*' can you do me a favor and at least try and look as if this is all news to you?" There was a hostility that she'd never heard Bee direct toward her before. Only to other people. And she in no way liked being on the receiving end of it.

"When exactly did you talk to Joseph about this?" asked Maddy. "It's not like he's been texting you. Or calling you." That much was true. She'd looked. Zero communication between Bee and Joseph. Not much new there. She knew that Bee was ultrasensitive about it, so it was a low blow, but given that Bee was suddenly getting an attitude with her, she felt like it was warranted. For a second, Bee's mask of polite suburban mom dropped, and there was nothing but naked anger. What was *that* about? Maddy had gone low, but not that low. And it wasn't anything that they hadn't discussed a hundred times before. And then the rage was gone, and normal Bee was back.

"I don't remember. I'd better get back in there," she said, with none of the regretful lingering she normally had when she said this. Bee was always trying to eke out one minute more with Maddy. One drink more. One more conversational topic. Not today. Today she was strangely eager to return to the hell of the bedtime routine.

"Okay," said Maddy.

"And don't forget," said Bee, turning back to face her. "Be surprised."

"I will," said Maddy, but she was saying it to an already closed door.

Maddy walked back down Bee's driveway toward her car, stepping over the crack in the shape of Africa that had been there ever since she could remember. She and Bee had had so much time together when they were younger. Thoughtless hours and days talking about nothing and everything. And now, when Maddy needed her and those rambling conversations more than ever, now that they actually had something of major consequence to discuss, Bee was never available. Or rather, she was available, but not in the way that Maddy needed her to be. Always one eye or one ear on the kids. The night out in Silver Lake had been Maddy's way of trying to get Bee to herself for a few hours, but even that had gotten kicked off course after Neb's random appearance and subsequent disappearance. And then, of course, incapable Sam had called her back home, and that had been that. And ever since then, it was as if the real Bee had disappeared into another dimension. It felt like she'd lost her.

She thought about Joseph's phone again. Emily's number was in his contacts, but under Sisu, which Maddy happened to know had been Joseph's name for her back in the day. She'd never heard him call her Sisu, but she'd read Emily's diary once, and so she knew that's what he called her in private. But the pet name hadn't been something she could have told Bee about. It was bad enough to fess up to digging around Joseph's phone, let alone Emily's teen diary.

There hadn't been any texts between him and Sisu and she hadn't featured in his call log either. Perhaps it was all fine and, like Bee said, nothing more than people having photos of people on their phone. Most likely he and Emily had just hung out in the city the day after Jodi Khan's party and had taken some snaps. But he hadn't mentioned the hanging out. Was that because he didn't feel like he could tell her about it in case she jumped to the wrong conclusion? Or the right conclusion. But it couldn't be the right conclusion, because no one would organize a surprise birthday party for their wife if they were hooking up with her sister. And even if they were down to throw a party, they definitely weren't going to submit to fertility testing. Because that was the other thing. Joseph had meant what he'd said about them starting treatment, and a couple of days ago they'd dropped off his sample at the clinic. They were scheduled for their consult next week. It was exciting, unnerving, but more than anything, reassuring. Because no one, *no one*, would be perverse enough to be trying for a baby with their wife when they were fucking someone else. Right?

CHAPTER 13

MADDY

Teaching wasn't the kind of job where you could slip in a little late and no one would care. Maddy's first class of the day was due to start in about one minute, and if she wasn't going to blow it, she needed to get out of the Jeep, walk around the block, and open the studio right now. Today's lateness was partly down to the fact that she'd eaten through her fifteen-minute buffer trying and failing to find her phone. But it was mostly because of the blank directive that Joseph had thrown at her as she was halfway out the door, to meet him at Embassy at seven for her birthday. It was in no way a suitable lead-up to a surprise party, and it had completely thrown her. Had Bee told him that she already knew about it? Or, even worse, had there never been any surprise at all. It was this last thought that had her sitting around the corner from her school for the last five minutes, trying and failing to convince herself not to cry.

She'd had a lot riding on this supposed surprise. It had allowed her to gloss over the unsettling pictures of Emily and to brush aside the fact that in the last couple of weeks, whenever she'd attempted to begin something in bed, he hadn't responded. He'd never rebuffed her before, but then she'd never made the first move before. She'd never had to. And as things had started to wane between them, she'd made a point not to. She'd wanted to see how far things would fall if left to their own devices. And now she knew. When he hadn't responded, she'd lain there, trying and failing not to feel rejected, but then she'd thought about the effort Bee said he'd put into engineering the perfect surprise for her. And about the fact that he'd delivered his sample to the clinic last week and that they had an appointment with the consultant tomorrow, and she had stayed sane. She had reminded herself that a good, solid relationship based on respect for each other's feelings, a long history of working through disagreements, an abundance of tolerance, kindness, as well as a healthy dose of basic adoration, didn't crumble overnight. They'd built this thing together, and it wasn't broken.

She'd had the mildest of crushes on Joseph when they were growing up. But back then he'd always been Emily's, and so she hadn't even let herself daydream it—she wasn't stupid. After Emily was long gone, and he'd moved away, she'd been witness to the endless stream of Eastside girls he brought back to the burbs to meet his parents. Each one skinnier, prettier, and with a bigger purse than the last. Bee and Maddy had had a good laugh about the most "Hollywood" ones. It was the beautiful-but-very-sincere ones that made them laugh the hardest. And then one Thanksgiving Joseph had come home without anyone on his arm at all, and that's when Maddy had stepped into the light.

By that time, she hadn't seen Joseph outside of a group setting or had much more than bare-bones interactions with him in years. But on that Friday, Maddy had gone over to the Moths', essentially to see Bee but really to check out their Thanksgiving leftovers. No one answered her knock, so she'd let herself in and helped herself to some turkey, cranberry sauce, and rolls. Which was fine. And the very last slice of their pecan pie, which probably wasn't fine. When Joseph had wandered into the kitchen wearing nothing more than a pair of boxers and had caught her in the act, she felt shot through with guilt and acted accordingly.

He said he'd keep her pie secret if she'd go on a date with him. She turned him down. She said it was because she didn't do "blackmail." But really it was because she knew that dating Joseph Moth was a bad idea. He'd let it slide, and then a year later when Bee and Sam had gotten engaged, Maddy had deftly sidestepped Joseph at the various family barbeques leading up to the big day, even avoiding him at Bee and Sam's rehearsal dinner. But then, at Bee's wedding, after he delivered the world's funniest, yet tender, best man's speech in a tux that effortlessly kicked his whole vibe up a notch, she realized she didn't feel quite as resolute about Joseph Moth being a bad idea. He tracked her down at the end of the night and asked her out again just as she was stepping into a taxi. He saw her waver, and he said that if she was worried about "the Emily thing," she needn't be. Because he was "done with all that." And she'd taken him at his word because she wanted to.

What followed was a campaign by Joseph to convince her that he was worth the risk. On their first date, he turned up with an actual picnic basket. The second date was horseback riding. The third date— the date where she'd finally been persuaded that, yes, he was worth the risk—had been at a rotating cocktail restaurant downtown. At this particular restaurant, the windows stayed in place, while the chairs and tables did a lazy three-sixty to take in the city views. Joseph wrote a series of notes and left them on the window ledge for her to discover each time they did a full rotation. "I really like you," "You have no idea how much I need to kiss you," and the final, "Will you be my girl-friend?" She nodded her head at that last one, and he'd leaned in and softly kissed her at the base of her neck. And from that moment on, she was utterly sunk. In that moment, he transitioned from being Bee's idiot big brother to someone she instantly fell so hard for that she was almost scared by the force of it.

They'd gone back to the cocktail restaurant exactly a year later, and the note left on the windowsill this time read, "Will you marry me?" She'd nodded again, and champagne had arrived out of nowhere, and a flurry of pictures had been taken—the waiters being in on it this time around. It had been a process. He'd won her over. He'd convinced her.

They hadn't just thoughtlessly drifted toward one other. Not like Bee and Sam who just kept getting drunk and having one-night stands that turned into one-month stands, which turned into forever. He'd intended for their relationship to happen, and if it hadn't been for his insistence, it would never have happened. And now they were in it. Eight years in it. And she wasn't about to hand him over to anyone, least of all her pathologically selfish sister.

By the time Maddy got to the studio, it was just as class should have been starting.

"Sorry! Sorry!" She smiled at the line of parents and Tiny Tutus toddlers that had already formed outside. She quickly unlocked the door and let them in, every last parent miserable at having been left standing out on the sidewalk in the intense sun without so much as a flicker of shade. Maddy's punishment was that seemingly every parent had an endless series of questions after every class, and she didn't get to go to the bathroom until the end of the day. She was used to it. The benefit was that between the teaching and the parents and the not peeing, she didn't think about Joseph and the unsurprising surprise party and all the rest of it for hours.

As she was locking up the studio that evening, her mind absorbed by a debate on which earrings would look best with the dress she'd bought for tonight, she felt a tap on her shoulder.

"You ignoring me?" asked Mrs. Trumbly.

"What?" said Maddy.

"I said, are you ignoring me! I just said your name twice and nothing."

"Sorry," said Maddy. "Mind in a million places. How are you?"

"I'm good. Just got back from Texas last week."

"How were the girls?" asked Maddy.

"Like two Tasmanian devils on crack." Maddy laughed at that; Mrs. Trumbly was not your typical adoring grandmother. "And Tammy's pregnant, again."

"Really?" said Maddy, suddenly getting the creeping feeling that this was all leading up to something.

"Did you listen to my message?"

"No. I've lost my phone. Did you manage to call someone about the air? I had a look, but I've no idea what's up with it. It's just not blowing cold. We should get it fixed before summer school."

"I'm selling the building." Maddy said nothing. Her mouth had completely dried out, and she wouldn't have been able to speak even if she'd known what to say. She felt the keys almost slip out of her slack hand but managed to grip them just before they fell.

"When did you decide that?"

"Recently. Property around here's worth a lot more than it used to be, you know."

"You don't say," said Maddy, not quite managing to drain her voice of what her mother would have called *a tone*.

"Yes. Real estate prices around here these days—I don't know how you young couples are supposed to survive!" She seemed less outraged at this than delighted at her own good sense to have been born thirty years before Maddy. "It's a scandal really when you consider what my parents paid for this place. All down to population density so I'm told."

"And you're just realizing this now?" It came out before she could stop it. But seriously, she hadn't known? Maddy had thought Trumbly was cutting her a deal because of the sweat equity she'd put into the place. She and Joseph had ripped out the old dive bar with their own hands and then transformed the shell that was left behind into a dance studio. They'd painted walls, affixed barres along one wall, wheeled in mirrors. Maddy had even inexpertly installed a vinyl dance floor over the old, cracked tile. She was well aware that Mrs. T. didn't have money to spare to fix the place up or even maintain it, but Maddy had been up to unsticking a window and persuading an uncooperative toilet handle to do its job, along with all the other things that cropped up. Least of all the dodgy air-conditioning. She'd figured it out on her own and spared her landlady the calls that most other tenants would have made weekly. But no, none of that counted for anything. Turned out Trumbly didn't have long-held beliefs in preserving local, small-scale business, and she hadn't been cutting Maddy a break for all the renovation work she'd done. She was just dumb.

"I bumped into your friend last week, and she brought it up," said Trumbly.

"What friend?"

"You know. That friend from when you were in school."

"Bee?"

"Is that her name? I see her around town with her boys all the time. She told me we were trapped inside a real estate bubble. She explained it all. The bubble keeps getting bigger and bigger, but one day it will have to pop." Trumbly clapped her hands together surprisingly aggressively.

It couldn't be Bee. Even if things had been stiff between them recently, she would never throw her under the bus like that. But outside of Bee, Maddy didn't have any friends around here. Not since she'd returned. But Trumbly, who knew Maddy from when she was a kid, probably thought she was still pals with the same crew she'd hung out with when she was a teenager. Rose had boys, and outing Maddy for having a sweet rent rate sounded much more her style. Making trouble for other people under the guise of it being "the right thing to do" was one of Rose's biggest joys in life.

"Okay," said Maddy, hating it but understanding. Maybe this could work out. She didn't know how much Trumbly wanted for the place, but with her recent cash influx, maybe she could swing a deposit and a small mortgage. It was just a large room after all, albeit in the center of town. Not like a proper house. "How much do you want for it?"

"Oh, honey, it's not for sale," she said.

"But you just said—"

"What I mean to say is"—and here her face changed from bland to softly smug—"I just sold it."

CHAPTER 14

EMILY

2002

It all started with the laughing. Maddy and Bee were always laughing, but today Emily could hear an edge to it. As if they wanted her to know there was a reason for the laughter, and that it was something to do with her. They wanted a fight. That was crystal clear, even all the way up in her room. Despite herself, Emily opened her door a crack so she could hear their voices more clearly. It didn't take long to get the gist of things. They'd been to some Red Hot Chili Peppers concert the night before. Did they really think she'd get all riled up over Maddy being allowed to stay out to go to some gig? And then she heard it. The thing they'd really wanted her to hear. Maddy said Joseph's name. Had *he* gone to the concert? Surely not. But then she heard his name again. Muffled and followed by more of those trying-too-hard giggles.

At that, Emily decided that what she really needed was a soda, so she left the safety of her room and headed down the stairs and into the kitchen. She was, of course, aware that she was walking straight into what they wanted her to. But that didn't change the fact that she had to know. Had Joseph gone to a concert with *them*?

"You like the Red Hot Chili Peppers, Emily?" asked Bee as soon as she walked in. Emily ignored her and opened the fridge to grab a Coke, but Bee, who'd followed her across the room, closed it before she could reach inside. Emily stared at Bee's hand on the edge of the door. It looked meaty, like one of the chops Sophie had stashed on the bottom shelf. Bee had thinned out over the past year and was all legs and eyes these days, but Emily had a feeling that she'd go the way of her mother later in life.

"I asked you if you liked the Red Hot Chili Peppers."

"Sure. I like them. Who doesn't?" she said, ignoring Bee's edge. She was here for the info, not a spat.

"Bummer you didn't come with last night, then," said Bee.

"Not that much of a bummer," said Maddy, and they both laughed again. When had her sister turned into such an epic bitch? Suddenly neither the soda nor the information seemed worth it, and Emily pushed past both of them, headed back for the stairs. It wasn't like she could trust a word that came out of their toxic little mouths anyway.

"Joseph went," Bee said. It was inelegant. But it worked.

"*What?*" said Emily, turning back around. In the few days since the Stone House, Joseph hadn't been at the skate park. He hadn't been anywhere at all. Emily had been giving him space, thinking that he might need time to get his head around what had happened. But perhaps it wasn't moping. What if he was pissed at her?

"He went to the concert," Bee clarified. "He didn't tell you? I thought you two told each other everything?" She made a face as if it was unbearably awkward that she had to be the one to fill Emily in here.

"I'm pretty sure he didn't miss you. In fact, it's probably safe to say he had a *much* better time with you not being there," said Maddy, and Emily could tell she wanted her to ask what exactly she meant by that, but she'd walked into enough traps for one morning.

"Honestly, I think it's probably healthier that you two aren't spending as much time together." The way Bee said "healthier" made Emily want to peel the front of her face off. Bee and Emily had been almost friendly the first couple of times they'd met. Bee had even waved to her once at school, albeit from the other side of the car park. But Emily had seen the look on Maddy's face as she'd noted that wave, and not long after that, Bee's behavior toward Emily had changed completely.

"Why's that?" Emily asked, all thoughts of escaping a brawl wiped away.

"You and Joseph are too young to be so involved." This sounded like parentspeak, and Emily wondered how much of Joseph's recent absence from her life was down to his parents actually having more of an interest in what he got up to than he'd let on. "Plus, there's the whole academics thing. You're bad news for his GPA."

She decided she wasn't about to stand in front of these two brats and try to explain what Joseph and she were to each other. It was beyond their experience and definitely beyond their imagination. Neither one of them had the mistiest of clues what true love was like, and her guess was that neither of them ever would. They didn't have hearts big enough to be capable of it. She turned again and headed back toward the stairs.

"Don't just walk off," Bee said, digging her fingers into the bone of Emily's shoulder and swinging her around. "You didn't hear the best part."

"You're definitely gonna want to hear the best part," said Maddy.

"What?" She immediately hated herself for taking the bait. But the truth was, she wanted to know.

"You think we should say? Or let my brother fill her in?"

"We should do it," said Maddy. "Just in case it slips his mind."

"Joseph kissed Maddy yesterday. At the concert." Before she'd made any conscious decision to do it, Emily reached out and slapped Bee across the face. Bee clutched her cheek and then doubled over.

"Bee, let me see," said Maddy, and knelt down on the ground trying to pry Bee's hands from around her face. Bee shook her head, and then the wailing started.

"If you can't take it, you shouldn't dish it out," said Emily, almost in tears herself.

"She didn't *hit* you, you psycho. Why don't you just go back to whatever sewer it was you crawled from? Nobody wants you here."

At that, Emily fled back up the stairs and into her room, where she threw herself on her bed, burying her face in her pillow in an attempt to muffle the tears. They couldn't know that they'd won. Maddy must have lied. There was no way Joseph could be even slightly interested in someone so different from her in every possible way. They'd only said it to trigger a reaction. Maddy was no longer the doe-eyed tween she'd been when Emily had first arrived. She'd turned. She was moody, territorial over everything—especially anything to do with her mother—endlessly jealous. Sophie and Emily didn't exactly have some huge mother-daughter relationship going on, but it was true that what they had was closer than not to friendship. Between shuttling her back and forth to her many doctor appointments and shopping for clothes Sophie insisted she needed, they'd spent a significant amount of time together, and Emily supposed that, yes, that came at a cost to Maddy. Albeit a small one. But more than the time spent, she knew what bugged Maddy the most was the fact that Emily wasn't Sophie's daughter, which meant that when they talked, not much was off the table. They'd discussed Maddy and her oddities. The baby talk. The crying fits. They'd talked about Sophie's mom going senile. Not that Emily was sure Maddy wanted to hear about her grandmother wandering into other people's houses and accusing her neighbors of stealing her underwear. But regardless, she knew that this thing with Joseph was nothing more than Maddy's return swat. That girl really never had learned to share her toys.

In the small hours of the morning, Emily still lay in the exact same spot. Still thinking. Not sleeping. The air all around her body like a hot fog. There was no special noise to alert her of his arrival, but one second she lay there alone, surrounded by heartbreak and heat—and the next, she just knew. She walked over to the window, pulled open the blinds, and there he was. Just the same as always. Just as beautiful as always. He smiled and gave her a wave, and she grinned back, pointing down toward the front of the house. Quickly she pulled on a T-shirt, snuck down the stairs, and padded through the living room. Then she unlocked the window, pushed the screen loose, and eased herself through the frame and onto the porch. Joseph was already standing on the front lawn, and within two seconds, she was in his arms.

"Where have you been?" she whispered.

"I'm sorry," he said, and pulled back to look at her in that way that no one else ever had.

"I smacked your sister pretty bad across the face," she said. She was worried about that. Ever since Bee had joined Maddy's general campaign against her, she could tell that Bee had fallen down in his estimation. Way down. He talked about her differently these days. Had called her a follower more than once. And so before today, Emily felt like she knew exactly where she stood in line for his affection. Number one. Way ahead of his sister and everyone else in his family. But since the Stone House, she wasn't sure anymore, and she needed to know. Immediately. She couldn't bear the suspense of not knowing whether she was still the most important to him. Because she had to be. Number two was no one at all.

"Maddy told me what happened. Sounds like Bee set herself up for it."

"She kind of did," she replied, relieved, but now wondering if Maddy and he were making a habit of having conversations about *things*. She didn't ask him about the supposed kiss. She wasn't going to make it that important. If it had meant anything, she would know. And from the way he was now smoothing her hair back from her face and looking down at her like she was a precious new discovery, she didn't think it had meant a thing. She was still his number one.

And then he kissed her, and they were back on. One of his hands quickly found its way under her T-shirt and then began its descent toward her hips.

"Come on," she said, and pulled him toward the huge oak in the front yard. Carefully she climbed the wood slats on the side of its trunk. Slats meant for much smaller fingers and toes. He crawled inside the treehouse right behind her, careful not to make any sudden moves. This was a structure built for one little girl to play house, not for two teenagers to thrash around in. The ceiling was so low they couldn't stand all the way up, so they took turns lying on the floor and wiggling their clothes off. Being slow and careful would have been torture on a regular day, but seeing as they hadn't been together in almost a week, it made everything almost too intense. Emily moved herself onto the bare planks underneath him, and he quickly worked himself all the way in. But within a few seconds he'd started moving too fast, and the whole house started to shift. Small movements at first. But then it started rocking, dangerously. Emily guessed that all that was holding the structure in place was about three thin planks and a few nails—none of it very new. If the house detached from the branch and fell, they could well be killed. But they kept going. They knew there was no stopping once they'd started. Nevertheless, when she heard one of the planks break away from the tree, Joseph felt her whole body freeze. They stopped, reworked their configuration, and figured out that if he lay the length of the treehouse and she pushed down on the frame of the treehouse window and slowly moved on top of him, it'd work. So that's what they did. All of it with a terrible forced slowness. None of their normal smash and grab. Before long he tapped her on the butt, which was her signal to get off him to avoid what was coming next. But Emily ignored the tap and started moving quicker. She could tell they were going to let go at exactly the same time. When they did, she closed her eyes and pinched her mouth closed to hold in the scream. He did no such thing, and if anyone on the street had had their window open, they would have heard someone shouting as loudly as if they'd just been drop-kicked in the stomach. When her eyes finally opened, she noticed a quick flash of white in the living room. She squinted her eyes and looked harder. Nothing.

He tried to sit up to kiss her, but she pushed him back toward the floor and then lay down beside him—the liquid he'd made half an effort at keeping out of her flooding down the insides of her thighs. They turned to face each other, and he pushed her hair off her face and then kissed her again, quietly.

"I'm sorry," he said.

"What for?" she asked, even though she knew. She wanted him to say the words. Joseph wasn't big on words. And the words weren't normally necessary. His eyes were simple for her to read, like two dark portals straight into the middle of his mind. She could understand those eyes better than any words. But today, she wanted to hear the words. To confirm that it all still meant what she thought it did.

"For not being around the last few days."

"Yeah. What's up with that?"

"I told my parents what happened at the house."

"You *what?*"

"It's fine. My mom could tell something was going on. And then she started poking and it all came out." So that was all it'd taken, she thought. A bit of attention from his laissez-faire parents, and he'd become putty in their hands. "They got me a guitar. I've been asking for one for ages. They gave me this crazy Les Paul one."

"Is that a special type?" she asked, amazed at how level her voice sounded. As if him ditching her to suck up to his parents was completely okay.

"You could say that."

"More special than me?"

"No."

"So your parents waved a fancy guitar in front of your face, and you forgot I was even alive?"

"That's not how it was. I just felt like I should make them happy for a while."

"Really?"

"The gun thing really freaked them out. They said if I stayed away from you, they'd get me a ticket to go to that stupid Red Hot Chili Peppers concert—"

"Really? That's all it took?"

"No! It didn't work. Because look where I am now. If I had to choose between having you or having music for the rest of my life, I'd pick you."

"Hmm. Thanks. If I had to pick between you and tuna for the rest of my life, I guess I'd pick you too."

"My music isn't your tuna sandwich. What's the most valuable thing you have?"

"You."

"Aside from me."

"Nothing. My mom was, I suppose."

"My music is as important to me as your mom was to you."

"My mom was *a person*. It's not comparable."

"I bet music makes me feel more whole than your mom ever made you feel." She could tell he was trying to make her see that she was important to him. But somehow, it still didn't feel like enough.

"I forgive you. But only because I love you." Only because she had no choice, which she supposed was what love was. Being unable to hate someone even when they failed to put you first.

"I love you too." He said it quietly and easily. Like he'd said it to her one hundred times before. Not like it was the very first time they were saying it to each other. Saying it ever. "I thought about you every day for a week, you know. I don't know why I didn't tell my parents to go fuck themselves."

"Because you wanted to keep your fancy guitar."

"I just want you," he said. "I missed you so much. The only time I felt normal was when I was sleeping, and that's because I had these endless dreams about you."

"What happened in the dreams?" she said, interested.

"Nothing. We just hung out. Walking. Talking. In one of them you looked kind of older, and I was watching you sleeping inside this vast four-poster bed. Just day-to-day crap. I had those dreams every night. And then the nighttime started feeling real, and the day started feeling like flat bullshit. And then I had to come and see you."

He started moving his hands over her hips and waist, but she didn't respond. Despite saying she'd forgiven him, she was still mad. Mad that he could be swayed by a concert and a guitar. And suddenly mad that he would even lay his lips on Maddy. Even if it was a nothing. So instead of sex, she let him stroke her hair while she thought about the dreams he'd had about her and wondered what it might all mean.

They stayed up in the treehouse almost till the sunrise, and Emily slept properly for the first time in a week. His body was her eiderdown, the crook of his arm the most restful pillow she'd ever had. When it started to get so light they could no longer pretend morning wasn't happening, they pulled their clothes back on, kissed one last time, and climbed out of the tree. Joseph didn't bother with the slats at the end of his descent, just dropped to the ground like a curly-haired monkey. When she reached the ground, he gently nudged her up against the tree with all of his body weight and then kissed her again.

"Same time tomorrow, Sisu?" he said, and she nodded.

"Same time, same place."

The sun was all but up, yet the morning was unusually cold and gray. He hugged her to him again but let go before she was ready. And then he walked away, not even looking back. The more air there was between them, the colder she felt. And as he turned the corner of the house and disappeared down the street, her teeth were practically chattering. Now that he was gone, it was as if he'd never been there. She needed him back instantly. One night was never going to be enough to make her feel better. She needed him for the rest of her life. To know that every time she arrived home he would be there. The only time she felt good and the only time she felt safe was when she was right up next to him.

She climbed back in through the living room window and half-heartedly tried to fix the screen back in place, but it wasn't going to happen, so she left it leaned up against the wall, not particularly caring if it was found or who found it. What was the worst they could do?

When she walked into the kitchen, Maddy was at the table. She had a glass of water in front of her, which she quickly picked up and took a feeble sip from.

"Enjoying your beverage?" Emily asked. The water routine wasn't fooling anyone. Maddy had been spying.

"Where have you been?" asked Maddy, louder than Emily would have liked.

"Shh," she said. "No need to wake the whole neighborhood. I just went outside for a walk before it gets too hot."

"You're lying," she said.

"Whatever." Normally Emily couldn't stand it when girls at school pumped that one out. But today it just seemed spot-on. Whatever. Anything Maddy said or thought or felt or was upset about didn't matter. *She* was Joseph's number one. That was all that mattered today. She opened the fridge to look for food. "It's none of your business what we get up to," she added. "You don't own every single person around here."

"Neither do you," she said. Emily looked up then, because Maddy's voice sounded weird and strangled. Her face was pink. For a second she couldn't work it out, and then she did. Maddy was jealous.

"Silly little girl." Emily had no idea why she said it. Perhaps it was the shock of seeing Maddy's face all pink and flustered. Or perhaps it was because she wanted her to know that if she thought she even had a chance, she was being ridiculous.

"Mom!"

"She's sleeping."

"Not for long," she said, and then as if it was nothing, Maddy grabbed a knife from the counter and sliced her own skin from the elbow to the wrist. It hurt her. Emily could immediately tell, and Maddy dropped the knife to the floor, then wrapped her hand around where she'd cut and looked up at her sister, surprised. Surprised by the pain or by the fact that she'd done it at all, Emily didn't know, but she expected her own face was echoing the exact same surprise right back at her.

"Oh my God, Maddy," she said. "Look." Maddy looked down at her arm and saw that blood was starting to creep between her fingers. "What have you done?" For a second, the kitchen swam, but Emily dragged her eyes away from her sister and grabbed a dishtowel.

"It hurts."

"I'm not surprised. Maddy?" She looked up, her huge brown eyes filled with tears, and in that moment Emily felt a reluctant swell of love for her. "Keep looking at me. Look right at me. I want you to take your hand away from your arm, and then I'm going to wrap this cloth around it." She moved toward her holding out the cloth, but Maddy flinched.

"Stay away from me." She picked up the knife from where it had dropped to the ground and thrust it out toward Emily.

"Whoa," said Emily, taking a step back. "Maddy, you need to let me help you. Look," she said, pointing to the ground. Maddy looked down, taking in the mess, then she put the flat of the knife to the blood and dragged it down through the dots, making a fat red smear. Emily felt her knees threaten to give, and she grabbed onto the edge of the sink. Maddy looked up at the noise, and they stared at each other mutely.

"Maddy. Something's wrong with you."

"What's wrong with me is *you*," she hissed, and then Emily watched as her sister opened her mouth as wide as it would go. And then screamed.

A few seconds later Sophie came running.

"Maddy?" As soon as she saw the blood, she dive-bombed for her daughter. "Ivan!" A second later he appeared.

"What happened?"

"She did it," said Maddy. Sophie ignored this and instead moved toward the sink. With a shaky hand, Emily offered her the cloth she was holding, and Sophie took it and then wrapped it firmly around Maddy's arm.

"We have to get her to the hospital," said Sophie.

"Maddy, what did you just say?" asked Ivan.

"I said, she did it!" This time it wasn't mumbled, her unsliced arm pointing right at Emily. "I saw her coming in from the treehouse. She was up there with Joseph. She said if I told you, she'd cut me. I said I wouldn't tell, but then she cut me anyway."

"That didn't happen," said Emily, her voice trembling. "Look, her blood's all over the handle. I didn't touch it." She saw them take in the blood all around Maddy, glance at Emily's clean hands, and then give each other a look that told Emily everything she needed to know. They knew it was Maddy. They knew she had issues. But there was no way they were about to verbalize any of that. They were going to let this one hang. Unaddressed.

After they bustled Maddy out the door and off to the hospital, Emily crawled into bed and fell asleep. As she slept, she dreamed about the Stone House. She floated down its wide staircase now carpeted in white silk and dusty peonies and swirled around and around a chessboard floor, naked but not caring. The dream had a happiness she wasn't used to, a gentle kind of warmth she didn't want to wake up from. But wake she did. At first the sound was just a mild whispering through the top of her dream. But then it grew louder and angrier, and her eyes opened. She was instantly blazing hot, the inside of her room as muggy as a greenhouse. She pushed back the covers, which didn't make her any cooler. Then the sound came again. It was coming from outside.

Roadwork? She looked over at the clock. Ten. Like it or not, her day had now started.

She pulled on the same T-shirt from last night and a pair of jeans and headed for the kitchen. The noise came again. A massive indignant whirring sound. What was it? She walked through to the living room and looked out the front window but saw nothing remarkable. And then, there it was. Something falling. She ran to the front door and pulled it open. Maddy and Sophie were on the front lawn staring up into the tree. Maddy had a bandage running the length of her arm, but otherwise seemed as good as new.

The whirring came again, and two planks fell to the ground. Emily could just about make out Ivan's shape through the branches and the leaves.

"What are you doing?" she yelled up at him. And then, as if it were being birthed from within the branches of the tree, she saw half of the treehouse emerge, before retracting for a second. And then with one more push from Ivan, it tipped right out and smashed onto the ground.

No one said a thing. Sophie was staring at the wood all over the lawn, and Ivan was still obscured by the tree. But Maddy looked right at Emily. And then she smiled.

"Why the fuck did you *do* that?" she screamed up at Ivan. Her last sanctum of imagined privacy, her last place to be alone with Joseph, destroyed.

"You know why," said Ivan, ignoring her swearing.

Having done its work, the chainsaw was now silent. Everything was silent, and in the quiet that its roar left behind, she was suddenly aware of every sound for about two blocks around them.

"Emily," said Sophie through the silence. "You and I need to talk."

The talking Sophie wanted to do, to Emily's boiling embarrassment, was about contraception. Sophie didn't bring up Maddy knifing herself in the arm, and Emily wasn't about to raise the topic. She presumed she'd gotten the truth out of her daughter at the hospital, which was why she wasn't interrogating her about it now. But in actuality, she'd have rather spent the next hour defending herself from the accusation of stabbing her sister than be subjected to the lecture she got instead. It wasn't the first time Sophie had talked to Emily about her relationship with Joseph and where it all might be headed, but it was the first time she made her feel dirty about it. And then, after her warm-up stint about what an adult undertaking sexual intercourse was, there followed a lecture about the consequences of unprotected sex and about sex being something special between two *married* people and how its sole purpose was for procreation. *But*, in spite of all that—Sophie said she was taking her to Planned Parenthood to get her a prescription for the pill. Like she was a feral cat that she was taking to a shelter to be spayed.

There was no judgment from the staff at the clinic. Just questions, the taking of weight and of blood pressure, and then the scribble of a prescription. But even so, by the time Emily got home, she was beyond embarrassed. Despite the long white box of pills now in her possession, she hadn't actually made her mind up if she was going to take them or not. At no stage had she been asked if she'd actually wanted them. It had just been assumed. When she got back to her room, she slipped one of the three blister packs out of the box. The pills were tiny and yellow. She thought it was amazing that such an insignificant chunk of material could halt nature in its tracks. The nurse had been clear. She was to take the one mammoth pill now—the morning-after pill—and then start on the yellow pills the first day of her next period. She slid the tiny yellow pills away and pulled the morning-after pill out of the bag. Emily was surprised how nonchalant Sophie seemed to be about her swallowing all these hormones. It was a strange stance for the wife of the principal of the local Catholic school. But then, she recalled, Sophie wasn't Catholic.

She went into the bathroom to get some water to take the pill. She filled a glass, admiring again the prettiness of the manicure Sophie had treated her to last week. They'd asked Maddy along of course, but she had turned them down. Emily's nails were still short, but they were no longer bitten into retreat with the top of her fingers bulging out around them, and dark magenta polish now replaced the Wite-Out she'd had daubed on there when she first arrived. The lines of dots and crosses she'd etched over her wrists had almost faded to nothing, and she had no plans to reink them. For the first time in memory, Emily actually liked looking down at her hands.

Emily took the water back into the bedroom, then popped the mammoth pill out of the pack and looked down at it, flat and white in her hand. Within seventy-two hours of unprotected sex—that had been the time frame she'd been given to take it. But she knew that the unprotected sex had been going on for much longer than that. What if she was already pregnant? What would the pill do to whoever was inside of her? She dropped the popped pill back into the bag and stuffed the whole thing inside her underwear drawer. She didn't have to do anything right now. She had time. What was important in this moment was space from this situation so that she could think. She looked down onto the street, which was quiet in the midafternoon heat. There was still enough light left in the day that she could head to the hills for a hike. By the time she returned to real life, she'd have her answer on what to do.

CHAPTER 15

MADDY

Maddy walked through the door of Embassy at seven on the dot. She'd been hanging around on Main for at least a quarter of an hour, not wanting to show up too early. She had wondered if—despite the way Joseph had served things up that morning—perhaps there would be some remnants of surprise when she walked in. She wasn't sure what she might be expecting. The lights to be off and then flipped on? That seemed unlikely in a public restaurant. A homemade banner, then? Perhaps he'd hired a mariachi band to burst into song. But when she walked inside, the restaurant looked exactly as it always had, the same dumpy blonde stationed just inside the door looking at Maddy blankly.

"Got a reservation?"

"What? No," said Maddy, her eyes moving to the corner of the room where she could now see Joseph at a table. "I'm with him. With them," she said, noticing that her husband wasn't alone. The blonde gave a half nod, which seemed to indicate that she'd allow it, and Maddy headed toward the table, passing a waiter who stepped urgently to the side to let her by. The waiters all had greased hair, long aprons, and recently inked tattoos on their forearms that no one expected them to cover up. The place was hip. Hip for Myrtlebury anyway.

Bee noticed her first. She sat at the middle of the table in front of a dark brick wall crisscrossed in naked bulbs and various metal sculptures. The harsh light gave the sculptures shadows and curves she hadn't seen on them before. During the day they were unremarkable, but now they had a Gothic edge. Greg turned to see what Bee was looking at, which caused Joseph to turn too. Who was that Joseph was sitting next to? *Emily.* There she was, sitting next to Joseph with an aura of absolute assurance, the two of them looking like they'd never spent so much as a day apart. They looked like a couple. Carbon copies of each other, like those two awful Staffordshire dogs she was hanging on to for no good reason—they were a pair. This was wrong. All wrong. Why had he invited *her*?

She'd wanted to text Bee before dinner to find out who was coming and what the deal was, but when she'd gotten home from work and had finally had time to have a proper look for her phone, she still hadn't been able to find it. The lost-phone phenomenon had turned into such a reoccurring one these days—even in the dinky guest house—that she'd been driven to download a finder app. Every time she'd accessed it up till now, it had unhelpfully told her the phone was at home, but not the specifics of under which cushion or on what shelf or in which drawer—which was what she needed. However, when she'd accessed the site from her laptop today, for the first time ever the site had given her a new location, and apparently her phone was already at Embassy. Joseph must have found it and, knowing she'd lost it earlier, brought it with him.

As she reached the table, she felt her last hopes for a fun evening dissipate entirely. Because someone—it must have been Bee; it wouldn't have been Joseph—had invited Rose. The very person who'd just managed to destroy Maddy's livelihood with one "well-meaning" comment. Rose was the first one up from her seat.

"Rose," said Maddy, giving her a wan hug. Rose gave her a quick kiss. Maddy managed to repress the urge to wipe away the outline of her saliva on her cheek.

"Look at you!" said Rose. "Happy birthday! How are you? James would have come, but it was all very last minute, wasn't it? We didn't have time to find a sitter." Last minute? The guise of this being a carefully planned surprise party was fading by the second. Perhaps Rose's invite had been the thing that was last minute.

"Good to see you, Rose," she said, and found it within her to return her peck on the cheek.

"Where's my kiss?" said Greg, his face full of faux indignance. Maddy smiled and carefully moved around the table to kiss him too. As her lips touched his cheek, she could feel how freshly smooth his skin was. Just-shaved smooth.

"You smell delicious," she said. And it was true, he did. He smelled exactly the same as he always smelled. The same as he'd smelled when she was fourteen. The scent of life before everything derailed. She could have happily sat there and sniffed him for the rest of the evening. "I blocked you in," she added. Space was a limited proposition on Greg's street, and their trio of cars coexisted in a delicate configuration of parking and reparking. It was an easy walk into town from Greg's house when the sun wasn't trying to fry you into oblivion, and as she felt she should be entitled to drink all the wine she wanted to on her birthday, she'd left her car at home.

"You get a free pass on your birthday." Greg said this right into her hair. If it weren't Greg, she'd have thought he was flirting. He sometimes went near the line, but for some reason, tonight he was bumping right up against it.

"Joseph stole my spot," she said back, not entirely unflirty herself.

"Joseph always gets first dibs on all the good stuff," he said, looking her dead in the eye, and despite herself, she felt a small pulse in that area that had been abandoned land for weeks now. Okay, now he *was* flirting. What was *that* all about? And as for Joseph getting first dibs. Well, they both knew that wasn't the truth of things. Was that why he'd said it? For a second she wondered what would happen if she grabbed

Greg by the face and gave him a second kiss, right on his lips. Just to see how it felt. Just to see what Joseph would do about it. Just to see if he'd even notice. But she didn't. Just smiled blandly in response and then moved back around the table to sit in the only empty seat, next to Bee. Chaste. Well-behaved. Just like she always was. She'd never seen Joseph jealous. She'd presumed because she'd never given him a reason to be. But perhaps because he thought she simply wasn't worth it.

"Where were you?" asked Bee. "We were worried."

"What do you mean?" said Maddy. In her opinion none of this was in any way a traditional opening to a "surprise" birthday party.

"You're quite late," said Joseph with a tight smile. "We called, but you weren't picking up."

"It doesn't matter," said Emily. "We're just glad you're okay."

"I'm not late. You said seven. And I wasn't picking up because I don't have my phone. You have my phone," said Maddy, thrown by what Emily had just said, or rather, how she'd said it. Was she acting? If not, Maddy thought they might be the first vaguely caring words she'd ever heard from her sister. That's what had always been so hard. Sisters were supposed to care. Even if they fought, underneath it all, they were supposed to care. But Emily never had. And the worst of it was, at the start, Maddy had cared a lot.

"No, Maddy, I don't have your phone," he said softly. "And it was six. But don't worry about being late, sweetheart. Like Emily said, the main thing is that you're okay." Sweetheart. That was new. She didn't think he'd ever called her sweetheart.

"Of course I'm okay," said Maddy, letting the phone thing drop. For now.

"This kind of thing's been coming up recently," he said to the rest of the table, and then to Maddy's mortification, he added, "We're keeping an eye on it." Five faces looked across the table at her with full-on pity. Particularly Rose, who was looking at her right now with so much sorrow it was as if she'd just received her diagnosis right there at the table.

"There's nothing wrong with me," she said, but was this more out of the habit of defending herself than her true belief? She was sure Joseph had said seven for dinner. Seven as in *Oh thank heaven for 7-Eleven*. But maybe it had been six. There had been a marked uptick in her memory failures recently. The new dress she'd bought especially for dinner had disappeared from the back of the closet where she'd hidden it. Joseph hadn't known about the dress. She'd wanted to wow him. When she couldn't find it, she eventually put on an old faithful instead, but then when she'd gone into the bathroom to do her makeup, there it had been, hanging in the shower. Had she done that?

"It's fine. You're here now. That's all that matters. There's no need to apologize," said Rose. Maddy was pretty sure she'd said that to underline the fact that Maddy *hadn't* yet apologized for her "late" arrival. "I'm all for an extra hour away from my children. And the guys are babysitting, which means the mommies can stay out as long as they like." She raised her hand to high-five with Bee, who was pecking something out on her phone but high-fived her back without even looking up. Without even *needing* to look up was what Maddy took away from that. As if they were one brain. She'd been mildly paranoid about Emily edging closer to Bee and taking over the top spot, but what if Rose had already beaten her to it?

"But seriously," Rose went on. "I was just happy to be invited. We haven't had a chance to connect since, you know, everything." Did she mean her parents or something else? There was an awkward pause, which Rose took it upon herself to fill. "So, how old are you today, Maddy?"

"Thirty-four," she responded. She didn't know why Rose was asking; they were exactly the same age.

"That's what I thought, but then I wondered if it was thirty-five or something. Thirty-four seems a weird one to celebrate with a big hoopla dinner. Not exactly a milestone."

"Neither's thirty-five," said Maddy. Unless you were into celebrating entering the "geriatric pregnancy" zone, which her ob-gyn told her she would be sliding into if she didn't get knocked up before then. And as for this being a "big hoopla" of a dinner, she had yet to see much evidence of that. Perhaps the mariachi band et cetera would feature later. Or perhaps there would be cake. Perhaps cake was the factor that tipped this whole event over into the "hoopla" territory.

"We're living for the moment," said Joseph, and reached across the table to squeeze Maddy's hand. "Living for the moment?" Hand squeezing? It was as if she were ninety-four, not thirty-four. She was saved from responding to Joseph's "living for the moment" comment by the arrival of the waitress. As everyone had been waiting an hour, they already had their orders pretty much memorized. Not wanting to hold up proceedings one second longer, Maddy ordered the first thing that her eye fell on. Lemon parmesan baked tilapia. Great. Embassy had recently reopened under new management, and the waitress was nervous, apologizing twice for not knowing what kind of whiskey they used in their sours when Joseph asked. Her nervousness rubbed off on Maddy, who asked for a Hanmattan instead of a Manhattan, triggering a new round of knowing looks around the table. Did they not think she could see them?

As the waitress was leaving, Joseph stopped her and asked her if the herb in the herb-grilled salmon Emily had ordered was actually dill. It was. Joseph asked if they could prepare it without the dill. Apparently this was all very possible, and as the waitress backed away, Emily looked at Joseph like he'd just saved her life.

Maddy tried to make eye contact with Bee to see what she thought about the whole herb-grilled salmon situation. She'd be able to tell from a fraction of a microlook, but despite the fact that they'd just ordered, Bee was still studying the menu as if she would soon be called to recite it from memory for the pleasure of a small crowd. Eventually she placed it back on the table.

"What?" Bee said, and then smiled a second too late.

"Trumbly came by the studio earlier today," said Maddy, pushing past Bee's *fuck-off* vibes. Perhaps she was hungry. Bee picked up the menu again. What was her deal? "Bee. She's selling the studio." Bee looked up. This had caught her attention. Finally. "Someone"—Maddy looked pointedly past Bee to where Rose was interrogating Greg on when he was going to get a girlfriend—"told her that she was sitting on a gold mine and that she'd better sell up before the market crashed."

"That was me, actually," said Bee. At first Maddy thought she hadn't heard right.

"Excuse me?"

"I didn't tell her to sell up at all. I just ran into her in the park, and we got talking about this and that, and I mentioned how good of her it was to give you such a great rental rate the last couple of years." What *was* this? Bee was always on her side. Right or wrong, she always was. "What? She's been giving you a stinking deal, right?"

"Well, she's sold the studio. So now there's no more deal. And most likely no more dance school. So I hope you're happy."

"Ecstatic," said Bee flatly. This was bad. She felt the rest of the table stop their conversations and turn to look at them. Maddy and Bee never fought. It was a known. Sometimes they danced around the edges of something. But always gracefully and always fully in consideration of the other's feelings.

"What's this?" said Joseph.

"Your sister told Trumbly she should sell my studio, and so she did."

"I didn't tell her to sell the studio. I was just honest with her," said Bee.

"This has nothing to do with honesty, Bee. This is about me trying to make a living." Maddy didn't remind her that the living in question was to support not only herself but Bee's own brother. She wasn't about to bring that up in front of Rose. She'd Facebook-stalked her recently and had seen that she was married to some sales director at IBM and lived in one of the new McMansions nestled at the foot of the hills.

"I know. I know. Good old capitalism. Winner takes all," said Bee.

"Bee, I'm hardly some international conglomerate bleeding the locals dry. If anyone's the victim of capitalism here, it's me!" Maddy gave a half laugh, incredulous, but also trying to melt this conversation back into something close to normal.

"Maddy Moth. Eternal victim."

"Bee?" said Maddy. This was serious. Not to mention excruciatingly embarrassing. "Is there something you want to say?" She'd seen Bee beat up on Sam before now and knew that this was how it went with her. If she was pissed at you, the last thing she was going to do was tell you what was actually wrong. Your only clue was going to be the passive-aggressive volleys coming your way, and in between ducking those, you had to do some quick working out as to what you'd done. But Maddy hadn't *done* anything.

"Emily," said Greg. "I hear you bought a house up on Devil's Gulch?" He was changing the topic pointedly. Bee crossed her arms and set them on the table, looking to Emily for her answer. But Rose, who'd been watching the argument wide-eyed, got there first.

"Wait. First off, I want to know where you've been all this time."

"New York," said Emily.

"Doing what, exactly?" Rose asked, downing the last of her martini. The strung-out waitress walked by, and Rose held up her glass. She was ignored, and Maddy was glad. If that was the end of Rose's second, and she hadn't eaten yet, any moment now she would be transitioning into Obnoxious Rose. She wasn't exactly the flower her name suggested when stone-cold sober. But drunk, even vaguely tipsy, she turned into a real drag. At least that was the way it'd been when they were seventeen and taking illicit swigs of Seagram's at the bottom of the graveyard.

"Working, living. The normal things," said Emily.

"So what made you come back?"

"I bumped into Joseph at a friend's party. He told me about Sophie and Ivan, and so I came back to take care of things. And then, you know."

"What?"

"I fell in love. With Myrtlebury."

"Is it really all that lovable compared with New York?" asked Bee.

"So what did you think when you saw Joseph at that party?" said Rose, a lascivious edge to her voice that Maddy didn't care for. The waitress approached the table, delivered Maddy's Manhattan, then swept Rose's empty glass away and set down a fresh martini. Rose had obviously primed her to "keep them coming."

"I was surprised. Pleased," said Emily. She glanced sideways at Joseph, and Maddy could see that her face registered something near pure pleasure. She had that look of that rooftop photo about her again. The glowy look. Maddy took a sip of her drink. It was too sweet.

"Did it all come back?" Rose didn't lay out precisely what it was that might have "come back" to Emily when she saw Joseph. She didn't need to. Everyone knew what she meant.

"One or two things crawled out of the crypt for sure," said Emily, and looked at Maddy as she said this, still smiling, though there was none of the glow of two seconds ago. And every trace of "just as long as you're okay" had completely drained from her expression.

"And how do you feel about your first love getting hitched to your younger sister?" said Rose. Greg gave a small shake of his head, and Bee dipped her face into her hands. Maddy just closed her eyes. "Oh come on. Are we supposed to not talk about it? Please. Like you haven't all been talking about it."

"It's not made our list of top topics, no," said Greg.

"Guys, that's not healthy. You need to talk about this. The three of you. Get it out in the open," said Rose. Her head momentarily bobbed backward for a second before she righted it and then hunched forward on the table by way of compensation. "I'm drunk. I can hear it in my voice. This is your fault, Maddy. Making us wait for an hour."

"Should I call—" began Bee.

"Joseph," Rose went on, her self-awareness about her altered state apparently not extending to the rest of her behavior. "And be honest here. Because it's important. Do you think you might have married Maddy, and I'm talking about subconsciously here"—she slurred so it sounded like *conshusly*—"because you couldn't have Emily?"

"Rose—"

"I'm not saying it's the case. All I'm saying is that you need to discuss these things, within a marriage. The two of them are very similar. In their . . . body." She swirled her hand vaguely in the direction of Maddy and Emily—binding them together in some kind of assessment. Maddy saw Greg take a microglance at her and Emily's chests and come to the tidy conclusion that perhaps Rose had a point.

"We'll be right back," said Bee, standing and pulling Rose up with her.

"Chill out. I'm just saying what everyone's thinking," said Rose, shrugging Bee off, then raising her hands in surrender to Bee's bathroom demand. Maddy watched them leave, struck by the potential truth of what had just been said. The plausibility of that fact that he'd only married her because at the time he couldn't have Emily. Though they looked completely different and had personalities that were as similar as stingrays and snowdrops, their bodies were absolutely cut from the same cloth. Was the reason Joseph had pursued her so determinedly because she'd reminded him of Emily? Perhaps that was why their sex life had trailed off entirely. Now that the real thing had shown up, the poor imitation held zero appeal.

But that couldn't be the case. Despite Rose's accusations that the topic needed to be discussed, the two of them had discussed this, at length—of course they had. They'd talked to the ends of it and back when they first found themselves entering into *something*, and he'd convinced her that whatever he'd been in with Emily had been relegated to nothing more than an intense memory from the past. No more note-worthy than any other deeply felt teen crush that ended up imploding. People moved on. People grew up. Next to no one stayed with their first crush forever, for so many obvious reasons. Not just because fledgling relationships were easily pulled apart by location shifts and new sets of friends, but also because people were ever-changing too—and at no faster time than in their teens and twenties. Married love, the love between Maddy and Joseph, was different. So much more substantial. The love that Joseph and Maddy had for each other was built on their true natures. That's what they'd decided. That's what they'd discussed. That was the conclusion that they had drawn.

Into the awkward and seemingly unbreakable silence that had set-tled in around the table, the food arrived. Everyone's dish clanking onto the table at the same time, borne by three separate waiters. Embassy tried to be fancy like that. Perhaps to make up for the lack-luster fare for which the place was famed. Stiff steaks, flavorless vegetables, toughened bread rolls. She saw a mild note of panic in the waitress's eyes when she saw that Rose and Bee weren't at the table.

"It's fine. Here they come now," said Emily, and nodded toward the bathroom. And true enough, there were Rose and Bee. Bee stony-faced, Rose defensive.

"I'm sorry," Rose said as soon as she was in her seat. "I didn't realize it was all so *sensitive*." She said "sensitive" in a way that was definitely the opposite of sensitive. Maddy wondered if she behaved like this around her husband's coworkers. She doubted it. Old friends were the worst. "Pretend I said nothing."

Maddy took a bite of her tilapia. Better than she'd expected. Emily poked at her salmon. Despite Joseph's request, it had arrived encrusted with dill.

"Do you want me to—" asked Joseph.

"It's fine," Emily said, and started on the dill's removal. As she sliced at the fish, the base of an image peeked out from the skin under her sleeve.

"Did you get a tattoo? What's it of?" asked Bee, clearly relieved to have found something neutral to talk about.

"This?" said Emily, putting down her knife and pulling her sleeve up. "It's an old one I got reinked." She extended the top half of her arm out toward the center of the table so everyone could get a look. Rose then started up with a story about a dolphin she'd had etched on her shoulder in her twenties, which her husband had recently said was dated and generic. He'd told her she should get it removed, but she hadn't wanted to because she still liked it, and now she was wondering if that meant that *she* was dated and generic. Then Greg told them about a tattoo he'd had done on some beach that had gotten infected. But Maddy could barely take in what they were saying. All she could hear was unfiltered noise, and all she could see was the waterfall. A bright blue waterfall, encased in rocks, all encircled in a rope pattern. So distinctive. She'd never seen Emily's tattoo before, even in its earlier supposedly more-faded state. Teen Emily had always been covered up from head to toe. Even in the summer. But that particular image Maddy had seen a hundred thousand times before.

She'd seen it on Joseph.

It was his only tattoo, and he never had explained the significance of it to her. And now she knew why. Sisu had a matching one. In a quick rush, she felt herself coming back to the surface. Back to their conversation. They'd moved on. Now talking about lasers and laser surgery. She watched her husband across the table, delivering a lecture on light refraction. She'd always thought he sounded so smart when he talked about things like this. Now he sounded hollow. Full of empty words. Empty echoing words that didn't mean a thing.

"Why do you have pictures of Emily on your phone?" she said, cutting across him.

"What?" he said into the silence.

"You have pictures of her. Tons of them. I want to know why." Most women would veer away from doing *this*, having this particular conversation in front of an audience. But Maddy knew that this was the only way she was going to be able to get something honest out of him. She didn't care about the embarrassment anymore. What was more important was to have witnesses. She needed other people to keep this on track. Other people to look at the snug selfie of the two of them cheek to cheek, the multiple pictures of Emily on a bridge, and pass judgment on what was happening here, publicly. She'd resisted confronting Joseph about the pictures for days. And she now knew it was because she needed other people there to witness exactly what this was. This needed arbitration. Because with just the two of them in a room, Joseph would explain it away. And she didn't want that anymore. She needed the truth.

"I don't have any pictures of Emily on my phone, Maddy," he said, and he was back to using that soft voice. The voice he'd used earlier when he called her "sweetheart." She recognized the tone now. It was the way her father had spoken to her mother right at the start, when she'd first started sliding. The voice he'd used when she'd accused him of having affairs, of taking her knitting needles and putting them in with the knives and then taking her knives and leaving them outside to rust.

"Give me your phone," she said. Doing as he was asked, he pulled his phone out of his pocket and handed it over the table to her. "Unlock it," she said. He took it back, unlocked it, and then handed it to her again. She navigated straight to photos, then his Photo Stream.

Nothing. There were photos from his last hike, snaps of the endless recording equipment he was eternally buying and selling on craigslist, photos of their last trip out to the beach. Even photos of New York. But nothing of Emily. Not one photo.

"You deleted them," she said, putting the phone back on the table.

"I didn't delete anything," he said, looking at her like he almost felt sorry for her. That was about to change. She almost felt embarrassed on his behalf.

"Hand over my phone, Joe," she said. He didn't have a clue that she'd sent the photos to herself. She'd deleted the text from his phone; she wasn't an idiot.

"Maddy. Sweetheart. I don't have it."

"Stop calling me 'sweetheart,' and give me my phone. I know you have it. I know that it's here. It's here!"

"I don't have it. You lost it earlier, remember?" said Joseph. His voice had turned hard. Because he knew she finally had him?

"I'll call it," said Bee. "And then if Joseph has it stuffed in his underpants or something, we'll soon find out." Maddy turned to stare at Bee. Why was she making this a joke? It wasn't funny.

"Go on, then," said Maddy. Bee, eyes still glued to Maddy's, picked up her phone and called her. Two seconds of silence passed before she heard ringing through Bee's phone. A split second later, an electronic tone sang out from Maddy's purse. She saw a mild flicker of something cross Bee's face, and then Maddy closed her eyes. The bouncy guitar rift twanging away was what was programmed for when Bee called. Her phone was in her purse. She'd checked it. She'd checked it twenty times. She fished her phone out and hit "Decline." Feeling the weight of all eyes on hers, she ignored them, tapped open her phone, and went straight to texts. They were open to her last conversation with Bee. She clicked off that and scrolled down to Joseph's picture. It was a picture from when they first got together. His boyish smile shone out from the image, even though it was no bigger than her thumbnail.

She opened it up. And swiped her index finger. There was their last text conversation. But above that, there was nothing. None of the images she'd texted herself from his phone. Just that conversation, which transitioned into the conversation before that, but with none of the images that she'd texted to herself in between the two. They were gone. Her proof was gone. She looked up. Rose had returned to her food. Everyone else was looking at her. Bee's face looked the same as when she'd just had a mouthful of sass from one of her kids. That wasn't right. Maddy wasn't being sassy. She wasn't behaving badly—she was trying to get to the bottom of what the fuck was going on. And if Bee was any kind of friend, she'd be helping her figure it out. Bee had seen the photos she was talking about, after all. She'd dismissed them as nothing. Though, of course, they weren't nothing.

"You told him," said Maddy.

"I told who what?" said Bee.

"You told Joseph about the photos. And he deleted them. And then he took my phone and deleted them from mine. You told him my passcode."

"What photos?" asked Bee.

"Jesus, Bee. The ones I showed you. On your porch? Remember? In the middle of bedtime?"

"You mean in the night or something?"

"No, Bee. Not your bedtime. The kids' bedtime. I came to your house. We sat on the porch, and I showed you the photos, and you said they were nothing. Last week? You said that people had pictures on their phone, and it wasn't a big deal. But it's *not* nothing."

"Maddy. You haven't been to my house in forever. And I don't know who you think you sat on the porch with and had some chitchat about photographs, but it wasn't me."

"We talked about tonight. You told me about the surprise party." Bee knew Maddy had been to her house. Why lie about something so stupid? She was probably trying to cover her tracks and not let Joseph know that she'd blown the surprise. Couldn't she see this was more important than that?

"Surprise party?" said Rose, pausing eating for a moment. "No one told me this was supposed to be a surprise party." Rose didn't know this was supposed to be a surprise? Maddy stared at Bee. What was happening here? Really happening?

"Bee, why are you doing this?" she said. Her throat suddenly felt like it was being squeezed on the inside from holding back tears that wanted out.

"Doing what?" said Bee. She'd dropped the sass and now just looked mildly alarmed, like everyone else at the table. "I'm not doing anything." Maddy pulled her eyes away from Bee and looked across the table to Emily, who looked back, blank-faced, before something close to amusement passed across her face. No one else would have interpreted it as amusement. But Maddy knew that expression. She'd seen that look before. It meant there was a joke, and Maddy was on one side and Emily, along with whomever else she'd hustled into a corner with her, was on the other. But Bee wasn't in Emily's corner. Was she?

"Are you on her side now?" Maddy asked Bee. She had returned to her food, signaling that she was ready to scoot by this whole conversation. To chalk it up to just another Maddy misfire.

"For God's sake, Maddy, grow up. No one's taking sides," said Bee.

"Ease up, Bee. It's not her fault," said Rose, and Maddy couldn't believe the surge of gratitude she felt toward Rose of all people. "Maddy, how long have things been like this? What does your doctor say?"

"She won't see a doctor," said Joseph. "I've tried."

"Oh my God. Because there is nothing wrong with me!"

"Maddy, you have to calm—"

Maddy stood up fast, tipping her chair back onto the floor. A baby-boomer couple who, having no conversation of their own, had been listening in now turned around to see exactly what it was they'd been tuned in to.

"Why are you doing this?"

"We're not doing anything," said Bee.

"Stop," said Joseph, standing up and coming over to Maddy's side of the table. "Stop picking on her."

"I'm not—"

"She's sick. The last thing she needs is—"

"I'm *not* sick! Stop saying that," screamed Maddy. *"If anyone's sick here, it's you!"* She stopped short, and so did Joseph. They'd both heard that phrase before. It was what her mom had flung at her dad whenever she'd felt backed into a corner.

"I'm taking Maddy home," said Joseph, righting her chair and picking her purse up from the floor. "This is too much for her. She's exhausted."

"I don't want to go home. Why are you talking about me like I'm ninety?"

"Because you're acting like it," he said into her ear. "Can someone cover the check, and I'll Venmo them tomorrow?"

"You're good," said Greg. "I got you." He nodded at Maddy, who stared back at him. He was the only one. The only one who hadn't piled on in the fight. The only one who didn't think she was insane. She didn't want to go home with Joseph. She wanted to go home with Greg. She wanted to reverse a whole life right now. Unpick it and start it again. But. She couldn't. Unless you swam out ahead of the current early on, life took you wherever it pleased. And hers had taken her here.

Joseph now had one hand at her back, propelling her toward the door so fast she could barely keep up. She used to feel so safe when he'd put his hand at the base of her spine. Now it felt borderline aggressive. Why did she get the feeling that the moment they got out of view, he'd drop the devoted-husband act and something real and unstoppable was about to begin?

CHAPTER 16

MADDY

The second they exited the restaurant, Joseph dropped his hand. His face had turned blank. When he looked like that, you were likely to get as much emotional reactivity as from a stack of tiles. She decided she'd let him have his sulk. When he was ready, he could be the one to try to explain what the fuck had just happened. She'd said all she had to say. Anything she added now would just be more of her asking why he was doing this and more of his denying that anyone was doing anything. If he'd even do that. When the blank face was on, words tended to become very limited indeed.

The two of them walked along next to each other, their footsteps in and out of an uneasy rhythm. For the main part, they were out of sync. Every now and then the sidewalk would narrow, and Joseph would hop down onto the street before stepping back up again. In the silence, she tried to unravel the knots. For what possible reason would Bee take things so far in pretending they'd never sat on her front steps and talked about those photos? She had to be lying. Maddy suddenly had an unwelcome memory of her mother mistaking Maddy for her grandmother and serving up long monologues about events and people from her school days. Could it be possible that she'd talked to someone who wasn't Bee about those photos? She didn't think so. But then, when her mother had talked to her about piano competitions and her crush on her biology teacher, completely convinced she was discussing it with her own mother, would she have believed anyone telling her the redhead in front of her was actually her daughter? It was the thing she kept coming back to that might make this all real. Her mother hadn't known. Her mother had never had a fully cognizant conversation with anyone about her illness. By the time it was so obvious that no one— not even her father—could deny what was happening, her mother had been beyond discussing it. Maddy had looked up the word that she'd only half remembered last week. Anosognosia. When you were too sick to know that you were sick. Too sick to know that you were lost to everyone around you. Lost to yourself. Was she really there?

The streetlights along the pathway were all out, and the night was lit by nothing other than the yellowing moon. No cars. No one else walking. As soon as they'd left the lights of Main Street, it'd been like they alone had owned the night. The air had finally given up the dragging heat of the day and was now cool with a nighttime breeze. If she hadn't been smothered in a blanket of misery, she'd have been exhilarated by the walk.

"You embarrassed yourself tonight," said Joseph, causing Maddy to stop walking.

"That's completely unfair."

"Do you have any idea how hard this is to watch?"

"What is?"

"You, turning into your mother."

"I *saw* those photos. Why would I lie about that?" She ignored the dig about her turning into her mother, even though it stung about as hard as an accusation could sting. Somewhere behind her, a window slammed shut. She started walking again; she didn't want anyone listening in on this.

"You're not lying," he said. She almost stopped walking again. Was he finally coming clean? "I believe you when you say you saw them. *You* believe that you saw them. But, Maddy, no one else did. Dents appear on car bumpers for no reason. Your keys grow legs and walk themselves off to every random spot in the house. Pictures disappear from phones. Is it really everyone else? Or is it you?"

"It's not me."

"Maddy, the first step with any of this is to admit that there's a problem here. Until you start to believe that there's even a possibility that you could be ill, no one can do anything to help you. All any of us can do is watch you spiral. It's painful."

"Is it Emily making you do this?"

"You should be focusing on yourself, not on Emily."

"Your first love." She said it to see if he'd deny it. He'd always denied it.

"You were my first love," he said.

"I don't think that's true." She'd said that before too, but this was the first time she'd really meant it. "You were obsessed with her. You were obsessed with each other."

"And then she left. And we weren't," he said neatly. Too neatly. There was something else under there, but she didn't know what.

"But you admit that you were attached. To one another," she said.

"Of course we were attached. Who knows how things would have turned out if she hadn't gone away. We were in something major." She didn't like hearing that. That sounded like regret.

"You could have found her," she said. He needed to acknowledge that not everything here had been swept up and out of his control. If he'd wanted Emily in his life all these years, he would have found a way. There was a reason he'd let it go.

"I wrote to her when she was in juvie, but she never wrote back." He'd written to her *there*? He'd never told her this before. "She never forgave me," he said.

"Forgave you for what?"

"For not taking her side. I think that's why she gave up. Why she pleaded guilty. She could handle everyone else giving up on her. But not me."

"She pleaded guilty because she was guilty," said Maddy. "She was destructive. Violent. She still is."

"She was complicated. The things she'd been through were complicated. But she needed me, you know. No one else seemed up to the job, and I think I just wanted to be the one to save her. I should have been the one to save her." Maddy stared at him. This was new. He'd never explained what had pulled him toward teenaged Emily before. In some ways she'd assumed it'd been as simple as someone letting him screw them. "And was she really ever that violent?" he added.

"She practically pushed you to the floor the other day. And she *cut* me. These aren't things that normal people do to each other. She's disturbed. She's done things that are disturbed all her life." He reached out and took hold of her wrist and then turned it over to reveal her inner forearm. The skin there was pale white, with one paler long line running down it. He pulled her close to him, turning her around so his body was directly behind hers. She twisted her head around to look at him. What was this? He still had hold of her wrist, but with his other hand he took hers and drew it slowly down and along the scar. The line started at the top, and as it drew closer to the bottom, curved toward the inside of her arm. As he drew the long line, it tracked perfectly with the angle he held her hand at. Too perfectly. When he finally reached the bottom, she shrugged him off and then stepped away out of his reach.

"You sure it was Emily who cut you?" he said. "I think there's a chance you could have been responsible for that one yourself."

She looked down at her scar and then brushed the palm of her hand along her arm, as if to wipe his insinuation away. And then she started walking, not looking behind her to see if he was following.

The cut. She had been so certain of the story she'd created that she'd forgotten about the other one tucked in right behind it. The real one. She'd blurred the truth. Edited it to make it what it should have been. And until that very moment, she'd forgotten that she'd done it. Did he know? Or was he guessing? Things between them had become fuzzed, but he was still the person who knew her best of all. And somehow, he'd figured this one out. He literally knew her better than she knew herself. Perhaps he was saying that he understood. That he knew that sometimes what was real and what you wanted to be real became the same thing. That sometimes we adjust the truth, just a tiny bit, just to make the truth what it should be. A simple rewrite of the parts that don't make sense, until you pull things around, and they start to align with logic.

But if this one fact she'd known to be a truth had just crumbled, what other parts of her reality were ready to cave in? She clearly no longer had a hold on what she'd done and what she hadn't done. And there it was. The first glimmer of proof that she might just be starting down the path her mother had gone down.

"I have to go to the Westside tomorrow. I'm meeting with Benny," Joseph said from beside her. She'd forgotten he was there. The least of the things her mind had recently betrayed her on.

"Okay," she said in a half whisper. Benny was a producer he'd worked with for over a decade. Meetings with him sometimes meant a new gig was brewing, but him dropping Benny's name hadn't sparked her normal surge of hope. She didn't feel anything. She could feel him waiting for her to say something else, and then she remembered. Tomorrow was their consultation with the expensive but competent fertility doctor she'd finally chosen. It had taken some searching. Not the expensive part, that was a given. But the competent part. She didn't want to be brushed off with an "unexplained infertility" diagnosis; she wanted results. Or at least, she had.

"We have our appointment with Dr. Drumgun tomorrow," she said.

"Oh right. I forgot," he said. He didn't sound like he'd forgotten. She waited for more, an opinion on whether he'd cancel Benny or if she should go ahead without him. They were getting results. His results. She already had hers, and she checked out. "Perfectly ovulatory" was the exact phrase. And then she remembered, if everyone else was right, and she was wrong, as must surely be the case at this point, then there could be no baby. It was selfish enough to bring a child into this world where great swaths of their home state were regularly engulfed in wildfire and all the topsoil would be farmed into oblivion by the time they hit middle age, but then to throw in an insane mother on top of that. How could she do it? If she already loved her child, which she undoubtably did, then how could she burden a new soul with this epic mess. Maybe the two years of trying and failing had been Mother Nature's way of making sure that she didn't.

"Do you think we still should?" she said, not bothering to explain exactly what they still should. He knew.

"Might be an idea to put things on ice," he said, and then surprised her by taking her hand. He seemed poised, waiting for her to contradict him. To tell him that there was nothing wrong with her and that she was pressing ahead with or without him. That's what she'd have said to him this time yesterday.

"I'll call and cancel," she said, and then it was he who turned to her in surprise. But then he took it in, the knowledge that she was as good as confessing that she knew. He had her. He'd broken through, and she believed him. The next doctor they'd see wouldn't be a fertility specialist. She'd call her mother's old consultant and make an appointment for as soon as she could get in. It was time.

CHAPTER 17

MADDY

Maddy looked around the waiting room, every last person with their head bent to their phone. There were no tattered magazines gracing the various chairs and tables of the room. No one wanted to read second-hand copies of *People* magazine anymore when they had their phone to gaze at, loaded with personalized content just for them. Maddy sometimes visualized people's phones swapped out for mirrors, a whole world of people staring in silent awe at digitized versions of themselves.

She glanced at the empty seat next to her and wished again that Joseph had come today. She didn't want to do this alone. It was too important. Despite what difficulties they'd been through recently, Joseph was still tied fast to her in ways that only married couples knew. He was obliged to care about her. And she was obliged to care about him. Which was the reason she was here.

A nurse opened the door and flung Maddy's name out into the waiting room. She felt the same shot of nerves she always did when this happened and obediently got to her feet. A few of the couples sitting around the room eyed her curiously. Probably wondering if she was doing this alone and thinking that, if so, she was clueless. She ignored the looks and followed the nurse through the door and down a corridor.

She suspected that, yes, what she was doing today could be classified as pretty clueless, but not in the way that those smug twosomes lined up along the walls of the waiting room imagined. What she was doing right now was either the best or the worst idea she'd ever had.

Early that morning, Maddy had changed her mind. She would visit Dr. Drumgun. She would hear the information. She would get this ball rolling. After all, a consultation was just that—a consult, merely a discussion about possibilities. No one was obliged to act on any of those possibilities. But how could it hurt to have all the information before them?

And as soon as she knew where they stood, she'd make an appointment with her mother's old consultant, and they'd talk it all through. There would be tests; Maddy would most likely get an MRI, and then they'd know where they were at. At that point they'd have the complete array of information before them, and they could make a plan. And even if after her MRI they found that the very worst was indeed true, there was every chance that Maddy would have years and years of life being more or less normal before things went downhill. Enough time to start a family, if not to see it all the way through. She could have her child. She could count each day with her son or daughter as an extra special gift, and then if she checked out early, Joseph would have something to remember her by. Someone to stand alongside him in life. Someone to take her place who was part of her. But how could she make any of these decisions if she didn't know what they were up against? She needed all the puzzle pieces before she decided what to do next. And whichever way the puzzle pieces placed themselves, she knew that whatever else was changing about her, one thing hadn't changed: selfish or not, she still wanted to be a mother. Desperately.

Dr. Drumgun's door was already open, and he smiled as she walked in the door, then got to his feet. Disappointingly for a doctor of fertility, the descriptor that came to mind once she was inside the office was *sterile*. There were the obligatory certificates on the wall. There was tastefully bland furniture. But no books. No family photos. No collage of babies he'd helped to manufacture up on the wall. A few ceramics in a display cabinet behind his desk were the only nod to style and warmth. And even they somehow looked like they'd been selected by someone who worked for a corporation.

"No Mr. Moth today?" he asked. Maddy closed the door behind her. As disinterested as the nurses probably were, she didn't want anyone overhearing any aspect of this conversation.

"He couldn't make it," said Maddy. "I hope that's not a problem." She sat down, and Drumgun sat too, not answering her question. Instead, he hit his keyboard a few times and squinted at his monitor, which was positioned so Maddy couldn't see what he was looking at. She presumed he was bringing up test results.

"So," he said, turning away from his computer, and even though Maddy barely knew this man, she already knew from that "so" he was about to deliver bad news. The very worst. But how bad, exactly, could it be? "I'll start by saying that it would be my strong preference to wait and reschedule this appointment for when your husband can be here."

"I know. He badly wanted to be here today, but he just couldn't get away."

"And there's no way he can be reached by phone?" Maddy shook her head with a smile. This doctor had a role to play, and he couldn't wiggle out of it just because one dude felt like he should have the back of another. It didn't work like that. Tests had been taken, an appointment had been scheduled, money had been dropped, forms had been signed, news was to be delivered. It was his job. Too bad if he didn't like the format in which it was going down.

"Okay." He took a breath apparently with which to steel himself and then rolled his chair back and forth a couple of times. Maddy felt herself fidget sympathetically. He looked uncomfortable in the extreme. Did they not get training on how to deliver sucky news at medical school? Why was he dragging this out like a high school drama student?

"So what's the deal?" she asked, clear-voiced. One of them had to take charge here.

"From your husband's test results, I suspect that he may be azoospermic."

"What's that?" she asked. She didn't like that Joseph had something with a name. She didn't like that at all.

"Has your husband—and this is where it would be useful if he were here so we could hear this information from him—ever had any significant injury to the testicles?"

"Recently?" she asked. She knew he hadn't. This doctor thought she was coming into Joseph's life at the last minute and demanding he fertilize her, but he was wrong. She'd known him all her life. Almost all.

"At any time. A flipped testicle in childhood? Sports injury. Mumps. Treatment for cancer. Anything like that."

"No," she said. She was going to say *not that I know of.* But she did know. There was nothing. She was also unimpressed at how he was leading with the follow-up questions. Clearly there was something major wrong with Joseph, and she needed to know what. "Can you tell me what's wrong with my husband? What's he got?"

"Azoospermia is a term rather than a condition. It means that there is low to no sperm production."

"So he has a low sperm count?" she asked. That didn't sound like such a big deal. Couldn't that be fixed? Baggy underwear, zinc supplements, and all that?

"We'll do another sperm test to get a second sample, but I have to say that in your husband's case it seems like it may be no sperm production at all."

"None?" No sperm at all? Could a person just walk around life looking totally normal and then have no reproductive technology whatsoever? "What do you mean, none? Why does he have none?"

"We don't know the answer to that yet. It's something to discuss in person with your husband, but options include genetic testing and then potentially exploratory surgery to check for the cause and—"

"What causes this?"

"There are different reasons. It's rare, but it could be genetic. Or . . ."

"Or what?" she asked, seeing something she didn't like flit across his face.

"Or there can be other causes, but we'd need to explore further."

"Could he be sick?"

"It's a possibility, but again, we can't tell unless we look further. The next step will be—"

"Could he have cancer?" she asked. "His mother had cancer. Breast cancer." She didn't know how she'd leaped from "other causes" to cancer, but from the way his face had looked, the C-word had jumped right in there. Having had the vague notion that whatever was stopping conception was coming from Joseph, Maddy had had a good Google as to the kind of things that could harm sperm production, and she'd learned that a tumor blocking the vas deferens did nothing to help fertility. She'd ruled it out as improbable. But now it felt very much ruled back in. She felt her breath start to come quicker.

"Mrs. Moth, we have no reason to think that your husband has cancer. It could very well be that he just has a zero sperm count. It happens. It happened to my cousin, in fact. As my aunt likes to say, they broke the mold when they made him. Literally. He and his wife conceived a beautiful baby girl with the help of a donor and—"

"I don't want to have a baby with the help of a donor, I want to have a baby with my husband."

"And we will do everything to find out if you still can. Have faith, Mrs. Moth. We have to take this one step at a time. First, a repeat test, and then if necessary, a blood test to see if he has anything happening genetically, and then we will move to exploratory surgery. We may also have the option of testicular sperm aspiration. That's sperm retrieval. All we need is one. But the first item on the agenda is for you to talk this over with your husband. We need to have him take one more test, and then when we have the results from the second test, I need you both to come see me so we can talk about his options."

"Why do you need to do a second test?"

"To see if we can get a better result."

"Does that ever happen?"

"Of course. One test isn't enough to make a call on this. This is a beginning of a journey you and your husband are on, and I am here to guide you. It's going to be okay. I know it's incredibly hard not to know. But we will know. We will find out what's going on."

Maddy began to cry. She wouldn't know, and she wouldn't find out. Joseph didn't even know she was here, and there was no way she could tell him.

"The good news is that you yourself are perfectly ovulatory, despite your advanced maternal age." She shot him a look that said *really*? He bowed his head, acknowledging that he may have used the wrong word there, and she realized that as well as being a doctor, this person across the desk from her was just a man. A man trying to give a woman some very bad news. "We just have to find you some sperm. Okay?"

He made it sound so easy. Find some sperm. As if by looking in enough of Joseph's creases and crevices they'd dredge some up from somewhere. But it *wasn't* that easy. If Joseph and she had been on the same page, then it might have been that easy. But the state they were in, with everything that was hanging over them. This may well never be resolved. The cold realization washed over her that despite her being the "perfectly ovulatory" Mrs. Moth, she may well never become a mother.

CHAPTER 18

MADDY

After the morning she'd just been through, if she'd had any other job on earth other than dance teacher, she'd have called out sick. But you couldn't just not show for dance class when you had a host of kids about to arrive and no guaranteed way of letting every last parent know you were canceling. And so to work she went. Maddy wasn't suited to teaching at the best of times, as her sister had pointed out to her a few weeks ago. Maybe if she'd been a teacher back when kids were still intimidated enough by adults to listen to what they said, she might have been passable at it. Maybe even slightly good. But teaching in an era where parents didn't believe their kids should be made to say "please" or "thank you" unless they genuinely felt it? Like, emotionally . . . She didn't stand a chance. She'd tried it all: mean teacher, nice teacher, silent teacher, chatty teacher. Nothing worked. These days she just alternately yelled and cajoled and then sometimes just went ahead and taught the class as if everyone were paying perfect attention. Today, she could barely even bring herself to do that. But for whatever reason, this of all things had seemed to work. Instead of the normal squealing and chasing and games of spit tag, she had somehow held their attention. When she'd asked them to, the students had grudgingly shuffled into lines and stood there awaiting further direction. When one student asked to go to the bathroom, there wasn't the normal chain reaction of another five wanting to go. And so there it was: depressed-don't-give-a-crap teacher for the win.

As she was locking up for the evening, she noticed an oblong plastic baggie containing a printout stuck to the front door. She didn't think it'd been there when she'd first arrived, but then she'd been in such a mental haze, she may well have just not noticed it. The bag was bright red, as if the news inside was so alarming it was important its envelope be colored a shade as disturbing as its contents. As if the sender wanted to alert everyone who passed by that there was *trouble within*. She took it down from the door and opened it up. The plastic wrapping was tough to rip open—clearly manufactured for keeping bad news fresh, no matter the weather. But eventually she made a hole big enough to retrieve the notice, and she dragged it out and scanned it.

Rent was going up. Ever since Mrs. Trumbly had dropped her bomb about selling the place, she'd been waiting for this. Waiting for the new owner to contact her. She knew she'd be getting either an eviction notice or a rental hike, neither possibility very appealing. What she hadn't expected was for the rate to *triple*. She'd almost expected it to double. She knew she'd had a super sweet deal with Trumbly, and she knew what current market rates were in Myrtlebury. She'd even done a financial forecast based on doubled rent and worked out that if that did happen, she'd still just about break even. Which wasn't great, obviously, but if she raised her rates again, she would have still been making something. But with this new rent, the triple deal, she was going to be heading into the negative just to keep the school open. No matter what she did. That was not sustainable. *In no way sustainable.* She read the note through again another four times. She had sixty days until the rent soared. That was something, at least. She'd have to find a new place before then. But where? Nowhere in Myrtlebury for sure. Would she have to *close*? Unless she could find somewhere else at a reasonable (very reasonable) rate, then the answer was: probably yes. Well, fuck. Maddy read the note again, her initial panic scan transitioning into a detailed examination—searching for the overlooked detail that might make this all not true. Who actually was it behind this bullshit? In the second paragraph were phone and email details for a Beverly Chen who appeared to work out of some office in Rancho Cucamonga. But the letterhead was for "Boa Development." And almost predictably Boa Development had its head offices in New York. A piece of an entirely different puzzle from the one she'd been trying to figure out that morning clicked into place. Wasn't Emily in property development? Even though she'd recently hopped state lines, her business base must still be back in New York. But for what earthly reason would Emily buy up Maddy's studio and then hike the rent on it? The answer came back instantly: because she could. An office being based in New York wasn't necessarily enough to pin this on Emily, but somehow all the logic was leading Maddy right there.

The best way to find out, of course, would be to ask her. Answers were needed. About the rent hike on her dance studio. About if those photos *had* been real. About all of it. And for once, she'd be able to rely on her sister telling her the truth. Because if Emily was behind the tripling of her rent, and if those photos of her on Joseph's phone were real, then ultimately she'd want Maddy to know all about it. Because where was the joy in taking something away from someone you'd hated all your life if you couldn't let them know that it was you who had done it?

Maddy scanned each and every window as she drove by Pile House. It wasn't hard to see inside. All the lights in the house were on, every blind open, and the house lit up its side of the street like an oversized beacon on the top of a lighthouse. She didn't see much of interest through the windows, though she fleetingly saw that where there used to be storage cabinets along one of the bedroom walls upstairs, now there was just bare wall. Maddy drove on and then pulled up halfway down the next block so she wouldn't be seen. Tonight, she wanted Emily off-kilter. Even if it was only for an eighth of a second.

She'd come straight from school and was still in her dance teacher's getup of jersey shorts over a catsuit. It was still hot enough not to need anything else on, but the ensemble had her feeling half-dressed and vulnerable, so she pulled on her wrap top. She didn't want to feel any more exposed than she already did for this conversation.

She closed the Jeep's door softly. Noise traveled this time of night. It wasn't until she had almost crossed the street that she saw it. Joseph's BMW. Parked outside Pile House. She stopped. Of course, his car parked outside Pile House meant nothing in itself. It was completely possible that he could have parked here while visiting Bee—even though outside Pile House wouldn't be the logical place to park for that. She reached for her phone. She'd text Bee and ask if Joseph was there. But in the middle of her half-composed text, she abandoned her message and slid her phone back into her purse. No good would come of Maddy's asking. Either he was with Bee and she'd look like she didn't trust her husband enough to directly ask him where he was—which she didn't—or he wasn't there. Which was, of course, much worse. Because then why else was he parked where he was parked?

As if in answer, the front door swung open and out walked Joseph, head down, eyes to the floor. He was wearing a hoodie. Universal uniform of the disruptive. He didn't see Maddy staring at him from across the road. But she watched him nevertheless. He didn't look guilty. He looked light. Was he not concerned who might see him? Joseph got in his car but didn't drive off immediately, and it took all Maddy's self-control not to rush over there and bang on his car window. Demand an answer. Demand his love. And then, for half a moment, Maddy second-guessed herself. Was that even him she'd seen coming out the front door? He had been in a hoodie after all, and it was dark—the streetlights on this corner of Peach hadn't worked since they'd moved in. But then he started the car, and the light from his taillight illuminated the curve of the BMW's bumper. And for the second time, she found herself watching that dent from an unobserved position. He drove off, and she watched his taillights journey all the way down the street. The traffic light at the end was amber, but he was in no rush to make it through before it turned to red. In no rush to get home to her.

Despite the growing list of hard evidence, she still wondered if there was a series of explanations for every red flag being waved in her face: the tattoo, this evening's visit to Pile House. Something simple. Explainable. Something less painful than what was becoming real. Because with every fresh second that passed, it *was* becoming more and more real. There was no way she could explain away what she'd just seen.

As soon as the light changed to green and Joseph's car turned the corner, she made a choice and crossed the street. Time to get to the bottom of this. She didn't pause to read the notice hammered into the lawn or take in the torn-up front yard or the contents of the dumpster. She walked past all of it. The only thing visible to her was the front door. The front door that used to belong to her. The front door of her childhood home.

She knocked. Nothing. She knocked again, louder. She was wondering if she dared to just turn the handle and walk in when she heard the thump of bare feet on wood, and the door opened to reveal Emily. Maddy watched as her face instantly went from hopeful to shut down.

"What do you want?" Emily asked, all the bounce of their encounters over the past weeks gone. This was the first time Maddy had seen Emily since her return without Joseph as a buffer. This was Emily unfiltered.

"Can I come in?" Emily opened the door wider but didn't stand out of the way. She seemed to be considering the situation. Then Maddy saw it. Emily was trying to work out if Maddy had seen Joseph leave.

"Sure," said Emily, eventually stepping back from the door, borderline hostile. She wasn't even going to pretend, was she? Even though they were adults. It was a smart move on her part. She knew it was the quickest way to intimidate Maddy: make her feel like a child again, remind her that Emily was the unpredictable *big* sister. Except these days, there were no parents to make sure things didn't get out of hand. Joseph was on Emily's side. And in the new grown-up world, Bee— Maddy's greatest childhood ally—had crossed over into Emily's world. She had no backup.

Maddy followed Emily into the kitchen, or what was left of the kitchen. All the cabinets had been pulled out, leaving great holes in the plaster, which revealed the ribs of the woodwork behind it. Emily was obviously in the middle of a truly epic refurb. So much for Emily fixing the roof and leaving the rest of the place untouched.

"I thought you were going to keep it the same," said Maddy.

"I changed my mind."

There was next to no furniture anywhere, but in the center of what used to be the kitchen, Maddy recognized the table from the house at Devil's Gulch. It looked even smaller now, sitting in the hollowed-out space. At the base of one of the chairs was a pair of sneakers, a pair of scrunched-up socks on the floor next to them. She resisted the urge to pick one up and see if it was a no-show sock. From here, it looked like it might be. The table hadn't been cleared of dinner, and the two plates left there bore the remains of Thai takeout. Maddy chose to ignore the evidence of Joseph's most recent meal and the socks and sat down at the table. Emily finished a text message she was pecking out and then sat down opposite.

"Who were you texting?" said Maddy.

"No one," she said. "So what's up?" Now that the moment was here, Maddy felt all the questions that had been stacking up in her brain over the past weeks leave her until all she had was the one. Was she still angry about it? That, of course, was the crux of everything. But there were entire worlds in the way of her being able to ask her sister that, so instead she decided to start with the studio.

"Do you work for Boa Development?"

"I own Boa Development."

"Excuse me?"

"It's my development company. I started it, in New York."

"So you bought my dance studio?"

"*Your* dance studio?"

"The unit on Main Street. I run a school out of that building. I was talking about it on my birthday, remember? You didn't happen to mention then that *you* were the one who'd bought the place."

"Didn't seem like it would add to the party atmosphere."

"So you know my rent pretty much tripled, right?"

"Just getting in line with current rental prices. Are you taking this personally?"

"Of course I'm taking it personally. You're buying everything that means something to me and then pulling it out of my hands."

"You agreed to me buying your dad's place. And if I hadn't bought your school, someone else would have."

"He was your dad too. And somehow this feels less like you randomly deciding to add some crumbling buildings to your real estate portfolio and more like a deliberate campaign to steal my life."

"What's your point?"

"My point is you need to get out of my town."

"So you get to tell me to leave because you lived here first? Because if we're going with first come, first served, I was with Joseph years before you were."

So that was it, then. Just thrown out on the table like that. Fine.

"I'm married to him, Emily. Married."

"Do you think he maybe just forgot that he's married?"

"That's not a thing you forget." Maddy pressed her thumbnail into the top of her index finger until she felt it slice the skin there. She wanted to know that this conversation was real. If the pain was real, then so was this conversation.

"It's amazing the things that people can forget when it's not convenient. Entire events just wiped from the collective memory. One person remembering something doesn't make it a truth, you know. Unless everyone buys into exactly the same story, a true thing sometimes isn't a true thing at all."

Maddy said nothing. She knew what Emily was talking about, but the only thing that mattered to her tonight was if Joseph was in love with Emily again. And what if he was? Joseph knew Emily. But so did Maddy. And unlike Joseph, she wasn't controlled by infatuation. If Emily really was Joseph's one true love, then maybe, *maybe*, she might have stood to the side to make way for his happiness. But it wasn't that way. There was nothing light about Emily. Nothing loving about her. Maddy didn't care how many years had passed; Emily was still broken. Maddy could see it hanging around her. In her very posture as she sat in the kitchen chair. Emily was still bruised. And now she wanted to bruise what Joseph had found with Maddy. To pull him back down into the swirl of her dark life. She wouldn't let it happen.

"It's not some kind of chaste union with separate beds and kisses on the forehead good night. We have sex. All the time. Good sex. It's grown-up, proper love." Her claims to this great sex she was having felt like a lie, but even though the passion had its ebbs and flows, the love was a constant. It could be counted on.

"You think that someone who loves you even slightly would be doing what he's been doing to you?"

Maddy wasn't brave enough to ask her outright what she meant by that. Was she admitting that they'd been sleeping together? Even though all the evidence was a sequence of flaming red arrows pointing that way, she still *couldn't* believe it. Joseph wouldn't humiliate her like that. But if it was true, all of a sudden, she didn't want to hear the truth from Emily. She wanted to hear it from him. It was time to ask. She'd only have to ask once, and whatever he said, or didn't say—she'd know.

"I need to go," said Maddy.

"Okay. Tell your *husband* hi from me." Emily smiled.

"Really? You're going to make fun of me now too?"

"Look. I just can't take your marriage to Joseph seriously is all. The only reason he married you, the only reason you've been having all this 'good grown-up sex' all this time, is because you reminded him of me," Emily said simply, as if this was a generally known fact that she was just bringing up now in order to be helpful.

"That's utter bullshit."

"Does he fuck you eyes closed or eyes open?" asked Emily. Maddy didn't say a word. And Emily had her answer. It was eyes closed. Every time. She and Joseph had argued about it more than once. But he had said he couldn't help himself. It was just what happened when he had sex. But now she knew he was lying. Every time they'd gone to bed, he'd deliberately closed his eyes so that he could think of someone else. Someone with the same body but with a very different face.

Maddy made it as far as the porch before her legs gave out underneath her. Thankfully, she'd managed to slam the front door behind her so Emily wasn't witness to her total collapse. She slid down the porch's pillar, her butt landing on the step with a rough bump. She couldn't cry. She could barely breathe. She was going to lose him. The last thing she had. The only thing that had ever mattered. And all she could do was sit there. She wrapped her arms around the pillar, then closed her eyes and leaned her forehead into its wood. This pillar was the only solid thing left in the world. The only thing that could be trusted not to dissolve as she held on to it.

It was only the thought of Emily opening the door the next morning to find her there still stuck in place that eventually got her to stumble off the porch and drift through the space between the house and her Jeep. She drove herself away from Emily and toward Joseph—to find out if there was anything that could be done about this thing of theirs they'd called a marriage.

CHAPTER 19

MADDY

Maddy pulled into the driveway, into the open spot next to Greg's car—the place where Joseph would have undoubtedly been parked had he been home. She walked down the drive toward the guest house, noticing that it was dark inside, then let herself in and flicked on the lights. It looked the same as ever. The bed, the kitchenette, the closet, the cluster of packing boxes piled against the wall. She pulled her phone out of her purse. Nothing from him or from anyone else. Had Emily warned him? She called Joseph. Straight to voice mail. She didn't leave a message. He was either out of battery or range, or the millisecond he'd seen it was her calling, he'd hit "Decline." Could a person just do that? Just decline their wife? Decline her right to an explanation, to an apology, to love? She realized that all the time he didn't come home, all the time he kept on "Declining," she had no real way of knowing where he was. In the end, all he'd had to do was step out of cell phone range and he was lost to her. Were humans really connected by nothing more than that one vulnerable line of frequency?

She opened the closet. His clothes were still there, as was his collection of Converses. She looked up to the top shelf where they stashed the duffel bags and saw that none were missing. A brief check of the bathroom revealed that his shaving gear and toothbrush were still there. He hadn't been here. So where was he? She needed to talk to someone. Someone who could view this situation from the angles that she couldn't. She felt an acute sadness pierce her chest as she suddenly missed her dad with such intensity that she gasped. That's who she'd be on the phone with right now—the one person guaranteed to always be on her side. If her parents were still alive, none of this would ever have happened. Emily would have stayed well away. What Maddy needed now, more than anything else, was the insulating bubble of her family. But her family had been Joseph.

But had she definitely lost him? Perhaps Emily had said all those things just to rattle her cage. Half of her believed that Joseph was going to walk through the door any moment with a bag full of groceries and dismiss everything she'd seen and heard that evening as a delusion. She looked down at the cut on her nail bed. The conversation with Emily *had* happened. She'd seen him leave the house. Hadn't she?

She sank onto the bed, unable to think. The only thing she could process was the pain in the center of her chest, which felt like someone had just sunk an ice pick into it. She needed information. Some facts that she could anchor herself to so she could unravel the rest. Her eye fell onto the desk underneath the window. Despite their having a storage unit crammed full of furniture, they'd had to go out and purchase a super narrow desk specifically to fit in the small space under there. *They, their.* Could she even claim those words anymore? She pulled herself up off the bed and walked over to the window. There sat their laptops side by side, silver and unassuming. She opened up Joseph's, plugged in the same password he used for everything, *EpicAudio1982*, and she was in. Despite sleuthing through his phone, she hadn't bothered going through his laptop before now. Everyone knew that the phone was where the goodies were. But as she had zero access to that and unrestricted access to this, it was a good place to start. Better than sitting on her bed staring at the wall and trying to work out what was happening from within the four walls of her brain anyway.

Unlike Maddy's desktop, which was a sea of folders, Joseph's desktop was completely clean, featuring nothing more than a picture of a pier leading to a glass-green lake. The bottom of the screen held a row of apps: Pro Tools, Logic Pro, Digital Pigeon. But where did he keep his *stuff?* She searched around for a few moments, trying but failing to find anything resembling a familiar file structure. Eventually she found a photos file, but it was empty, as if Joseph had never saved a picture of anything in his life. Thinking she'd check his search history, she launched Chrome, and there she hit gold. Joseph's entire world was digital. Of course it was. There were a series of folders on his browser, and she opened each one up, scanning the bookmarks inside, each one less interesting than the one that came before it. Drum stores, hiking sites, 3D printing, gear exchange. She clicked on his finance folder. Only two links. Their joint account and then QuickBooks. QuickBooks being the closest thing to personal he had in here, she clicked it open, then entered his email and good old *EpicAudio1982.* It didn't work. She added a dollar sign to the end, which she knew he sometimes did when a site required a symbol. That didn't work either. She followed that with various uppercase and lowercase configurations of the same thing. Nothing. The boys' names and birthdates. *EpicAudio* with their wedding anniversary date optimistically added. Nothing. On a whim she added *Sisu* and was relieved to see that that didn't work either. Then, just to try it, she added *Sisu* and a dollar sign and felt her heartbeat ramp up to triple time. She was in.

As unfamiliar as she was with the software, the picture it painted of Joseph's finances was instantly clear. She scanned through the rows in front of her, and a vastly different story from the one Joseph had been presenting over the past couple of years became quickly apparent. Were these his accounts? If not, then what were they doing on his laptop? She scanned the amounts again. The transactions ranged from tens of thousands to hundreds of thousands. The highest for just over three hundred thousand. She clicked on the three hundred thousand line and saw that it had tags. "Apple." "Mohawk Inventory." "St. Nov FF." She recognized Mohawk Inventory. Joseph had talked about them before. They were a band from San Diego that he'd dug up at South by Southwest. But why was this file tagged with "Apple"? Apple *computers*? Bands didn't rack up these kinds of figures with streaming agreements. She thought about the most recent Apple ad she'd seen. The one for AirPods with that girl who was clearly in love with her cat. Was the music by Mohawk Inventory? She Googled *Apple music ad Mohawk Inventory* and there it was in black and white. Various articles about the tune that was now an undeniable part of everyone's internal landscape. The article wasn't wrong. Maddy had sung it in the shower herself before now, or the first two lines anyway. But she hadn't known it was *them*. Then there was information about how they'd been spotted by Apple scouts and the rights had been scooped up, which had led to commercial fame. Was Joseph an Apple scout, then? But it wasn't just Apple. As she dug through more files with more five- and six-figure deals she saw Target, Old Spice, Audi.

She then opened the "Taxes" tab and saw the tax calculation for this year. An eye-watering amount. She searched but couldn't see any actual tax documents uploaded anywhere. Was this perhaps just the equivalent of a vision board for QuickBooks? Fantasy figures that he hoped would melt into a reality. But Joseph wasn't the type to believe that imagining a shiny future was the springboard to diving into it. That was Maddy's realm. *She* was the one with the vision boards. Vision boards that she had to admit painted a picture radically different from the life she was currently living. A life lived in a tall, skinny house by the ocean, a loving spouse she'd snipped straight from the pages of one of her old surfing magazines, who it had to be said looked nothing much like Joseph. Long tables piled with homemade dishes; a tribe of friends as close as family crowded around them. The vision board hadn't worked so far.

No house by the ocean, no big group of friends. As of today, perhaps not even a spouse.

She went back to browsing the transactions again. As well as the entries being tagged with various corporations, each one was also tagged with "St Nov FF." It couldn't be a nonprofit for the school; he would have told her. But what else could "St Nov" possibly stand for other than St. Novatus?

Emily would have told him her version of things by now. Of course she would have. When Emily was first found, Maddy had known that there was every chance that would happen, but she'd trusted that if and when it came down to it, he'd believe her. His own wife. After all, he hadn't believed Emily last time. No one had. But that couldn't be what this "St Nov" tag was all about. Even if he'd switched sides and now bought Emily's side of the story, "St Nov" had been all over Joseph's accounting for the last year. Emily had only shown up a few weeks ago. And Greg wouldn't have, literally *couldn't have*, told him. Unless the guilt had finally got the better of him and he had. She felt an ugly knot of panic pull tight in the center of her chest and slammed the laptop shut. Then she opened it again and took a snapshot of the QuickBooks screen. She was going to have to do something she'd successfully avoided doing for about two decades. She was going to have to talk to Greg about what they'd done.

As she approached Greg's back door, she could hear Radiohead playing. She also smelled cooking and was instantly hungry. Her hunger surprised her. She'd forgotten to eat lunch that day, sure, but given what the day had wrought, she was amazed her body still had the wherewithal to make all its usual biological demands. She knocked on the back door. No response. She knocked louder in order to be heard over the thrum of "Creep," and a second later he pulled open the door. The first thing she noticed was that he was wearing an apron.

"Hey," he said. And then noticing her noticing the apron, "I'm making schnitzel. Messy business." He held the door open for her, and she walked inside. Despite her frazzled state of mind, she noted the radical improvements made to the kitchen since she'd last seen it. The wood-effect tile was now an actual floor instead of a series of boxes. The cupboards were a cheerful blue; there was a white marble countertop where before there had been flimsy corkboard, and he'd added a compact diner booth. She moved past him to slide onto the bench there. Cute.

"Looks good in here," she said. "If the firefighter thing doesn't work out, I think you might have a future in interior design." It was a joke, but given what she was here to talk about, joking about his future as a firefighter was a lousy way to ease into this conversation.

"Wine?" he said, washing his hands and ignoring her commentary on his future career options.

"Always." He poured her a careful glass from the open bottle of red he had on the counter, then put it down on the table in front of her.

"So what's up?" he said, sliding onto the bench opposite hers, the bashed-up pork chops abandoned on the countertop.

"You making all this just for yourself?" she asked. She was impressed. She found it a hassle to cook just for her and Joseph, and so she rarely bothered. Joseph was more of the chef in the relationship. She corrected herself, *had been* more of the chef in the relationship.

"Not just me, no," he said.

"Who else, then?" said Maddy, before she could suck the words back in. It was beyond ridiculous. She had no right to be territorial over Greg. She'd always had hazy ideas about keeping him in her back pocket as her ultimate backup plan. Wouldn't it just be the way that the minute she actually needed the backup, he got attached. She shut down this line of thought. She hadn't even split up with Joseph, and she was already trying to line up his replacement. What the fuck was wrong with her?

"Just work people," he said, and Maddy tried not to show that she was relieved. "You and Joseph want to join us?" he asked. "There's already too much food. And I know there's more on the way."

"I don't know where Joseph is," she said, jolting the conversation back to where she needed it to be. Greg didn't respond, and she saw it immediately. He wasn't even going to pretend. "You already know, don't you."

"All I know is that you two seem off. What happened?"

"I'm going to ask you something. And I need you to tell me the truth."

"I always tell the truth," he said.

"Not always," she replied, and he slid backward on his bench, genuinely offended.

"There's a difference between honesty and truth. Have I always been completely transparent with everyone I've ever met? Neither of us has. But if someone asks me a direct question, I don't lie."

"Okay, fine. You're not always transparent, but you don't lie," she said. It sounded like she was agreeing to split hairs, but she wasn't. She was trying to ask him where his loyalty lay. She paused before asking it. She had to know. But it was one of those life-changing questions. One of the ones you couldn't take back. "Did you tell Joseph about the fire?"

"No," he said. "Of course not." She felt her whole body unclench, the wood of the bench suddenly hard against her sit bones. Of course Greg hadn't told anyone. The consequences would have been as dire for him as they were for her. She picked up the glass in front of her and took a solid mouthful of the wine inside. It was a malbec. Something she'd taken a fancy to drinking a few years ago after she'd had a good one at a party. She'd never quite reached that first malbec high again afterward. But this mouthful was close. "But Maddy."

"What?"

"It's making its way out there."

"What do you mean?"

"People are asking me about what happened."

"Who's asking?"

"Bee."

Maddy felt the skin at the base of her skull contract as if someone not of this world had just blown a puff of air there. So Bee knew. This was why she'd been so vile toward her recently. But Bee wasn't just going to believe some wispy rumor she'd heard about something that went down a thousand years ago. She would believe it, however, if she'd heard it from her brother.

"Emily," said Maddy. "She told Joseph. Joseph told Bee." Emily still couldn't prove a thing. But Maddy knew better than most that it wasn't always proof that won out. The winning was in getting people to believe.

"I'm sorry." He slid out from behind his side of the table and came over to join her. "You've no idea how much I've wanted to talk to you about this. Not just for the last two years, but for the last twenty. But you haven't let me get near enough to you to have a decent conversation about anything, let alone this. How come you want to talk about it now?"

"Because I'm pretty sure Joseph's been lying to me. And I want to know why. I saw something on his laptop."

"What?"

"You know how broke he's been?" she asked, and Greg nodded. "Turns out, actually not the case." She picked her phone up from the table and then brought up the image she'd just taken of Joseph's QuickBooks. Greg took the phone out of her hands and zoomed in on some of the individual figures.

"Those are some big numbers for sure."

"And then look," she said, taking the phone back from him. She blew up the image bigger and pointed to the "St Nov FF" "St Nov. What is that? St. Novatus?"

"Maybe? Might just be what he called the company."

"But why name it after the school? And Greg, look at all that money. He's been telling me he's broke."

"I mean—"

"What?"

"Could be that it's not all profit, you know? Perhaps those are just accounts for this St Nov company, and he gets a fraction of that. You should see the financials for the fire department. Those figures are huge, and it's not like we're seeing that money. It's just passing through."

Maddy considered this. Could that be true? The money was just passing through from corporation to band, and Joseph wasn't seeing any of it. Or just a fraction of it. It was possible. But then why not mention it?

"You need something stronger than this," he said, facing her and holding up her wineglass.

"No," she said. "This is fine." She took another sip of the malbec, hoping to be transported again at least for a second, but what a few moments before had tasted like raspberry and cherry and joy now just tasted sour and overspiced.

"If Bee has this figured out, it's only a matter of time before everyone knows," he said.

"But people won't believe it. It's just an unfounded rumor."

"Not so unfounded. Even if it was, you so sure no one in this town ever believed an unfounded rumor before?" He was right. Life in this town could be about to get pretty brutal for the both of them. But the fallout couldn't last forever. Scandal faded. All scandals faded in time.

"How bad do you think it'll get?" she asked.

"It happened too long ago for the police to get involved again, but I don't know if there could be a possibility of a lawsuit. There's every chance things get majorly ugly before they even out."

She folded her arms and lowered her head to the table. A lawsuit? She hadn't even thought about that. She couldn't deal with this on top of everything else. She moved her head from side to side, brushing the skin of her forehead against the back of her wrist. Something she did when she was strung out after teaching. It provided zero comfort.

"I'm shipping out before it gets bad. Out of sight, out of mind, you know."

"You're leaving?" she said, and abruptly sat back up, her heart suddenly beating too hard and too fast. Was he seriously going to leave her to deal with this on her own?

"I just got offered a job—out of state," he said. He looked her dead in the eye as he said it. He wasn't shying away from this. There was something else in there. Something he wanted to let her know.

"Where out of state?" she asked, a flicker of a possibility already building.

"Small town in Idaho. About two hundred miles east of Boise. Not so far from Montana. I already rented a condo there." He broke off eye contact. "I'll hold off selling this place till you can find something else."

"Gee, thanks," she said. She was wrong. There was no flicker here. He was straight-up abandoning her. Illogically, this hurt . . . She'd relied on Greg—and she was just now realizing how much—to put her above everyone else in their circle. Even when she'd despaired of having one last person on her side, she'd still presumed she'd had Greg. She hadn't even counted him. But she'd always counted on having him.

"You'll find something else," he said.

"Will I?" she asked. With next to no income and no one to cosign a lease with, she wasn't so sure she would. Her parents dead. Joseph on the way out. Bee on the other side. It was the most alone she'd ever been.

"You want to buy this place? I'll cut you a deal." The possibility scuttled across her consciousness but extinguished itself immediately. If things really were over with Joseph, she was going to need every penny she had to start again. And the budget in no way stretched to a house purchase.

"I have no job, Greg. And the very last place in the world I need to be buying a house right now is around here." As soon as she said it, she realized that like it or not, she was going to have to move too.

Greg watched her face as the realization sank in, then went over to the counter, grabbed his laptop, and slid back onto her side of the bench.

"Take a look," he said. He opened up his computer, loaded a site, and angled it toward her. She could see an artful photo of a log cabin that looked like it'd been plucked off the side of Mont Blanc and dropped into the middle of a meadow of wildflowers. She wasn't in the zone for oohing and aahing over the details of his new life. But she found herself drawn in anyway.

"It's pretty," she said. And it was. Despite herself, she listened as he flicked through the images, zoomed in and out on floor plans, and told her how his new life was going to be. He'd put a deposit on a plot of five wooded acres with a river running along its perimeter, with plans to build his very own cabin. From a kit, of all things. And then, after he'd constructed this haven of timber, he was going to stay there for the rest of his days in peace and tranquility, putting out fires as required and generally being the local hero he'd always wanted to be. The cabin had four bedrooms, and he didn't say, but she guessed he had plans on marrying some local beauty and filling those rooms up with mini Gregs. It felt beyond surreal to be sitting at this table in the wake of her husband leaving her, looking at the building blocks of someone else's dream. Eventually she could hear no more.

"So good for you." She didn't bother to keep the snip out of her voice. He was flashing his beautiful future in front of her face one second after he'd told her he was abandoning her to be ravaged by the wolves. "If you'll excuse me, I have to go see if I can track down my alleged husband." She half rose, expecting him to slide out of the bench to let her out. But he didn't.

"Come with me."

"To . . . the cabin?"

"Why not?"

She sat down on the bench again. Could it be that easy? Just run off into the wilds of not-so-far-from-Montana with her husband's best friend.

She could do it. She knew she could. But the question was: Did she want to? He hadn't said that he loved her, but she knew that he did. The truth was she wasn't ready to let go of Joseph. She'd been in the doctor's office trying to find out why she couldn't conceive his baby *this morning*, for God's sake. She couldn't unloosen the ties that fast. Greg saw her waver.

"Maddy. You and Joseph aren't going to make it. Bee told me. He's out."

"I'm sorry, but since when did you and Bee start having heart-to-hearts?"

"Just the one heart-to-heart." He closed the laptop, but as he did so, she caught something in his face. Greg was terrible at lying. Was he lying about talking to Bee? That made no sense.

"And when exactly was that?" she asked slowly.

"I'm not sure. Recently."

"Before or after my birthday?" She suddenly thought of that text she'd seen on Joseph's phone. The one from Greg. *Bee knows.*

"A little before," he said. She watched him take his laptop back to the counter, then she slid out from the bench and followed him. She needed him looking her right in the eyes for this one.

"Greg." She paused, waiting for him to turn to face her. Eventually, he did. "Did you tell Bee what we did?" He didn't say a thing. He didn't have to. It was right there on his face.

"It was going to get out anyway," he said eventually. She stood there staring at him, wondering how she could make him stuff the words back into his mouth. But it was too late. The exact people she'd been hiding this from for more than half her life now had the facts about what they'd done. Greg had confessed, and his doing so would make everything Emily said from here on out irrefutable. Emily had her proof. She'd finally won. He pulled her into a hug, and even though he'd just effectively turned her whole life on its head, she let him.

"It doesn't matter. Maddy. Who cares who knows? We can leave all of this, tonight. We just need to make the decision to do it. It's as easy as that." Greg had held her life in his hands all these years, and he'd waited until now to snap it in two. She tried to back out of his hug, but instead of letting her go, he pulled her in closer.

"If you knew you were going to tell the whole world about this one day, you should have done it before I married him." She could hear her voice shaking.

"I'm not the one who busted up your marriage. He'd already decided to leave you way before I ever talked to Bee." She looked up at him then to see if he was attempting another lie. He wasn't.

"He doesn't want to have to go through everything your dad went through with your mom. That's why he's out."

"That's not it. He's not like that," she said, pulling herself out of his grip.

"He's just like that."

That didn't feel true. That didn't feel like Joseph, but then she realized she had no way of measuring what was or wasn't true about Joseph anymore. She no longer knew who he was. But what she did know was that she didn't need any more secondhand opinions.

What she needed was concrete information on all of it. And then when she had it, she'd find her husband and squeeze the truth out of him. And when he tried to explain and duck, she'd have him. There were, after all, some things that weren't down to opinion. As much as people might try to fudge events and feelings, there *were* knowns.

She walked out into the night, not bothering to close the door behind her. She didn't need Greg. As easy as he'd made it sound for them to walk out of this life and into the next one, she knew that if she went with him, it would only be because she'd been backed into a corner. And that the only reason she'd found herself in this corner was because of what *he'd* done. She didn't need another person in her life who pretended to have her back only to let her fall the minute they thought she wasn't looking. What she really needed was proof. And she knew where she had to go to get it.

CHAPTER 20

MADDY

A car blared its horn hard as it overtook her, shocking her out of her mental haze. She ignored it and kept on driving. She'd only had half a glass of wine, but with the lack of food, she could feel that it had gone to her head, so she was driving slower than was advisable on the freeway. Cars swept by her on either side. Occasionally they honked. It wasn't like she was swerving, so she had no idea why people thought the honking was justified. She hated nighttime driving; she could never see properly. She squinted at the road in front of her, only now realizing the reason she was having trouble seeing this particular evening. She flicked her headlights on. The freeway in front of her became instantly clearer. She sped up, silently berating herself. She was the first to admit that she was a scatterbrained driver—she tended to zone out, especially on the freeway. Sometimes she'd come back to earth to find herself driving north, well on the way to Sacramento. She probably shouldn't be driving given everything that had happened in the last few hours. But she didn't have a whole lot of choice. She had to know.

She glanced at the end of the hammer she'd snatched from Greg's shed, sticking out of her purse on the front seat. She'd taken his screwdriver too. She cracked the window slightly to try to dissipate the smell of his aftershave that was somehow still all around her. The same aftershave as when he was a teenager. Who did that? Someone who hadn't moved on with their life, that's who. It wasn't her fault that he'd wasted the last twenty years of his life in the throes of unrequited love. She'd married someone else; that should have been a clear enough indication of how she ultimately felt about him, despite how things had been back then. But she wasn't that fourteen-year-old girl anymore. That girl was an entirely different person. That was what was so difficult about all this. She knew what she'd done back then was wrong. Of course she did. But it wasn't *her*. Teenaged you was still you, of course, but an insane and irresponsible version of you. The things she'd done that she thought were no big deal back then. The way she'd thought of people and treated people. The way she'd treated Greg. It was appalling. But really, was it exclusively *her* fault? Because if Emily hadn't been in the mix, none of it would ever have happened.

She could see her past motivations for what they were now. Childish, petty jealousy. But back then the things that she'd done had been the only way to make herself seen. For months it had felt like she had been disappearing next to *The Emily Show*. Compared with her messed-up sister, she was the easy one. The low-maintenance one. The forgettable one. Whereas Emily had the doctor visits, the trouble at school, which no one talked about in front of her but that her parents talked about constantly when Emily wasn't there. And of course, there was all the sex she was having with Joseph. It had been all her parents had talked about toward the end. She knew that Emily hadn't been dominating their focus because Emily was more lovable than she was. But specifically because she was *less*. And at the start, when Emily was a pile of silence and bruises, that had made sense. Despite being suddenly out of her parents' spotlight, Maddy had never doubted her number-one place.

Until suddenly she did.

She couldn't pinpoint exactly when the shift happened. But as time went on, Emily had transformed, in her mother's eyes, from an unpleasant-but-necessary long-term lodger to someone who might just turn it around if she got some nurturing. Maddy began to notice that Emily and her mother had what could definitely be described as a *relationship*. And seemingly that relationship came with a price tag, which apparently it was up to Maddy to pay. Or at least, that was what it felt like. It had started off small. Emily being driven to appointments and Maddy left at home alone. Her mom coming home bearing shopping bags full of new clothing to plug the imagined deficit in Emily's wardrobe. And then it moved on to conversations between the two of them where Maddy was not included, which eventually evolved into Maddy being asked to leave the room lest the adult nature of what they were saying sear her infant ears. As if she was a child and they both were the grown-ups. She'd left the room, as asked. But that hadn't stopped her from standing just outside the door, listening to every word that was said. These—the conversations where she was asked to leave—were the conversations about Emily's relationship with Joseph. All the skipping school, all the hot and horny making out that Emily and Joseph were doing, and the consequences it might eventually lead to. The conversations were also sometimes about her. Her own mother talking to Emily about how childlike Maddy had become. Emily empathizing about how hard it must be to have a "child like Maddy." Like she knew a thing about it. Like she was such a treat herself. Those conversations had been hard to hear, but she'd listened to every word anyway.

Gradually the tide of emotion shifted, and where it had been Emily on the outside, it was now Maddy. As if her mom had room for only one daughter at the center of her universe. It happened slowly over the months, in a series of small doses, but there was one specific incident that was the catalyst for all the trouble that followed.

It was something about the way Emily's face had changed the second she saw Maddy that day. Like she'd won a race that Maddy didn't even know she'd been competing in. In Emily's hand was *the bag*. White and oblong and important looking. What was inside ostensibly a private mystery. Though Maddy had a pretty good idea what was in there.

"Hey. What are you doing sitting on the stairs like that?" This had been the way her mom had greeted her. Like she was an untidy puppy instead of her actual daughter. Though to be fair, she had probably looked a bit like an abandoned puppy, sitting halfway up the stairs, picking at the bandage tight around her arm, staring at the front door. Waiting.

"Where were you?" said Maddy.

"Nowhere important," said her mom breezily, in a way that told Maddy that that was all she needed to know about the situation. A look passed between Emily and her mother. Part amusement at Maddy's nosiness, part acknowledgment that where they had been and what was in the white bag was beyond her childish understanding. But Maddy did understand. Her mom had taken Emily to the doctor for a prescription of the pill. And now Emily was slinking off past her up the stairs, package in hand. Off to do God knows what with its contents. Did her father know about this contraceptive situation, or was he turning a blind eye?

She found her mom in the kitchen, pouring a cap of vodka into a glass of orange juice. She seemed to do that more often since Emily. Maddy moved over to the kitchen table and slumped into her chair. Her mom didn't ask her if she wanted a glass of milk like she normally did. Too busy lost in her own thoughts. Thoughts about Emily.

"You don't need to treat me like a four-year-old. I know where you and Emily went today," said Maddy, pulling both feet up onto the seat of her mom's chair. She had boots on; she was waiting to see if her mother was going to tell her to get her feet down.

"Then maybe stop talking in a four-year-old voice," she said. *Had* she said it in that voice? She didn't even realize when she was doing it anymore. What had started as a joke now just came out unbidden. Some weird habit that had erupted not long after Emily had shown up.

"I didn't!" she said.

"Okay, Maddy. If you say you didn't, then I'm sure you didn't." Her mother opened the fridge, blocking Maddy's view of her. Patronizing cow. Her mother was useless. Useless. She hadn't believed her about Emily and the cut on her arm. She was pretty sure her dad did, even though he hadn't said much about it, but not her mother. She had been turned. What was the point in even having a mother if she wasn't prepared to unquestioningly take your side? It was as if the whole thing hadn't happened at all.

And so she dragged her boots off the seat with a clunk, and a few seconds later, she was out the back door with her father's school keys in her pocket and a plan swirling. She'd give them a scare. Not the type of scare that Emily gave them. Just a small, Maddy-sized one. Both of them had a curfew. Ten o'clock. Emily ignored it; Maddy never bothered to challenge it. Well, tonight, she would. Come ten thirty, she'd be out. She wouldn't be at Bee's, she wouldn't be at the park, she wouldn't be anywhere they'd look for her. She was going to go to the school and stay there until at least eleven. Maybe even midnight. And then, when they started debating whether to call the police or not, she'd come home. And then they'd notice her. Not enough to make up for all the lack. But enough. Her point would be made.

By the time Maddy got to the school gates, the sun was down and the wind had picked up, causing the gates to rattle slightly against the chain and padlock at their center. Stupid. She felt completely stupid. Was she really going to go and hide on school property for hours just to freak out her parents in some kind of little-girl protest? She spent enough time bored at school during the semester without spending holiday hours there. Plus, she'd been so scared of being caught rummaging through her dad's jacket pockets that, as soon as she had the keys in her hand, she'd just shot out the door, which meant she had nothing with her to help pass the hours. Not a flashlight or a book or even a snack. This was going to be the opposite of fun. She looked at the keys in her hands. There were at least a dozen of them. Experimentally she took one and tried to fit it into the padlock. She managed to ram it about halfway in before she gave up and yanked it out again. The next one didn't fit. Or the next one. The one after that slid all the way into the padlock but wouldn't turn.

"Hey."

Maddy half dropped the keys at the voice, and a series of unlikely excuses as to why she was trying to unlock the school gates flooded her brain: a forgotten textbook for a summer project, somewhere private to practice a dance routine, somewhere quiet to think.

"Shit, it's you," said Maddy. The zip of fear that had just shot across her stomach was already fading but was quickly being replaced with something else.

"Nice to see you too! I didn't know you knew swear words like that," said Greg. "What are you doing?"

"I bet I know more swear words than you do," said Maddy, not looking away from the gate and letting her hair fall forward over the right side of her face to hide the fact that she was now blushing. And not blushing because she'd been caught in the middle of initiating her stupid plan. Blushing because it was Greg. Up till this moment she was certain she'd been able to keep her annoying feelings about Greg an iron-clad secret. No one would have guessed from the way she spoke to him, or rather, avoided speaking to him, avoided sitting near him, avoided looking him in the eye, that she had an epic-sized crush on him. Whenever he turned up at Bee's house to hang out with Joseph, it was as if whatever part of the room housed Greg suddenly fuzzed into black. She blocked him out. It was how she dealt with the Greg thing. Because the alternative was to look at him and talk to him, and if she did that, then he'd know it all.

"Are you trying to break *in* to school?" he asked. Maddy had gone back to rattling the key inside the lock.

"Kind of," she said. Short. That was how she spoke to him when she absolutely had to. In as few words as possible. As if that would make his presence less.

"Want me to have a go?" asked Greg, moving in a little closer. "What happened there?" He went to touch the bandage over her forearm.

"Nothing. And it's fine," she said, her whole body tensing up. That was the last thing she needed in this moment, to be in key-handing-over proximity. She knew that he liked her too. That's what had triggered the whole thing. That look. She'd caught him staring once. She'd been wearing a new black T-shirt instead of one of her normal pink or pale blue ones, and when she walked through Bee's front door that day, he'd stared at her as if she was suddenly the most intricate and captivating object he'd ever seen. That one drawn-out look was all it took for her crush to take hold. And now she couldn't shake it.

Channeling all the force of her embarrassment into her right hand, she tried to rotate the key again, and this time it grudgingly gave a fraction and then turned all the way. Quickly she pulled off the padlock and eased open the gate. She turned back to close the gate behind her, a half smile ready for him now that she knew escape was near. But. He'd already followed her through. "What are you doing?" she said.

"I'm coming with you," said Greg. "You have no idea how intrigued I am about what you're about to get up to."

"I'm not about to get up to anything."

"Why not? You've got the keys to everything there, right?" He nodded at her hand, which still held the keys, the one she had opened the padlock with clenched between her fingers.

"I'm just picking up a book I forgot. For a summer project," she lied.

"All right, then," he said. "Let's go pick up some homework. I've never been inside a girls' school."

"I'm sure it's not that different from your school," said Maddy, even though she knew that wasn't true. She'd never been inside the local high school, but she could tell from the outside that it was nothing like St. Novatus with its wood-carved interiors and cherubs and gargoyles everywhere you looked. She realized she'd stopped blushing, which instantly made her blush again. Greg noticed.

"I'm bugging you," he said.

"It's okay. You're not bugging me," she said, and tucked a sheet of hair behind her ear, bravely revealing her burning cheek. Maybe if she simply ignored the red heat all over her face, then he would too. "Come on. I'll show you what a *girls'* classroom looks like, and then maybe we can wrap my dad's office chair in toilet paper or something."

"Now you're talking," he said.

As they walked toward the ancient gray-stone stairs that led up to the front door, Greg pulled a pack of cigarettes out of his pocket and lit one. He took a drag and then offered it to Maddy.

"No thanks. Gross," she said, waving at the puff of smoke filling the air next to Greg, and then flushed even darker, realizing that she'd just called him gross. As they started up the stairs, he took another firm drag, then threw the cigarette down onto the stone below and crushed it with his foot.

"There," he said. "That was my last-ever cigarette."

"Yeah, right," said Maddy.

"I mean it. I'm giving it up for you. That was it." He took the pack out of his pocket and placed it neatly on the smooth-tiled floor next to the front door.

"Litterbug," said Maddy, thrilled that Greg would be giving up smoking for *her.*

"Can't win with you, can I?" said Greg as he picked it up again and put it back in his pocket. "That *was* the last one, though. I've been meaning to give it up for a while. You can be my inspiration."

She wasn't going to get very far in working through this crush if he kept doing things like this. Feeling another flush come to her face, she got busy sorting through the keys in her hand, praying to whoever might be the saint of embarrassed teen girls that the first key would be the right key. She picked an ugly large iron one from the bunch and slid it into the lock. The key slipped all the way in and then practically turned itself. Bingo.

"All right," said Greg as the door swung open. "Time to see how the other half lives."

"Shut up," she said, giving him a smile.

Greg walked past Maddy into the hallway and stood gazing up at the huge wooden staircase that filled the right half of the hall and led to a long gallery that wrapped all the way around the space. Maddy followed his gaze upward, seeing it all through his eyes. It was beautiful, she supposed, if for a moment she could forget that this was school.

Greg was already off, down the stone-carved corridor leading off from the hallway. "What've you got stashed down here? The knights of the Round Table?"

"Come back, Greg," she called after him. "That's just the chapel."

"So let's check out the chapel," he said from the depths of the corridor.

She saw the lights flick on from the depths of the corridor. "Turn the lights off, Greg," she called out. He didn't respond, so she crossed the hallway and started down the corridor after him. She could see he was already at the end, trying the doorknob. The door was ancient, made of heavy-looking dark wood and set back into a stone archway; it looked like a portal to another century.

"It's locked," said Greg, looking back at her. "What's it like inside?"

"Nothing much. It's just a chapel," said Maddy. "Come on, let's go back. I need to turn these lights off before someone sees."

"I just want one quick look inside," said Greg.

"Why? It's really not that special."

"You can only say that because you've already seen it. I will literally go to my grave not knowing the secrets of what's behind this door unless you show it to me now."

"Fine," said Maddy, handing the keys to him—he could fuss with them this time. Who was she to deny Greg a glance at a chapel? He was probably the only person under forty who'd *actually wanted* to go inside the place in decades. "Knock yourself out."

"Cool," he said, and took the keys from her hand. His fingers bumped against hers when he took the keys, but instead of a full-on flush, she just felt a small pinging burn hit the tops of her ears. She even managed to look him in the eye briefly. It was working. Greg unlocked the door and stepped into the chapel. Maddy flicked the light switch off in the corridor and then walked in behind him, the normal chapel smell of old hymn books and slightly molding kneeler cushions masked by the light trail of Greg's aftershave.

Maddy had only ever been inside in early morning, and seeing it lit by nothing but what moonlight could filter its way through the stained-glass windows was a vastly different experience. During the day, the place seemed miserable and utilitarian. But this night, everything took on a new quality. The statues of the saints looked wistful, and the way the white moonlight hit the center of the altar, like some kind of reverse shadow, transported the room back to its original purpose—inspiration. Because that's how Maddy felt as she walked up the aisle. Inspired. And ever so slightly mystical.

"Whoa." Greg came up behind her and then walked past her to stand on the altar, in the middle of the white patch of light. He carefully reached out his hand as if he were trying to grab a handful of moonbeams, like a child. Maddy was about to tell him to get down from there, but then stopped herself. Why shouldn't he stand in that spot and try to catch the moonlight? Greg pulled out his lighter, and she felt a jolt of what was either panic because he was about to smoke or despair that he was smoking again so soon after he allegedly quit "for her." Much to her relief he simply lifted the flame to the candle wedged into the top of a brass stand. She walked over to join him and looked out over the rows of pews. So this was what it felt like, to stand at the front. She'd only ever looked the other way.

"It's not bad, is it," she said, feeling a kind of heavy peace descend around them. It was quiet. Truly quiet.

"Do people ever get married in here?" he asked, turning to look at her.

"I don't think so," she said, annoyed with her heart for turning itself inside out with squeezing when Greg had said the words *get married*. Jeez. "I think there might have been a nun who left the convent and then—" She stopped. Greg had stepped right in front of her. She looked up at his face. There wasn't anywhere else to look. She felt panicked and ecstatic all at once. Was this it? Was she going to *kiss* someone? She knew that Greg's pupils normally had a series of black flecks around the irises, but she couldn't make them out by this light. All she could see was the pale blue green of them. And their expression.

"Did you follow me to school?" she said.

"Kind of," he said, looking down again off to the side. "I was heading over to Joseph's and saw you walking off down the street without Bee, and I guess I thought I might get a chance to talk to you, away from the others."

"Well, if you want to say something," teased Maddy, "you'd better say it now."

He looked back up at her, staring in silence, and Maddy wondered if she'd taken it too far. And then he moved his arm around her waist and up between her shoulder blades, and before she had a chance to ask him what he was doing, he'd placed his lips on top of hers. And then there was no more talking. Only hard kissing followed by rapid movement that turned frenetic in a matter of seconds.

Maddy was the one who took her T-shirt off first. Afterward, she reflected that she hadn't known why she'd done it. Because that was the moment when everything became unstoppable. After her T-shirt came his, and then her bra. It felt surreal to have his skin against hers. Their mouths hadn't left each other the whole time. And without saying anything, Maddy gave the button of Greg's jeans a soft tug. He pulled back for a second and looked at her.

"You want to?" he said. She nodded. Wanted *what*, she wasn't sure. But she knew that she didn't want to pause or hold on or have a considered conversation about what it was they were doing. She knew she wanted his jeans off and her jeans off and everything that might follow. She took her jeans off first, to show him she was serious. And then, because he wasn't moving a muscle, just staring, she took her underpants off too. He broke eye contact to unbutton his jeans, which in the middle of that very grown-up moment, Maddy found amazingly childish and sweet—as if he had to look down to work out where the button was. And then, when he was completely naked, he stepped back toward her. She briefly wondered what on earth she was doing, standing here stark naked in the chapel with a boy. With Greg. And then he kissed her again. He nudged her up against the altar and started to lift her up onto it, but she moved him backward and pulled him down onto the mat in front of it. Down on top of her. She felt the cold stone under the softness of the thin carpeting, but there was more of the firm kissing to compensate. And then she could feel him pushing up against her and incredibly, going inside, just a little bit.

"We should stop," he said, not stopping at all but edging farther inside instead. It hurt. It hurt a lot, a raw pushing and separating sensation.

"You don't need to stop," she said. "I'm on the pill." She had no idea why she said it.

"What?" he said.

"I said, I'm on the pill. You can keep going."

"There's no way you're on the pill," said Greg.

"Why wouldn't I be?" she said.

"Because you're fourteen. It's okay. I'll pull out," he said, and sank himself in farther. She held in a small yelp of pain. And then he started moving harder, and the pace of everything changed.

"Greg," she said, pushing against his butt with her hands, suddenly wanting to slow it all down, but it was no good; he'd already gone somewhere else. She tensed up and tried to pull backward a little bit, but doing that only seemed to speed him up. And then quite slowly, but noticeably, the sensation changed. The raw tearing turned into something else, and she found herself moving her pelvis back and forth, trying to catch up with him. Her whole body had moved about half a foot across the floor with the effort of his pushing, and now she found herself half underneath the cloth covering the altar. She grabbed onto the material to move it away from her face just as his whole body went rigid. There were four sharp stabs; on the last one he shouted, and suddenly it hurt again. Reflexively she pulled on the cloth flapping around her head against the pain, and a second later she heard a hard clatter. And then he fell down on top of her. For a second she was completely squashed by him, all the air pushed out of her, and then he came back to living and quickly lifted his torso off her.

"Oh God," he said, realizing. "I'm so sorry."

"For what?" she said. She'd said he could, after all.

"For coming inside. I was going to pull out. But I couldn't." Maddy opened her mouth to say something, but before she could say another word, Greg had leaped off her like she was as hot as the surface of the sun and was on his feet. The second he left her, she felt a rush of cold air hit in between her legs, and she was instantly allover freezing.

"Shit!" he said, running past her and grabbing up the flimsy material that had just been flapping around her face a second ago.

"What?" she said, and flipped herself over to see what he was doing. "Oh *God*!"

Flames. A river of orange flames undulating so hard it actually swung the tapestry it was consuming. The face of Mary was just about still visible, but the rest of the picture was swathed in fire. Greg, still naked, was beating at the flames with the altar cloth, but the fussy lace was rapidly turning into a ball of fire in his hand.

"Drop it!" yelled Maddy, furiously searching for a fire extinguisher, even though she knew there wasn't one in here. For a second Maddy hoped that the tapestry would be the only thing that took. But as Greg threw the bundle of flaming lace to the ground and tried to stamp on it, the flames found their way to the base of the altar, and its varnished, dried-out old wood enthusiastically lit with a huge *woomph* as if it had been just waiting for the opportunity to do exactly that all these decades. Maddy started backing off from the heat just as the floating droplets from the flames found their way onto the floor. The carpet joined in the party instantly, the flames leaping up from the material like someone had turned a gas stove on underneath it. She knew that at this rate the fire would be over to the wooden pews within a few seconds, and at that point it would be game over.

"Just leave it," said Maddy, throwing Greg's clothes at him. She'd already pulled on her jeans and T-shirt. She didn't know where her bra was, and she didn't care. "Greg! Come on!" Greg pulled his clothes on and then stood in front of the flames. He took a couple of steps forward, like he was trying to figure out what it was he could do to tamp them back down and then backed away again. Maddy grabbed him by the hand. Dirty gray smoke was billowing upward and outward, and it was becoming hard to talk. Instead, she pulled him toward the exit, then led him out the chapel door and halfway down the corridor. Just before they got all the way to the hall, Greg left her side and ran back toward the flames—simply disappeared back off into the dark.

"Greg!" It was so dark that she couldn't clearly make him out once he stepped away from her. She coughed and then fumbled her hand along the wall until she hit the light and saw what he was doing. He was pulling the hefty chapel door shut. That door was thicker than any modern fire door. Closing it might just save the rest of the school from getting burned down to nothing.

"Come on," she yelled at him as he ran back up the corridor toward her. The ceiling above her was tinged with haze now. "We have to get out!" They ran alongside each other up the rest of the corridor until they burst out into the hall, their eyes blinking and their mouths searching for clear air.

"Where is there a phone?" asked Greg.

"A phone?"

"We have to call 911."

"Greg. We're not calling 911. They'll know it was us."

"Where's the phone?" he repeated.

"God, Greg. There's one in the school office."

"Where's that?"

"In there," she said, pointing to a door off the hallway. He ran to the door and tried the handle. Locked. Maddy instinctively felt at the pocket of her jeans for the keys, but they weren't there. Probably somewhere on the chapel floor. Greg pulled off his T-shirt, wrapped it around his fist, and smashed at the frosted glass of the door. It took four tries, but he managed to poke a hole through. Then he reached his hand in and tried to open the door from inside. He couldn't do it. He pulled his hand out again and started trying to push in the rest of the frosted glass.

"Leave it. We'll call when we get home," said Maddy.

"Then they'll definitely know it was us," said Greg. A second later, from somewhere above them, a piercing shrill bell started to ring. The sound instantly filled her head, like she was being simultaneously drilled through both ear canals, and they both instinctively put their hands over their ears, and then in silent mutual agreement, they sprinted out the front door and down the steps—something about the bell clearing them to make a run for it. Maddy headed straight for the gates, wanting to put as much space between herself and the accusatory noise as possible. Greg didn't seem to be in such a hurry and stopped halfway across the entrance to look back at the school.

She went to take his hand to pull him back through the gates, but then a thought that the panic and the noise had, up until this moment, pushed out of her head surged forward. Sister Ida. Sister Angela. Were they inside? They didn't always stay at the convent when school was out. Most years they spent summers at a mission in Mexico, but she hadn't heard anything about a trip that year. Greg turned to look at her.

"What?" he asked. She opened her mouth to tell him what and then stopped. No good would come of it. He'd only run back into the school in some useless attempt to try to get them out. They probably weren't even there, and then they'd get found out for nothing. And if they were there, it was likely already too late.

"Nothing," she said. "Come on. We need to go." She stepped through the gates, and a second later, he followed her. "The alarm goes to the fire department," she said as soon as they were about half a block away. She could still feel the throb of the alarm ricocheting over the top of her eardrums. She didn't know if what she'd just said about the alarm was true. But it *felt* like it would be true. Surely her ever-sensible father would have made sure this was the case? And even if it wasn't the case, the alarm was so loud, someone else would call 911 sooner than later. Surely.

"I should be there when they arrive," said Greg, and stopped walking. "I should let them know where the fire is." He squatted down on the ground with his hands crossed over his head. Maddy didn't know whether he was trying to get some breath or was just losing it. Considering everything that had happened in the last half an hour, she felt surprisingly little.

"I'm pretty sure they'll be able to work it out for themselves," she said. "You know that if we fess up to any part of this, we'll both be kicked out of school at the very least."

"No. No we won't," he said. He stood up. His face and hands were black, his eyelids dark pink. He looked wired. "It was an accident."

"An accident while we were having *sex*," she said. Something about the word *sex* quieted him down. They'd had sex, and Maddy understood that because of that, she now had some kind of hold over him, some new ability to make herself understood. "If my dad knew we were on school property during the holidays, he'd ground me for the rest of my life. Let alone the sex part. And now a fire? *You* want to explain it all to him?" She could immediately see that Greg did not want to have to explain to her father that he'd set his school on fire while having unprotected sex with his fourteen-year-old daughter. "If we tell anyone about any part of this, it'll follow us around for the rest of our lives. Going to college. A decent career."

"But we can't just walk away from it," said Greg.

"What good will it do? Letting everyone know it was us won't reverse the damage. It won't make a difference. The only thing it'll guarantee is a whole ton of trouble." In the distance she heard a small whoop followed by the desperate wail of a siren. They were coming. *"We have to go,"* she said again. She noticed blinds starting to open in the apartments across from the school. "Please, Greg." If he went back to the fire and told them everything that had happened, she would be screwed. Emily would be the least of her problems. "If you care about me even a small amount, then you have to come away, *now*." The sirens wailed again. "Come," she said, half pulling him toward her. "Just walk. We have to start walking." He was almost there, almost with her. And then he started to walk.

They walked all the way to Pile House, where he softly kissed her goodbye. On the cheek this time. And then after that, because of all the things that happened next, Maddy made sure Greg never got close enough to her to kiss her ever again. It was why things would never be fixed between her and Emily. Why Emily had spent so many years in the wilderness. And why, despite their desperate teenaged infatuation with each other, she and Greg had never gotten back to being closer than friends of friends. And now they never would.

CHAPTER 21

MADDY

Maddy punched numbers into the keypad and watched as the gate rattled back from across the entrance. As soon as the gate opened enough for her to pass, she drove across the parking lot and then around to the rear of a cinder-block building. She turned her engine off, and she watched as some guy walked inside his unit then pulled the door firmly down behind him. She had no idea how he could do that. The lights were operated from a box on the wall outside, and the thought of being in there with the door closed, unable to access the dial, made her breath come fast and light. Maddy wasn't claustrophobic, but you didn't have to be to be freaked out at the thought of being trapped in a storage locker in the pitch black.

She made her way over to their unit, flipped open the box at the side, and turned the dial as far around as it could go. Then she unlocked the door, hauled it upward, and there it all was. Everything that had once filled Pile House now rammed inside this box full of hot air. It wasn't exactly crisp out, but the inside of the locker was pure magnified heat.

None of these items made sense out of context. Instead of her parents' beloved furniture, it now just looked like junk. It smelled like junk. Like a secondhand clothing store. She wondered if there was a way for rats to get in despite the tightly packed cinder-block walls and sturdy door. Was it rats or mice who were able to squeeze through impossibly small gaps? She would get rid of it. All of it. As soon as she got to the bottom of what was happening with her husband and her sister, she would call a broker and ditch the lot.

The overhead lighting was not subtle—two long lines illuminating everything within. But despite the abundance of light, she couldn't see what she was looking for. The right side of the unit was a wall of boxes, and as far to the left as possible, which wasn't very, were the stacks of furniture. Carefully, with the boxes at her back, Maddy squeezed her way through. All her own tax documents, medical bills, and general paperwork were in the same file box they always were, now underneath the extra narrow desk in Greg's guest house. But Joseph's items had always been stored in his monster of a filing cabinet that had followed them through all their moves. Greg's guest house was the first place they'd lived where there'd been no room for it, and so it had been relegated to the storage unit. This was where she'd find the tax documents that would make Joseph's income over the past year real or not real. It seemed a small detail to be clinging on to in the midst of everything, but if she could have one piece of real, irrefutable evidence, if there was *one thing* she had that he couldn't brush away or blame on her failing mind, then she had him, and the rest of the truth would fall into place from there. When the time came to confront him, she would need possession of facts. And stashed inside his Big Bertha of a filing cabinet was where she'd see whether the three quarters of a million that had passed through this "St Nov" last year had been his or just something he'd shuffled around on behalf of other people. Of course, in a normal marriage you could ask this question of your husband and expect a pretty straightforward answer. But as Maddy was learning, her marriage was anything but normal.

She was almost to the end of the narrow pathway when she saw it, all the way at the end, pushed slightly back behind a stack of dining room chairs. Why had he put it all the way back there? As soon as she reached it, she gave its top drawer a tug to see if it would open. Locked. Of course it was locked. She didn't have a whole lot of room to maneuver, so she pulled Greg's hammer and the screwdriver out of her purse, which she then dropped on the ground. Realizing she had no idea how to do this, she nestled the screwdriver into the line where the drawer met the top of the cabinet and gave it a couple of taps with the hammer. All this did was chip off some paint. She'd had vague ideas about levering the drawers open, but now that she was here, she could tell simply busting them open would require brute strength that she didn't have.

She put the tip of the screwdriver into the lock to see if she could somehow turn it. Unsurprisingly, there was no way, so she tapped the end of the screwdriver with the hammer to see if that did anything. A bead of sweat escaped from around her throat and ran down in between her breasts, so she pulled off her wrap top and dropped it on the floor next to her purse. She *had* to do this. The answers were in here. She hit again. Less cautious this time. And then again. As she smacked the back of the screwdriver, some of the anger she'd been keeping tamped down over the last few weeks started to surge, and she sped up—barely flinching when she missed her target and hit the tip of her thumb. Eventually, she saw that the lock was retreating into the cabinet. Three more hits and then the lock shot backward, useless, and the drawer rolled a couple of inches open.

She dropped the tools and pulled the cabinet all the way open. As she had expected, there was a mass of hanging folders and files, but in the space to the right of that, she saw something else that made her breath stop. Newly ugly in the harsh light, she could see two items that had exactly no place being inside Joseph's filing cabinet. Her father's barometer and her mother's hairbrush. She picked up the barometer first. It was a lighter color than she remembered it being, the wood not as sturdy. Its arm pointed toward "Change." *No shit,* she thought. Why had she been so attached to this item? It was just a thing; it wasn't her father. She put it down and then picked up the hairbrush. She turned it over in her hand so that the bristles tickled her palm, then she lifted them to her nose. It smelled like nothing. If it had ever held the last few traces of her mother's scent, it was now gone. But what were these doing in here? When she'd accused him of taking them from her car, she thought he'd just absentmindedly moved them somewhere. Not stashed them away. And if he'd found them later and put them in here for safekeeping, why hadn't he told her? But then, as she put down the hairbrush, she saw one more item in the bottom of the drawer, and she realized exactly why he hadn't told her. Her stomach lurched with a wave of hatred toward herself for how willingly blind she had been, and then she picked up her mom's bracelet from the bottom of the cabinet, its heavy metal warm in her hand.

He had taken these items and hidden them. For the sole purpose of fucking with her grip on reality. To make her think she'd already taken the first step on a jagged path of decline that would eventually kill her. The dents in the cars, the photos, her keys, the dozens of other items eternally misplaced and endlessly missing. Each incident on its own, meaningless—but stacked one on top of the other, a portfolio of errors that had convinced everyone, including Maddy, that she was losing her mind.

She attached the bracelet to her wrist and then reached back into the cabinet, feeling the links slip down her arm and make the same slight jingle-jangle noise they always had. This was real. She didn't need any more than this. She didn't need to wait for anyone else, especially not Joseph, to assure her that she wasn't going insane. He didn't hold that kind of power over her anymore. Now she knew.

She brushed her hand over the labels of the hanging folders, flattening them so she could read them from her cramped position, and quickly found what she was looking for. She pulled out a folder labeled

"1099s" and flipped it open. And there it was. Another piece of the puzzle falling into place with a sickening clunk. Her eyes went to the name first. Emily Grisanti. And the name of the company? The St. Novatus Fire Fund. She picked the first one up and read it all the way through. It told her everything she needed to know, but she wasn't about to stop at one. At first, each document tallied perfectly with the transactions she'd seen on Joseph's desktop. But then as she moved back, the date jumped a year. There had been two years of this. He'd been hiding all his money in Emily's name for the last two years. With shaking hands, she held the folder to her chest, picked her purse up off the floor, and then squeezed back through the corridor of her parents' crap to reach the outside.

Finally free, she sat down hard on the gravel, taking deep breaths in until the world took on a semblance of normal again. Behind her, the lights of the unit shut off. The papers she now held in her arms may have had Emily's name on them, but Maddy knew this wasn't Emily's money. This was Joseph's money in Emily's name. And it was no big mystery as to why.

He didn't love her anymore. That was beyond clear. The love that she'd relied on for the past eight years had gone. Evaporated as if it were never there. She expected the realization to hurt more. The betrayal hurt, but not the removal of the love. She realized that she'd been hardening her heart against this exact loss ever since they'd moved into Pile House. While her mind had been oblivious to everything Joseph was doing, her heart had known one hundred percent that his love was on the move. This final piece of evidence was all she'd needed to detach from him completely.

But why had he tried to make her think she was going insane? She put a hand around the bracelet on her wrist again. Firm, undeniable evidence. He'd hidden it to paint her as crazy. Just like her mother. It was beyond cruel. This wasn't what people did as a precursor to divorce. Pulling the wool over her eyes about the money was one thing. But this was something more than that. This was about revenge. This was about the fire. And about Emily.

CHAPTER 22

EMILY

2002

Emily's walk came to a premature end before she had an answer on her morning-after-pill quandary. Her grand error had been leaving the house without taking so much as a water bottle, let alone anything to eat. She didn't even have a sweater. At first, she pushed through the thirst and hunger, but when it started getting dark and then turned cold, she gave up and headed home. It was late when she got back to Pile House. So late she wondered if they might have already locked up for the night. Perhaps that would be the beginning of the end of her living there. She'd try the door, find it locked, and just keep on walking. Where to, she didn't know.

But when she got home, she saw the lights in the house were still on, which was strange for that time of night. She didn't know exactly how late it was, just that it was late enough for it to be an issue. She bypassed the front door and slipped around the back of the garage with plans to look over the fence and see if Joseph was still awake. His house was on the other side of the block, and there were trees between the back of his house and hers, but if the light was on in his bedroom, she'd be able to see it.

Emily took two steps into the alley before she saw her. It was the whiteness of her skin that she saw first and then the bright white of her bandage. Maddy was so pale she looked like a teenaged ghost slumped up against the fence, and she was crying so hard she didn't even notice Emily as she walked over the rubble and leaves, down the alley toward her.

"What's wrong with you?" she asked, and watched as Maddy's whole body gave a start as if she'd just heard a gun go off.

"Nothing," she growled, and wiped her face on her knee.

"If there's nothing wrong, then why are you wiping snot all over your jeans?"

She had no answer to that, just gave her damp knee a little wipe with her thumb. Emily slumped down next to her and leaned back against the fence. Maddy smelled weird. Like sour chemicals. But then there was already a smell of smoke and ash over the whole neighborhood, so her smell mixed in.

"Want to talk about it?"

"Nope."

"Fine. I'll leave you to it, then," she said, pulling her feet underneath her to stand up. "You need to tell them that it wasn't me who cut you. You know that, right?" Maddy ignored her. "First of all, I don't appreciate you painting me as a knife-wielding psychopath. Second of all, I think you probably need help. Professional help, I mean. I know I'm messed up, but at least I have an excuse. You're just . . . disturbed." Maddy said nothing to this. It was literally as if she hadn't heard a word. Emily could tell she wasn't faking it. It was as if she were somewhere else. "Should I get your mom?" she asked, wondering if she was perhaps actually in shock or really sick.

"No! Don't get her. I'm fine. I just had sex is all." Emily immediately shot out an involuntary gasp of laughter at the thought of it. Maddy was barely more than a tween.

"With who!" she said, sitting back down. This she had to hear.

"With Greg."

"Greg? I didn't think you were into him. What happened exactly, and why are you crying about it? Did he *rape* you?" As much as Emily wasn't Maddy's biggest fan, she wouldn't wish a forced hymen breaking on anyone.

"No!" she said forcefully enough for Emily to know she was telling the truth.

"So, what happened?" Emily didn't have Maddy down as the unplanned-underage-sex type. It was actually all pretty ironic given the fact that she'd ratted her out that very morning for exactly the same thing. Was that *why* she'd slept with Greg? Surely not. "Come on. Where did you do it?"

"At school."

"You did it *there*? Why there?" Joseph and Emily had done it in some pretty dank and unromantic places, but she couldn't imagine a place less conducive to losing your virginity than St. Novatus.

"Just *fuck off*, Emily." She wondered if she thought her new non-virgin status made it okay for her to talk like that. She'd never heard Maddy swear before, and her doing so seemed to sharply reinforce the evening's learnings: Maddy was no longer a child. Perhaps that was why she'd said it—so her sister could understand that she was only a hair behind her in the sprint toward womanhood. "I'm sorry," she said, burying her face in her knees again. "It's been a rough night is all."

Emily thought about her own "if it happens, it happens," Russian-roulette attitude toward conceiving a baby. A pregnancy wouldn't ruin her life. In fact, she had the feeling it might even be the beginning of her being taken seriously. But if Maddy got pregnant, that would be another thing entirely. She was precious. She was treasured. She didn't need to create a whole new wing of a family in order to be in the center of a world. Surely she knew that. A baby would be a disaster for her.

She was only fourteen, for God's sake. How had she even known what to do?

"Did he use a condom, at least?" she asked. No response. "Maddy? Did you—"

"No. No, we did not use a condom. And no, *no*, I don't know what I'm going to do about it."

Emily could hear the panic in Maddy's voice, and she wanted to take Greg by the shoulders and shake him senseless for leaving Maddy to cry it out behind her parents' garage with a bundle of his DNA swimming around her middle heading straight for the target. Because somehow Emily could almost feel Maddy getting more and more pregnant as each second passed—could almost see what was happening inside her. One ripe, dainty egg spinning slightly as it got battered by a storm of iron sperm. The insistent path of the winner as it burrowed its way through to the heart of things. Stop it. She had to stop it.

"Listen. Come inside and take a shower. You stink like a campfire. And then, I've got something that I think might help."

And so, Emily gave Maddy her morning-after pill, her decision made for her. Maddy didn't stop to ask if *Emily* needed it. Just swallowed it down eagerly. Instantly absolved of her sins. Then she said thank you, quietly, back to her normal meek self. And for a second they felt more like sisters than not sisters. Emily had saved her. And Maddy had let her.

Emily left her bedside lamp on when she went to bed that night, but a few hours later, she woke to darkness—hungry and strangely cold. Someone had turned out the light. She stumbled out of bed and went over to the window, wondering if Joseph's arrival was what had woken her, and sure enough, there he was. He pointed at the gnarled wood on the ground, his face a show of mock horror at their middle-of-the-night hangout being obliterated, then he leaped onto the bottom of the tree and started climbing the rungs that had yet to be removed. For a moment she couldn't work out what he was doing. And then she realized. He was coming in. Emily slid her window all the way up and then manically searched the room for something that might help him bridge the gap between the tree and her window. Joseph was level with her now and was shimmying his way along the branch that almost, but not quite, reached her room. He got to the end of the branch and made his way up into a shaky squat. There was probably about a five-foot gap between the edge of the branch and her window. Doable but risky.

"Don't," she hissed, but he just waved her backward. She moved back to give him space, knowing that the leap was more or less inevitable. For a second there was silence, then a rustle of leaves as the branch rebounded against his push off and a thud as Joseph's feet knocked against the clapboard, the top half of his body miraculously curled over the bottom of the window. She grabbed him by a belt loop on the back of his jeans and helped him over the windowsill and down onto the floor. "Don't ever do that again!" she started, but he was in no mood to talk. He pulled her down next to him and her tank top was stripped off before she'd even finished her sentence.

They kept things eerily quiet; the illicit threat of being discovered meant that things finished more or less as soon as they started. Afterward she climbed back into bed and immediately turned on her side, ready to sleep again. But instead of making another flying leap out the window, Joseph crawled into the bed too and cuddled up behind her, his arm finding its way over the front of her chest, hugging her to him protectively. The security of his body up against her back sent her helplessly spiraling down into sleep, but just before she shut down, she gently knocked her head five times on the pillow. Joseph's wake-up call.

The wake-up call didn't work.

The next thing she felt was a rush of cold air around her body as Joseph leaped out of bed and then dive-bombed for the floor to grab up his clothes. She turned over, groggy. Sun was up, but barely. Emily sat up in bed a little, pulling the duvet up around her chest, and that was when she saw her, and despite her professing not to care what they thought, she felt a thousand tiny daggers of fear pierce the underside of her stomach. It was Sophie. They'd been caught.

"Get dressed," Sophie said, eerily calm. This wasn't the calm of a woman about to deliver a lecture on boundaries being violated and the resulting consequences. This was the calm of a woman who was so angry that the anger had boiled over and turned into something else. "Downstairs in four minutes. Both of you." Sophie left, closing the door quietly behind her. She'd never seen Sophie like that. Why did people have to get so freaked out about sex?

They dressed silently. Not caring but still caring about what was going to happen next. Before they walked down the stairs, Joseph pulled her to him and kissed her on the top of her head.

"It'll be okay," he said. "What's the worst they can do?" Emily silently agreed. It wasn't like they could physically keep the two of them apart. It wasn't possible.

She walked into the living room a step behind Joseph. Maddy and Sophie were both on the couch. Maddy didn't look much better than she had yesterday. All the bouncy red that normally flushed her cheeks was gone, and her eyes were desperate. Her normally sleek hair was puffed up at odd angles. Probably a result of her sleeping on it wet. Emily wondered if they'd figured out what Maddy had been up to yesterday. Perhaps Greg was scheduled to arrive any minute, and they were all going to get the second installment of the shame talk.

"Sit down," said Ivan, gesturing to the two unoccupied Queen Anne chairs on either side of the fireplace. They both sat. Emily always thought either side of that fireplace was an especially awkward place to put a pair of chairs, and it didn't feel any less awkward now that she was sitting in one. She glanced over at Joseph. He had his eyes on Ivan, which was pretty brave, as she could already tell that Ivan was in full-on principal mode. Her father's chin had retracted into his neck, and his mouth was turned down in a perfect U. Folded arms. Eyebrows bunched up over the top of his eyes like two angry pyramids. Joseph looked back at Emily and reached for her hand across the fireplace. Emily took his and held on, the heavy weight of the hold pulling gently on her shoulder socket.

"Emily," said Ivan. "Did you take a set of keys from my jacket pocket yesterday?"

"Your car keys?" she asked.

"You know the keys that I'm talking about," he said. And it sounded to her like he'd already made up his mind about whether she'd taken his keys or not.

"I don't know what keys," she said, looking him dead in the eye. In the past, Emily had lied to make things sound lighter than they were. She'd lied to smooth things over, to liven things up. She'd lied about the small things as much as she'd lied about the big things. But this she wasn't lying about. The problem was, she'd so perfected the performance art of lying that now no one knew when she was being genuine and when she was making it up. She'd fuzzed things.

"Emily, there was a significant fire at St. Novatus last night. Sister Ida and Sister Angela are both in the hospital. Sister Angela is in the ICU."

Her hand suddenly swung toward her chair as Joseph let go of it in shock. She blindly went to reach for his again, but it wasn't there. She turned to look over at him, but he was staring at Ivan. Less bold now.

"What happened?" asked Emily. She'd never met Sister Ida, but she remembered Sister Angela. In Emily's first week at the school, Sister Angela had asked to meet her, and halfway through a math class, the school administrator, Mrs. Murphy, had escorted her up to the top floor. Mrs. Murphy had told Emily no less than three times that the nun's quarters were normally strictly out of bounds, but Emily hadn't needed to be told. A soft smell of aging books and dried flowers filled the corridors, and there was a quiet peace that wasn't present in any other part of the building. This was a different realm. Sister Angela had immediately smiled when she laid eyes on Emily, unbothered by her haphazard hair or the pinprick tattoos scattered over her wrists and arms. She'd simply taken Emily's cold hands in her dry ones and held them. Then she'd said a short prayer asking the archangel Gabriel to keep Emily safe from harm, reached up to touch her cheek, and then Emily had been spirited straight back to class. It'd been a simple event, but one she thought about often.

"Sister Ida helped Sister Angela down the stairs, but she collapsed before she could move her outside. By the time the fire department got to her, she wasn't conscious."

"Is she going to be okay?" asked Emily, her throat suddenly tight.

"We don't know yet," said Ivan. "So. Where were you last night?" Emily saw that this question was directed at her. She glanced over at Maddy, who looked like she was slowly dying of not wanting to be there. Unlike Emily, she hadn't perfected the art of lying. Emily remembered what Maddy had said about being at school yesterday and immediately knew that whatever had happened there last night was down to her sister.

"I was out, walking, and then I was in my room." After a detour via the side of the garage, but she reasoned that there was no need to throw that in the mix—yet. "Joseph was with me all evening," she said. Instantly, she knew she'd blown it. Evening. Why had she said *evening*? He hadn't shown up till the middle of the night. Now she knew she'd forced him to either lie to cover for her or correct her to cover his own butt.

"And were you with Emily? All evening?" Ivan asked Joseph. Emily could tell her father already knew what the answer was. Joseph seemed to be stuck on what to say, which wasn't helping matters.

"I didn't mean *evening*," she said at the same time Joseph said, "I don't know where she was during the evening."

"I came up to her room about two," said Joseph.

"And don't think that any of *that's* okay either," said Ivan, staring directly at Joseph, who was cowed enough by now to look at the floor, all of his earlier "What's the worst they can do?" drained away. "Aside from the fact that you're having premarital sex with each other. You are also both technically minors," he added. "That's statutory rape."

"Rape? Joseph never raped me."

"You could *both* be charged with statutory rape," said Ivan, looking entirely serious about the whole thing, even though the notion that they were both simultaneously busy raping each other at the same time was clearly ridiculous. "But that's not what we need to talk about right now. Sister Ida and Sister Angela are fighting for their lives. The school chapel is destroyed, Emily. Hundreds of thousands of dollars' worth of damage."

"Maybe no one took your keys. Maybe you just lost them somewhere," she said.

"My keys were on the chapel floor. Next to what was left of a *bra*."

"What do you mean, 'what was left of a bra'?" Emily asked.

"The wire part," he said, not even slightly embarrassed. As principal of a girls' school, he'd had more than his fair share of dealing with tampons thrown up onto the ceiling and bras catapulted onto the light fixtures.

"My bras don't have wire in them," Emily said. "I'm not the only person in this family with boobs, you know." She could feel Maddy trying to make herself less visible. Maddy had developed quickly in the last few months and had much more in the way of breasts than Emily did. Even at fourteen.

"Maddy. Do you have an underwire bra?" Emily asked.

"I don't want to talk about my bras," said Maddy. It was pretty clear to anyone who could read facial expressions that, yes, she did have underwire bras. Emily could see that Sophie had noted it too. Ivan as well. For four whole seconds it looked like the line of attack was going to pivot and land squarely on Maddy. But then he turned back to Emily.

"Bras and keys aside, the state we found the bathroom in this morning makes it pretty clear that someone in this house was near a fire last night." Emily looked over at Maddy, who was now looking at the floor. Could they not see how guilty she looked? All they had to do was glance her way.

"What's wrong with the bathroom?" asked Emily.

"It was left in quite a state. Soot trod into the bathmat. Towels that reek of smoke on the floor."

It was well known in the household that, out of the two daughters, Emily was the towel dropper. Maddy always hung hers on her hook on the back of the bathroom door, but Emily didn't have a hook, and the drop of the towel on the floor was a sort of protest that there was yet another thing that Maddy had that no one had ever thought to give her. But Emily hadn't had a shower last night. Maddy had. And obviously, rather than run the bathmat and the towels through the laundry to cover up what she'd done, she'd left a mess on purpose. She'd figured out that someone was going to take the blame. And she was making sure it wasn't going to be her.

"It's one too many signs pointing to this house, Emily. Is this all because of the treehouse?"

"You seriously think I'd start a fire because you took down a treehouse?"

"I don't know. You set fire to your uncle's motorcycle because, what, he annoyed you? You tell *me*. If not because of the treehouse, then why? After everything we've done for you."

Emily's mouth dropped open. Setting the motorcycle on fire hadn't been some kind of generic teenage rebellion. It'd been a primal scream for help. How did he not know that?

"Um," she said, her voice helplessly filling up with sarcasm. "I didn't do it. I wasn't there. My bra wasn't there. I didn't take your keys. And if we're going there, I'm not sure what it is that you think you've so specially *done for me*. I'm your daughter, not a refugee."

"Emily. Clean up your attitude and start talking truthfully. We can't move forward with any of this if you're just going to sit there and throw out lies."

"Why are you so certain it's me? Why don't you ask the person in this family who actually has boobs that need a bra what she was doing at St. Novatus yesterday, *with Greg*." For a second he looked confused, and then she realized he couldn't begin to conceive that his other daughter was just as much of a woman as Emily was. "Maddy was with Greg yesterday, at school. I found her having a nervous breakdown by the garage. They had sex. She told me."

"I did not!" said Maddy, sitting up now at the edge of the couch, as if she'd been just waiting to jump in and defend herself from this exact accusation. From out in the hallway the phone started ringing.

"Why are you saying that, Emily?" said Sophie. "Maddy doesn't even like Greg in that way."

"Definitely not," said Maddy. "Greg and I are barely friends."

"I'm saying it because it's what she told me. She was a mess. They didn't even use a condom, so I had to give her my morning-after pill."

"Your *what?*" said Ivan.

"The morning-after pill," Emily said. "Sophie and I went to get the pill yesterday. And I gave Maddy my morning-after pill."

"You're on *the pill?*" he said.

"Not yet. But next month, yup." Ivan looked at Sophie, who looked back at him with an empty expression before lowering her eyes and then turning away from him. That gesture somehow confirming that, yes, she'd taken Emily to get the pill and, no, she hadn't told him.

"And Maddy, you *took* Emily's morning-after pill?" said Ivan, having difficulty with all of this.

"No!" she said. The ringing phone stopped, and the aftersilence was suddenly the loudest thing in the room. Ivan opened his mouth to speak again, but before he could, the phone started up again.

"Hold on," he said, and moved off into the hallway. In the silence that followed, Emily thought again about Sister Angela. It would have been easy for her to have dismissed her as an antiquated religious crackpot from another era, but there had been something special about her. She was a genuinely good soul. A person with no other agenda than to give. She hesitated to use the word, but perhaps even someone close to *sacred*.

Emily stared out the window at the oak that Joseph had climbed up early that morning. The top branches of the oak were completely naked of leaves and pure white, like jagged broken fingers reaching for the sky. The oak was sick. She'd heard Sophie and Ivan talking about it. The dead branches needed cutting back before a storm came through and the whole tree came crashing into the house. It should be handled as a matter of urgency, they'd said. But still, in the weeks between that overheard conversation and now, no one seemed to have done a thing about it.

Ivan walked back into the room. All the accusatory heat of earlier had drained out of him, and he somehow looked gray.

"Sister Angela just passed." Emily's guts flip-flopped, and she put her hands to her stomach to try to calm a sudden swell of nausea. Dead. A woman had *died*, and her father thought she was responsible. If she couldn't convince her own father she was innocent, how was she supposed to convince anyone else? "I have to go to the hospital. And then the police want to talk to me. Emily, Maddy, neither one of you leaves this house until I get back. This isn't going to go away. Joseph, I'll be speaking to your father later."

He turned and left the room, and in the vacuum that was left, Emily wondered if she'd finally get a chance to state her case. She needed to set things straight before they unraveled any further. But Joseph was headed for the front door, Maddy was already halfway up the stairs, and Sophie, refusing to even look in Emily's direction, was right behind her. No one wanted to hear it.

Ivan didn't come home the rest of that day, and Emily spent the next few hours perched by the open window in her room, thinking it through. She'd pushed the window all the way up and was considering how all she'd need to do was tip her body a few inches to the left and her life would either be over or radically different. Neither of which seemed a bad proposition. As she sat there, she saw Greg walk up the drive. He had flowers. Decent ones, not some bunch of stringy pink carnations. Looked like someone was in love. Joseph had never brought her flowers. The front door opened. Emily couldn't see who'd opened it, but she hoped it was Sophie. Those fancy flowers would blow Maddy's cover story about her and Greg barely being friends.

"You need to leave, now." This was Maddy, crushing his hopes and dreams before they ever got going.

"Why?"

"Are you completely stupid? You know why."

"No I don't. No one knows we were there yesterday."

Then the chatter became whispered, but she could make out her name being thrown around. *Emily*, said with a hot hatred. The discussion swirled for another minute or so, and she leaned out as far as she could to try to hear better, deftly catching herself each time she almost fell. She heard the front door close and saw Greg walking back the way he'd come. He still had the flowers. She wondered if Maddy had told him about the morning-after pill. She wondered if it would actually work. The nurse had told her that it didn't always. Maddy would definitely have some explaining to do if the pill wasn't able to weave its magic and that fertilized egg burrowed its way in. Greg looked up at Emily's window as he walked back down the sidewalk, and she gave him a half wave and a smile. She'd seen him, and she'd heard their conversation. More to sling on her growing dump pile of evidence. Not that anyone was interested in looking at it.

She waited till the moon was up and the house was quiet before she padded down the stairs to dig some food out of the fridge. She rummaged around until she found a Tupperware dish with that evening's mac-and-cheese dinner inside, soft and still slightly warm in the middle. She ate most of it, then chucked the container in the sink. She walked into the living room, worried they might have somehow secured the front window to try to shut down her nighttime escapes, but when she tried it, it opened as smoothly as it always had. They hadn't even bothered to put the screen back on. She climbed through the window, jumped onto the porch, and then started down the drive.

Joseph's bedroom window was closed. She knocked quietly on the base of the frame. Nothing. There was no light on inside the room, but it was only eleven, it wasn't like he would be sleeping. She knocked again, louder. And this time the light went on within about two seconds. He twisted open the blinds and then pulled up the window.

"Hey," she said.

"Hey."

"I didn't do it." She could feel the cool air from his bedroom spilling out through the window.

"Do what?" he asked blandly.

"Start that fire." His face was a blank, but she could still see exactly what was going on inside his head. He didn't believe her. He thought she'd done it because she'd done it before. "Joe, do you really think I'd steal my father's keys, let myself into that creepy chapel, take my bra off, and then light the place on fire? It wasn't even the type of bra that I wear! It was Maddy's."

"Yeah, Maddy says she's missing a bra."

"What?"

"She said she had a pink one, with underwire, and it's missing." So she'd spun it. Spun it around so her bra was *missing*, not left there by her. A missing bra that was in all likelihood a *taken* bra. Her sister was banging a boy she wasn't even dating, and now she was twisting facts to make it look like Emily was an arsonist. Emily had completely underestimated her.

"First of all, when were *you* speaking to Maddy?" Knowing that she was on shaky ground, Emily had complied with Ivan's order and hadn't left the house all day. Maddy had obviously ignored his decree.

"Today. She was down at the skate park. We got chatting about things."

"'Chatting?'" she asked, her heart going cold. "Did you kiss Maddy at that Red Hot Chili Peppers concert?"

"Who said that?" he asked.

"Bee."

"It was more of a lip bump than a kiss."

"Explain."

"We went to go and get some water. We were talking about 'Californication' and what the lyrics meant, and I just kissed her. I don't know why. The music was loud, I could feel it buzzing in my chest, and I wanted to see if I'd feel it vibrating in her lips. I know that sounds weird. But it's the truth." So there it was. He liked her. Even if he didn't know it. Emily knew a boy didn't kiss a girl he wasn't at least attracted to—even with a backstory of wanting to see if her lips were vibrating. She had a sudden urge to pull the window down over his skull and crack it in two. "Emily, I'm sorry if you're pissed about what happened at the concert, but you have to stop saying Maddy started that fire. There's no point in ruining her life as well as yours."

"Why is my life ruined?"

"I don't know. Juvenile detention?"

"I'm not going to juvie, because I didn't start that fire. It was Maddy. She practically told me she did it."

"Maddy's *practically* a little girl. Arson's not really her style," he said. *More your style* is what hung in the air between them. "She told me what happened with the knife. She said you looked at her like you wanted to kill her."

So there it was. He believed Maddy over her. But even with the accusations hanging in the air between them, she could tell from the way that Joseph was looking at her lips that he still wanted to kiss them. And not just to see if they were vibrating. She knew that if he opened his window all the way, and she climbed in, she'd find he was painfully hard already. He'd be so sensitive that he'd barely get inside her before he came. The thing that drew them together was still there, unfaded. He stood back from the window to let her in, thoughts of what would come next already swirling between them, but instead of scrambling up onto the sill, like she would have this time yesterday, she turned, and then she walked away.

As she crossed the lawn, she heard the definitive thunk of Joseph closing his window behind her. He wasn't even going to try to appease her. He genuinely believed Maddy's screwed-up story about her arm, and he unquestionably believed that Emily had started that fire. He didn't even want to hear her side. This boy, who she'd thought knew her in ways that no one else had, didn't know who she was at all. All the hours they'd spent supposedly falling in love had meant nothing. He was just another human ready to drop her the moment it looked like knowing her was going to be difficult. Just the same as Sophie. She was back to having no one. Her sister had taken the lot. In all the time since her mother had been gone, Emily had never wanted her as much as she did in that moment. And if she couldn't have her mother, she wanted to be somewhere safe and dark where she didn't have to deal with any of this. Somewhere quiet where nothing mattered anymore. No hatred, no disapproval. She realized she was sending up a silent prayer for death.

Emily made her way back around the block, climbed in the front window, and went straight upstairs into Maddy's room. It was one thing for Maddy to turn her parents and the rest of the world against her, quite another when it came to Joseph. Emily closed Maddy's bedroom door behind her and then sniffed to see if she could detect any trace of smoke. Nothing. Emily's room had the bathroom, but Maddy's was the bigger one. It was also the one without a funky stench of mold coming from the closet. She silently picked through Maddy's laundry hamper to see if she could find anything smoky lingering in there, but someone, either Maddy or perhaps even Sophie, had emptied it out. She looked down at Maddy as she slept, willing her to wake up. She didn't even stir. Emily knew that if she'd done even one of the things her sister had done over the past couple of days, she wouldn't have been able to sleep at all. But Maddy was out. No guilty conscience whatsoever.

"Hey," she whispered eventually. Nothing. She gave Maddy's shoulder a nudge, and that did it. Her eyes half parted and then flew open the rest of the way. She drew in a breath to scream, and Emily clamped her hand down over her mouth, but a second later she felt pain slice through her hand, and she pulled it away again. Maddy had bitten her.

"What's wrong with you?" said Emily, rubbing her palm.

"Get out of my room."

"No. You have to tell them it wasn't me. You have to tell Joseph."

"Oh, Joseph, of course," she said. "You're obsessed. Everything's about him."

"No, Maddy. It's about you telling the truth for once instead of blaming me for all your bullshit."

"I have no idea what you are talking about," she said. Prim and smug, just because she could be.

"Tell them."

"Mom!" she screamed. There was deathly silence. And then she went again. "Mom! Dad!" And then the screaming started. Emily jumped up from the bed and ran for the door. But before she could get there, it smacked opened, and in they both ran. Ivan in nothing more than his underwear.

"What's going on in here?" he said, though from the way he was looking at Emily, he'd already made his mind up about what was going on. Maddy pointed at Emily.

"She was trying to suffocate me!"

"What? How exactly was I suffocating you?"

"She had her knees on my chest. I couldn't breathe."

"Okay, young lady, that's it," said Ivan, and for half a second Emily thought he'd seen through her ruse and was talking to Maddy. But no. It was her. She was the "young lady." He moved toward her and clamped his fingers around her arm.

"Get off me," she yelled, and kicked him in the shin. She lashed out again, and he grabbed her under the arms and began to drag her across the room, but before he could get her out the door, she twisted back around to face Maddy.

"Hey, Maddy," she said. Maddy looked up, her eyes full of caution. "You should watch your back." She saw Maddy bury her face in her mother's shoulder, then Ivan hauled her across the landing and none too gently threw her inside her room and slammed the door closed. She sat there in the darkness, watching his feet move back and forth across the line of light coming under the door. A minute later she heard him haul the ancient armoire that lived next to her door across it, effectively trapping her in. She ran into the bathroom and tried the door that opened onto the landing. Locked from the outside. All possibility of escape finally shut down. And at that she gave up, crawled into bed, and slept.

When she woke, the armoire was still across the door. Emily had no clock in her room, but it felt late. Midmorningish. Thirsty, she drank some water from the bathroom faucet, then opened her bedroom window to see exactly how far it was from the ledge to the branches of the oak. If Joseph had managed to make the leap from the tree to her window without a running jump, surely she'd be able to make it in reverse with a few feet to get some impetus going. She felt her palms turn cold at the thought of what might happen if she didn't make it to the tree. But it was either stay in this room and face everything headed her way or take the risk. She'd almost psyched herself up to jump when she heard the thud of footsteps heading up the stairs and then the heavy scrape of the armoire being pulled back.

Ivan opened the door, his eyes searching the room for her as he walked in. When he saw her, she couldn't tell if he was relieved or pissed that she hadn't tried to run away in the night. If he'd wanted to be rid of her, all he'd had to do was leave her door unblocked, and she would have taken care of the rest. Ivan moved all the way into the room, and that was when she saw the two police officers behind him.

"Dad?"

He looked at her then. As if he had no clue as to why she'd just called him that. She didn't know why she'd said it either. Perhaps a sad attempt to remind him that regardless of what he thought she'd done, she was still his daughter.

"Emily Grisanti." The first officer, a squat guy with a snubby nose, took a step toward her. She caught sight of the cuffs hanging from his belt, and for a second she stopped breathing. "I'm arresting you on suspicion of—"

"No! Dad?"

"Of arson with intent to endanger life."

"*What?* I haven't done anything!"

"We'll get to all that. But for now, you need to come with me. You have the right to remain sil—" He saw her make the decision a split second after she made it. Without looking back, she sprinted toward the window. If she made it to the tree, she'd head straight to the Stone House. And if she didn't reach its branches, then none of this would matter anymore.

She didn't even get as far as the ledge. Both officers were on her before she took her second step, and her entire body hit the floor, chin first. In a blind panic, she drew both knees up to her chest—one hand on her chin to try to shut down the pain now ripping through her jawbone, the other over her eyes in an attempt to make everything stop.

She felt two sets of rough hands on her wrists and legs trying to pry her legs away from her chest, but now she was frozen rigid.

"Help me. Help me," she heard someone whispering before she realized it was her own voice.

"Stop resisting," said the second cop, his hot breath hitting the center of her ear. She opened her mouth to tell them she wasn't resisting, but no words would come out.

"It doesn't have to be this hard." She felt her body lift inches off the ground as she was picked up by one arm. At this, the pain in her jaw doubled up, and her body jolted back to life. The second her body opened up, they laid her facedown, arms behind her back, and seconds later she felt the cool metal of cuffs around each wrist being drawn tight. Then there was a pointless pat down and she was dragged to standing.

The last piece of her to come upright was her head, and when she finally lifted it, she felt a soft trickle of blood escape her nose and run down her lip. She went to wipe the blood away but then realized she was no longer free to touch her own face. One of the cops nudged her toward the bedroom door, and her legs obeyed. Ivan was still in the bedroom, his expression unreadable, but she could see Sophie and Maddy standing on the landing, clinging to each other. Sophie in tears. Maddy so white she looked halfway dead.

The officer walked her along the rest of the landing and down the stairs intoning the rest of her truncated Miranda rights before she was hustled out the front door and into the back of the cop car. The snubby-nosed officer got into the driver's seat a second later. He didn't say a word, and she definitely wasn't in the mood to chat. Instead, she stared at the crisscross of the cage in front of her and tuned in to what the cop outside was saying to Ivan.

"You have a family lawyer?"

"Won't she get a court-appointed one?" This was her father. The cheapskate.

"Not if you have the ability to pay. That'll ultimately be up to the court to decide, but it'll delay things if there're questions over who's funding this."

"I'll send someone," he said, and she could tell he was mad. Mad about providing a lawyer to defend his own daughter, as if she were a defective car engine that was costing him more than she should.

"As she's got a prior, she'll likely be detained at juvenile hall until we can get her case to court."

"Fine," he said. Fine with her too, Emily thought. Even if he wanted her back, which he clearly didn't, she would never set a foot inside Pile House again.

"You want to follow now or—"

"No. I have the insurance people arriving at the school any minute. I'll come down later after the lawyer's been."

"I know this was hard, Mr. Doyle. But it was the right thing to do."

"I know."

And there it was. Her own father had done this to her—reported her to the police for a crime she hadn't committed. She slumped back as far as she could, the cuffs digging into the base of her spine. He must know she could hear him. Did he just not care? Perhaps the tinted window meant that he'd forgotten she was there. That was no excuse. He'd still said what he'd said. He'd still done what he'd done. The officer got into the passenger's seat, and she looked out the window at Ivan, who now stood on the front porch next to Sophie and Maddy, arms around both of them. The people who were supposed to care most about her, abandoning her to the care of the state. Again. She wasn't surprised about Ivan, this was after all the second time he was effectively washing his hands of her. And in that moment where Sophie had to choose between Emily taking the hit or the axe falling on her own daughter, of course she put Maddy first. But Joseph. If Joseph didn't believe her. If he didn't love her anymore or, worst of all, if he never had, then what was the point of any of it? This town, this family, and this house were over for her. If it wasn't within her power to be free, she could at least control the fact that she never had to see any of these people again. At least she could escape from *them*. Whatever lay ahead, it was somewhere else. And that was what she needed; to be anywhere that wasn't here.

CHAPTER 23

MADDY

Maddy stood across the street from Pile House in the dying light of the day. Her grandmother used to call it wolf light. The time of day between dog and wolf. The time when all that's familiar becomes wild. Maddy looked up to the windows of Emily's old bedroom, its peony-print wallpaper softly faded. This was the first time she'd looked properly at Pile House since she'd moved out. All the blinds were gone, and she could see into every single window. And what she saw through each window was the same, no matter which room she looked in. Echoing emptiness. Nothing but wood panels and walls. No furniture. No light fixtures. The house was a blank. Maddy's eyes moved toward the grass where tire tracks had ripped the lawn to reveal the yellow clay below. Tire tracks from what?

She crossed over and this time stopped to read the sign rammed into the lawn. Looking now, it wasn't a sign at all, but an artist's rendition of five generic townhouses. All identical except for their individual shade of pastel. Bedrooms looked onto bedrooms. Bathrooms onto bathrooms. One set of blinds raised at the wrong time could spell disaster. If these neighbors weren't as close as family when they moved in, it would surely only be days before they knew one another's most intimate rituals. But there was no way Pile House's walls and ceilings could be reworked to represent what she saw on this drawing. It wasn't possible. Emily was demolishing the place. To build this rats' nest.

Her childhood home was about to be torn in two. And there was no way for her to stop it. All she could do was take one last mental snapshot of the house before it was gone forever. But as she took in the bare porch and the fresh stump that was all that remained of the old white oak, she knew that these weren't the final moments of her parents' home but an empty husk of it. This was nothing more than a house with the soul sucked out. Emily had been sucking its soul out in front of her all along, dismantling it piece by piece in front of her very eyes. And now that she had all the pieces positioned exactly as she wanted them, she was ready to send in the machinery and demolish the thing entirely. She looked again at the drawing of what was about to be built here. Pile House ripped apart so that five families could pack into this dirt patch in the sun and listen to each other fucking and fighting for the next thirty years. She pushed down the scream that wanted to escape and instead gave the bottom of the post a heartfelt kick. It hurt her foot, but she did it again, harder, and then again, until she'd left three dirty dents in the white wood. It felt insignificant in the face of what Emily had done. She felt insignificant in the face of what Emily had done.

Maddy trod over the mud to reach the living room window, where she pressed her face up against the glass. No lights on anywhere. No one was home. But the empty feeling echoing back at her from the darkened rooms was more than a not being home. The house had a feeling of abandonment it hadn't had a couple of hours ago. She climbed up onto the porch and rang the bell. Then knocked. But it wasn't going to bring anyone. Emily was gone.

Maddy was barely thinking as she put the Jeep in drive and headed toward the hills. Toward Devil's Gulch Ridge. With a jolt of panic, she realized that the only reason Joseph had found Emily's place before was because he knew the house and knew the hills. The last of the day's light was gone now, and the first stars were showing, small prickles of white light against the dark sky. Not quite enough light to see by. She was going to be driving blind.

Maddy drove up the last suburban street and then slipped onto the lane that led up to nowhere. Within two minutes she was driving on a dirt track and putting the Jeep's suspension to the test. The road felt bumpier than it had last time. This wasn't the route they'd taken before. Last time they'd come in from another direction entirely. She should probably head back before she got irretrievably lost. These matter-of-fact thoughts came to her. The sensible thoughts. And yet she ignored every last rational one of them and kept driving forward.

She took a left and drove upward, over a hill that was so steep she thought the Jeep might fall backward. Despite every cell in her body screaming at her to carefully reverse back down the slope, she made it over and followed the road as it twisted to the right before losing all sight of the sky under a canopy of dense tree coverage. Twice she almost stopped to think it all through. The third time she felt like stopping, she deep-breathed through it and pushed the gas pedal down harder. There would be no sensible retreat from this situation. She wasn't driving back having not found him. She couldn't rationally believe that he could slip out of her life as simply as he had done. She would have a conversation with this man. He was obliged to explain himself. Did he really feel like he was justified in everything he'd done to her because of something that had happened when she was fourteen years old? No one stayed the person they were when they were fourteen. To be held accountable for something you'd done, or rather something you hadn't done, back then was ludicrous. She needed him to see that he was the one in the wrong here. Not her.

As she drove on, she began to let instinct steer the car. Some unknown internal sensory system now at the wheel. She was getting closer to him—pushed forward by the silent spirit of all strong women everywhere. Whatever it was that everyone was made up of on a fundamental level—the things everyone was, beyond flesh and bone. She was being helped. She would find her husband. It was going to happen.

She was in a partial daze when she turned the corner and found herself on a smoother road. It was a road that she thought she faintly recognized. Very faintly. She drove along a little farther, finding herself preemptively slowing down. And then within a few seconds, the trees finished and there it was. Emily's house. She'd found it. Without a second's pause, she drove up onto the gravel, the undulation of it under her wheels feeling like nothing after the crazy paths she'd driven on to get here.

She didn't have to wait. He was at the top of the stairs before she had even turned off the engine. She wondered if he'd been waiting for her, or if he had felt her reaching out for him as she fumbled through the canyons. He came down the steps, two at a time. She lowered her window as soon as he got to the car. She'd intended to get out, but he was already right up by the door and didn't look like he was going to step back in order to give her the room to do so.

"What do you want?" he said. Not even a flicker of remorse. "You should go. Emily doesn't want you up here."

"Joseph, I made one mistake when I was fourteen years old. It doesn't mean you get to throw our entire life away. And it doesn't justify what you've been doing to me."

"And what exactly do you think it is that I've been doing to you, Maddy?"

She held up her wrist with her mom's bracelet on it and felt some satisfaction in watching him pale a little as it slid down her arm. "I saw what else you had stashed in there." She grabbed at the folder, the papers inside sliding out onto the front seat. She picked the first two up and read them out loud.

"Target, eighty grand. Audi, almost a quarter of a million dollars. Everything in Emily's name. Divorce courts tend to not look favorably on a spouse trying to hide assets, Joseph. You told me you were broke." Her heart was beating fast. She'd mentioned the divorce word. Because of course she was going to have to divorce him; anything else was unthinkable. But even so, she wanted that word to wake him up. To snap him out of the bewitched haze her sister had pulled him into. She wanted him to hear that word and then beg her to forgive him for everything.

"I haven't tried to hide a thing. When your lawyer talks to my lawyer, I will be nothing but transparent. Take as big a chunk as you want, it's just money." The Joseph she knew would never say that hundreds of thousands of dollars was just money. But he'd been found out—so what else could he say. And what did he care about money now that he had access to Emily and her millions.

"Why did you do it? Those goddamn stupid socks, my bracelet." She was glad she hadn't asked him *if* he'd done any of those things. She was beyond giving him any room to wiggle out of it. Incredibly, she could see that he was debating whether to come clean, even now. She silently willed him to talk. As much as she'd told herself earlier that she didn't need him to tell her she wasn't insane, she needed this admission.

"Because I wanted you to know what it feels like to have someone mow down your own definition of who you are and what you've done, and make up bullshit in its place. And then I wanted you to stand in the middle of that and see your world fall apart because of it. Because that's exactly what you did to your sister. And it ruined her life."

"Jesus Christ, Joseph, I wasn't trying to define who she was! I was fourteen. I was scared."

"Why did you tell everyone that the fire was Emily?" he asked.

"I never told anyone it was Emily. I never said a thing! They all made their own assumptions."

"Maddy, I don't think you realize how much you fucked up Emily's life. Juvenile detention destroyed her. She's still in therapy over it. I don't think she'll ever not be. You did that to her. And you've taken away twenty years of our lives."

"What's that supposed to mean?"

"Twenty years where we weren't together. But I tracked her down, and thank God I did because this is where our real lives begin. We just need you to stay away from us." She couldn't believe what she was hearing. When had *she* become the one everyone needed protecting from?

"What do you mean, you tracked her down?"

"When Ivan died. While you were dicking around doing half-hearted searches on Facebook, I hired someone to do the real thing. Your dad said something to me when he was in the hospital."

"What?" she asked.

"He said he'd been too hard on her. I thought he was talking about your mom. But he wasn't, he was talking about Emily."

"How exactly was he too hard on her?"

"He said he hadn't listened when he should have. That he'd let her take the blame for things that weren't her fault and that it was the biggest regret of his life. So I found her. And then she told me the truth."

Maddy felt herself already dismissing his words. Her father had never really said that. This was another lie to make her feel terrible. But then a soft memory floated up. Hadn't her dad said something similar to her? When he was so weak that he could barely keep awake long enough to have a conversation. He'd wanted her to find Emily. He'd said those exact same words—that he'd been too hard on her—that he'd wanted to make things right. And she'd assured him that she'd been looking for Emily ever since he got sick. A lie. But a lie to help him. Because who would want a person like Emily showing up on your deathbed to make your last few days miserable with recriminations? But now it seemed that even though she thought she'd smothered the truth, her father had already had it. Somehow he'd figured it out. Her lies had been to protect his notion of who she was. So that he'd still love her in exactly the same way. And seeing as the truth was all it had taken to pull Joseph out of love with her, it was just as well she had.

"When did you find her?"

"Just after your dad's funeral."

"So you've been in a thing with her for two years."

"I'd hardly call it 'a thing.' But, yes, since I found her, we've been together."

And there it was. Confirmed. Ever since they'd moved into Pile House, every second of her life with him had been pure fabrication. Her thoughts rushed forward in a hundred thousand fragments as she tried to flip back through everything that had happened in that house since they'd moved in. The endless confusion, the endless lack of money. Misery stacked on top of misery, lies on top of lies. He'd done it just to be cruel. Just because he thought that she'd somehow earned it. Every time they'd had sex, every time they'd had a conversation, he'd been somebody else the entire time. She didn't know who this man was, but she knew she didn't want him.

Joseph, seeing that she finally understood everything, stepped back, his body language saying what he wasn't: they were done.

"So that's it?" she said. "You're just going to live up here in this dump now?" She looked at the house, her eyes landing on the huge latticed window looking out over the drive. Moonlight shone directly on the glass, but it was black and reflective, and Maddy couldn't see what was on the other side—but she could make a substantial guess. *Her.* Joseph turned to look at the house and then smiled.

"It'll do." And the way he said it made Maddy wonder if it wasn't just Emily who was the draw. Perhaps it was also this place.

The grandeur of it. The way it promised to elevate you, to turn you into something you weren't. She had one thing left in her arsenal. It wouldn't pull him back, but then, she didn't want him back. It would, however, sting.

"I hope you don't have some big plan to fill this ugly house up with kids. I went to see Drumgun this morning. You're firing blanks. It could be cancer—he doesn't know." She looked at him; he was completely unrattled. How could he be unrattled?

"I had a vasectomy." For a moment, she didn't understand the words. And then she did. This had to be another lie. She'd have known if he'd had surgery. "I got it done in New York. After I found Emily."

"Why?"

"She had a miscarriage when she first got to juvie. After that, she never wanted to put herself in the position of being pregnant again. As I said, what you and Greg did fucked her up in ways you can't even begin to imagine. So I got the snip." Two years of trying for a baby, and all along he knew it was never going to happen. Months of passing her the thermometer and then writing down her temperature after she called it out every morning. Months of him happily jamming two pillows under her butt every time after they had sex to help his aging sperm win out against the ravages of gravity. And there they'd both sat, their legs propped up on the wall, talking about their future, their baby, their family. And all along, he'd known it was for nothing. Maddy thought of the catalog of pictures of Emily that she'd seen on his phone, and her mouth turned completely dry. All the time she'd been focused on the house and her school and trying to conceive a baby, Emily and Joseph had been becoming a living thing. And then when it was fully formed, it had risen up and destroyed her marriage. Destroyed her entire life. And it was nothing more than her father's doubt in who Maddy was that had triggered the whole thing. She opened her mouth to tell him that he could go fuck himself and his invalid sperm and his money too, but before she spoke, her eyes moved to straight behind him—to the top of the stairs. Emily. There was no gloat in her face. No fear. No triumph. None of the normal emotions of the woman who's won. Just hate.

Emily walked down the steps, and then out onto the drive to stand next to Joseph. Maddy waited for the smug smile. The smile that would confirm that all of this had been about taking the last thing Maddy had. But it didn't come. Emily just stood there, waiting for Maddy to say something. And then Maddy saw Joseph reach to the side, take Emily's hand, and gently squeeze it. And Emily squeezed back. The two of them were on one side, and she was on the other. Everything that he'd done to her and all he could see was what had happened to Emily half a lifetime ago. They honestly thought they were the ones who'd been wronged here. The pious fucks.

Maddy threw the Jeep into reverse and swerved it wide to the right. Her chest was tight and raw with hurt, her hate for Emily throbbing vigorously at its center. Pulsing. Time to go, before she did something stupid. She put the Jeep in drive and spun the wheel the other way, but when she felt her foot connect with the power of the engine, something inside said no, and she turned the wheel hard back to the right and charged forward, five thousand pounds of steel underneath her foot. Joseph had seen what she was doing and had already jumped up onto the steps, but Emily hadn't moved. Did she *want* to die? She'd almost reached her when Emily snapped out of it and threw herself up onto the steps after Joseph. Maddy shot past her and then slammed on the brakes, the wheels grinding into the gravel. Joseph and Emily looked at her from the steps, breathing hard. Horrified. She quickly reversed again, and then, not stopping to look behind her, turned the wheel one more time and shot out of the driveway.

She drove back down the trail she'd just driven up. Her sister brought it out in her like no other human had before or since. And what did they expect? They'd labeled her a monster—this was the result. She'd shown them what they'd wanted to see. What they believed she was. Who they had turned her into. And now she had to live out the rest of her life. Pushing down the thing she knew about herself. Knowing that she'd been ready to kill them both. Pushing down the fact that underneath the shock and the denial and the hate, she loved Joseph more than she'd ever loved anyone in her life. But knowing that he was Emily's again. Just like he always had been. He'd been nothing more than on loan to her all these years. And the only one who hadn't really known it was her.

ACKNOWLEDGMENTS

It takes so very many people to bring a book to life, and I'm grateful to all of the talented team at APub for the effort they've put into launching *Half Sisters*.

A never-ending thank you to Fiona Pearce for reading the very first draft and then getting in touch every few weeks to ask when the novel was coming out. Her persistent belief in Maddy's story is what convinced me it might actually be worth doing something with. A big thank you to Emily Milon for all her ideas and enthusiasm. Also to Jamaal Pittman and Greg Sullivan. Henry Auerbach, you are a star for answering all my copious, specific, and often intrusive questions about fires and the firefighting life!

Thanks to Mr. Todd Burke for defending my writing time from the demands of domesticity, for silently bringing me cheese on crackers when I'm heads down and forgetting to eat, and for telling me that it's all going to be okay, even when it most looks like it isn't.

My fantastic agent, Liz Parker, brought this book to life in so many ways, and I will be forever grateful. And finally, thank you to my wonderful editor, Danielle Marshall, for her professionalism, tenacity, kindness, and editorial vision. You make it feel easy.

BOOK CLUB QUESTIONS

1. Throughout this story, Maddy's husband tries to convince her that things that aren't true are true. Do you think this can happen to anyone or only someone who has certain vulnerabilities? How would you advise a woman to guard herself against gaslighting?

2. Maddy has rewritten her past so much that she almost believes she isn't guilty of things she's done. Have you ever known anyone to make such selective edits to past events that they become a new truth?

3. As Emily says: "Unless everyone buys into exactly the same story, a true thing sometimes isn't a true thing at all." Do you think truth can be moved entirely if enough people choose not to believe it? Or is truth ultimately a thing that can never be moved?

4. Myrtlebury, where this story takes place, is in the grasp of gentrification. Is the community where you live unchanged or becoming gentrified? What are the advantages and disadvantages of your community's unchanged or gentrified status?

5. The sibling rivalry between Emily and Maddy starts before they reconnect as adults. What role do you think

Ivan and Sophie play in triggering the rivalry between them?

6. Joseph and Maddy have known each other since they were children and spent their teenhood in each other's lives. What advantages and disadvantages do you think preadult years spent together have for a marriage?

7. Ultimately, Bee takes her brother's side over her oldest friend's. Do you think it was the right thing to do? Why or why not? Would you have done the same thing?

8. Rank Emily, Bee, Joseph, Maddy, and Greg in order from most villainous to least. Look at the character at the start of your list. Why do you think they were the worst? And the character at the other end of the spectrum: why do you think they were more sinned against than sinner?

9. Revenge is a dish best served cold. Do you think that by the end of the story Emily is completely satisfied by the revenge she's served? Does she feel any better for it? Is her revenge complete?

10. After Maddy drives off at the end of the story, what do you think her next moves will be? What would you do in the same situation?

11. A couple of the characters in this book talk about "the one who got away." Do you know of anyone who had someone who "got away"? Did it affect their consequential relationships?

12. Toward the end of the book, Maddy snoops on her husband's laptop. This is after she's looked in his phone. She also mentions having read her sister's teen diary. Is it ever okay to snoop? Ultimately, have any of these snoopings given Maddy information that's helped her?

ABOUT THE AUTHOR

Photo © David Muller

Virginia Franken was born and raised in the United Kingdom and is the author of *Life After Coffee*. She graduated from the University of Roehampton in London with a degree in dance and worked on cruise ships as a professional dancer before changing tracks to pursue a career in publishing. Virginia currently lives in suburban Los Angeles with her family. She gets most of her writing done when she should be sleeping. For more information, visit www.virginiafranken.com.